One True Path

Other books by Barbara Cameron

ONE TRUE PATH

Book 3 of the Amish Roads Series

Barbara Cameron

Abingdon fiction

a novel approach to faith

Nashville

One True Path

ISBN: 978-1-4267-6622-0

Published by Abingdon Press, P.O. Box 801, Nashville, TN 37202

www.abingdonpress.com

Macro Editor: Teri Wilhelms

Published in association with Books & Such Literary Agency

Library of Congress Cataloging-in-Publication Data has been requested.

Printed in the United States of America
1 2 3 4 5 6 7 8 9 10 / 20 19 18 17 16 15

For
my daughter, Stephany

Acknowledgments

One True Path is the third book in the Amish Roads series—the third Amish series I've been asked to write for Abingdon Press.

I love writing novels about the Amish because I love stories of faith and hope and family—and romance. Thank you to readers who have embraced all three series. I am humbled that you enjoy reading them and often write me to say so. Thank you to Pamela Clements and Ramona Richards at Abingdon Press for their encouragement and faith in my writing. I hope we work together for a very long time. Who knew where this journey would lead when Barbara Scott bought that first series years ago. . . .

Thank you to senior editor Ramona Richards and editor Teri Wilhelms for helping improve my books, to Cat Hoort in marketing, Katherine Johnston in the proofreading department, and many, many people like the cover artists, printers, and distributors I have never met. I always say that it takes a village to create a book. One day I hope to meet this wonderful team.

I also want to thank beta readers Kimberly Taylor, Anne Martin Fletcher, and Linda Tuck-Jenkins for agreeing to read a rough draft of *One True Path* in a hurry for me. Their input was invaluable, and I appreciate them so much.

On a personal note, while I was writing this book my daughter, Stephany, came to my aid when I experienced a health challenge. I want to thank her for sitting with me for hours in the emergency room, for taking care of my pack of Chihuahuas—including one who went straight for her ankles in front of me—and in general for providing emotional support when I occasionally switched roles with her and needed her to care for me. She has a big and generous heart, and I am so grateful to have her in my life.

And above all, thank you to God for this amazing journey called life. I believe there are lessons in every situation and person we encounter, and while I hope never to have such a severe health challenge and healing process again, I do find myself more grateful than ever for every day I get to be here.

I hope you enjoy this book about Rachel Ann and Abram who find out that they want to be more than friends. . . .

Blessings!

Be ye not unequally yoked together with unbelievers:

for what fellowship hath righteousness with unrighteousness?

and what communion hath light with darkness?

2 Corinthians 6:14 KJV

1

*R*achel Ann Miller watched her *bruder* Sam dig his hands into his oatmeal and lick it off his fingers.

"Sam! Use your spoon or I'm going to feed you like a *boppli*," she said sternly. "You're four years old now. You need to behave and eat like a big boy."

"You want some oatmeal, Rachel Ann?" her *mamm* asked as she put the teakettle on the stove.

She watched Sam grin at her, exposing a mouthful of gooey cereal. Rachel Ann should have been used to it, but her stomach rolled.

"*Nee, danki*," she said. "The toast was enough."

She used a wet washcloth to wipe Sam's mouth then reached for his chubby little hands. Before she could grasp them Sam clapped them, sending little globs of cereal and fruit flying.

Rachel Ann ducked, but she felt something wet hit her cheek and after she wiped it off she found several other globs of oatmeal on her skirt.

"I'm going to get you for this," she threatened Sam as she wiped his hands carefully.

He just laughed and rubbed his gloppy hands on the table, then reached for Rachel Ann.

"*Nee*, Sam, don't do that, you'll get Rachel Ann all messy!" their *mamm* chided.

But Rachel Ann saw her mother trying to hide her smile. No one could be upset with the adorable Sam for any length of time. He was so loved and so loving.

"Don't worry about getting him cleaned up," her mother said with a sigh. "I'll dunk him in the tub after everyone's finished with breakfast."

Rachel Ann handed Sam a piece of toast and, with an eye on the time, opened the refrigerator and pulled out the makings for lunch.

"Do you need some money for your driver?"

She shook her head as she wrapped her egg salad sandwich. "He said he could wait for payday." She waited, and when her mother turned her attention back to Sam, she quickly made a second sandwich.

She put the sandwiches, two whoopie pies, and an apple in her insulated lunch bag and added a plastic bottle of iced tea she'd made up the night before. The lunch bag bulged with the extra food, but her mother hadn't noticed before, and hopefully she wouldn't this time.

"I'm glad you're happy working at Leah's," her mother said as she sat at the table with a cup of tea.

"It was that or take the job Mrs. Weatherby offered." She shuddered at the narrow escape she'd had. Elizabeth, one of her closest friends, had heard about an opening at Stitches in Time, and Rachel Ann had been lucky to get the job.

"You'd have been a great mother's helper for her," her mother told her. She poured a glass of juice for Sam and put it in front of him. "I don't know what I'd do without you."

She found herself thinking about Elizabeth who was married to Rachel Ann's cousin Saul. Elizabeth had shared with her that she'd been the oldest *kind* in a large family and felt stifled.

Somehow, it helped to know someone else experienced the same feelings of wanting to do more than care for *kinner*. Elizabeth's family had been bigger and her *mamm* sounded like she wasn't as good managing her job as a mother as Rachel Ann's, but still, they had found they had much in common since they had gotten to know each other better.

Elizabeth had suggested she talk to Leah about working at Stitches in Time after saying Saul didn't need anyone at their store. Since Anna, one of Leah's granddaughters had had her *boppli*, she had moved from full-time to part-time for a while. Thanksgiving was over now, and with the Christmas season looming, the timing was perfect for Rachel Ann to step in to help.

She wanted full-time, of course, not part-time. But Elizabeth told her it's how she'd started at Saul's store, and now, not only did she work full-time, she and Saul had fallen in love and gotten married. So Rachel Ann held out the hope maybe part-time would turn to full-time in the future at the shop.

Rachel Ann glanced up as Sam banged his spoon on the table and she frowned. It was so sad Elizabeth had suffered a miscarriage. Sometimes, when she thought no one noticed, Elizabeth looked so . . . lost and Rachel Ann suspected she'd thought of the *boppli* she miscarried. Try as she might, she never felt she offered the comfort her friend needed—even though Elizabeth said people didn't need words, they needed someone to listen, and Rachel Ann had listened when she needed it.

She slung the strap of her lunch tote over her shoulder, grabbed her purse and jacket, and walked over to the table to kiss everyone good-bye.

"I won't be home for supper," she reminded her mother as she bent to give her a hug. "Mmm, you smell like apples."

"Not from rubbing applesauce in my hair," her mother said with a laugh. "Look at this. I may still be getting it out of Sam's hair when you do get home."

Sam heard his name and giggled. His hair—golden blond and straight—stood up in stiff little peaks full of oatmeal and applesauce.

"I hear some *Englisch* women pay a lot of money for facials with oatmeal," Rachel Ann told her. "Have a *gut* day. Tell *Dat* I'm sorry I missed him."

"He'll be home from the auction when you get in this evening."

"I might be late."

"Not too late." Her mother gave her the look mothers seemed so good at. It spoke volumes.

"*Mamm*, I'm twenty-one—"

"I know how old you are. I was there, remember?" her mother said dryly. "And you know it's not safe to be out too late. Drivers aren't always looking out for someone walking or even riding in a buggy."

"I know, I know." She bent and hugged her mother and then her *bruder* before she walked out the door.

Even though she knew her *dat* wasn't in the barn, she couldn't help glancing that way as she walked down the drive.

A movement caught her eye. Abram Lapp stood watching her from the porch next door. He lifted a hand in greeting, and she waved back. She liked him—they'd been friends since they were toddlers. They'd sat near each other in *schul* and even attended a singing together once.

But now they were in their twenties, and their friendship hadn't turned into something romantic the way some had in her community. She felt Abram was too serious for her. Too . . . settled. Rachel Ann liked *rumschpringe* and didn't want to settle down yet. And she didn't think she wanted to date an Amish man.

As a matter of fact, she knew she didn't.

She stood at the bottom of the drive for only a few minutes when a car pulled up and the driver leaned over to grin at her. "Hey, babe, been waiting long?"

Rachel Ann opened the passenger door and got in quickly. She glanced back at the house as she pulled on her seat belt. "Please hurry up and get going. I don't want *Mamm* to see."

Michael leaned over to kiss her cheek, and then he straightened, checked the road, and pulled out, tires screeching.

"Don't do that!" She slumped down in her seat and prayed her mother didn't hear the tires—or look out the window. When she glanced over her shoulder she saw Abram still standing on his porch looking in her direction. She frowned. Why was he watching her? She hoped he wouldn't tell her *mamm* what he'd seen.

"Make up your mind, babe. I make a quick getaway, it's gonna be noisy."

Rachel Ann bit her lip and frowned when she looked over and saw how fast the car was going. Maybe instead of praying her mother didn't see her, she should pray God would slow down the car.

She pulled the visor down and checked her reflection in the mirror. Her starched white *kapp* looked slightly askew. It must have been bumped when she got into the car. She straightened it, fastened it more securely with covering pins, then smoothed her blonde hair worn center parted and tucked back in a bun. Her blue eyes sparkled, and color bloomed on her cheeks even though she didn't wear makeup.

She folded back the visor, leaned back in her seat, and watched Michael as he drove. The fall breeze coming in the window tossed his black hair away from his lean face, the bright morning light giving it a bluish gleam like a raven's wing. He must have felt her staring at him because he turned and winked at her.

Life had become exciting lately. New job. New boyfriend. She felt like she was going down a new path for her, one she hadn't ever dared to dream.

"Got something good to eat in there?" he asked, gesturing at the lunch tote.

She nodded, got out one of the sandwiches she'd packed, and unwrapped it for him.

He took it and bit into it. "Mmm," he said as he took a bite. "Way to a man's heart."

"So what are we doing later?"

"How about pizza and a movie?"

"Sounds *gut*—er, good. I get off at 5:30."

Michael finished the sandwich in a few bites. "Anything else in the bag?"

"A whoopie pie."

He took his eyes off the road for a moment. "I love those."

"I know." He loved her baking. She unwrapped the big cream-filled cookie and handed it to him.

"Fabulous things," he said, licking his lips after biting into it. "They're the best I've ever had, and I've been eating them for years."

She glowed at his praise but shrugged. Her whoopie pies were good, but so were those made by many of her friends and women in the Amish community.

He dropped her off at the shop, promising to pick her up at closing time. She drifted inside on a happy haze.

"*Guder mariye*," Leah said, looking up from paperwork spread on the front counter.

"*Ya*, it is," Rachel Ann said. "A *gut* morning!"

Abram stood on his porch and watched Rachel Ann hurry down her drive and stand there waiting at the bottom of it.

She seemed awfully eager for her ride to her new job. He'd managed to get it out of her—she had found a job—when he talked to her the night before.

As usual he'd found an excuse to take something over to her house and get himself invited to supper. Yesterday he'd visited a friend who had produced a bumper crop of pumpkins so he'd carried a few over to Rachel Ann's *mamm*. He and his *mamm* had decided they had more than enough for the two of them.

Now, finished with morning chores, he stood drinking his coffee on the front porch and watched Rachel Ann impatiently tapping her foot; he knew he had to figure out some way to get himself invited to supper again tonight. He wanted to find out how her day had gone . . . how she'd liked working in a shop when she'd been so afraid she'd have to take the job offer from an *Englisch* woman to work as a mother's helper. He just plain wanted to be near her, even when she had never looked at him as more than the boy next door who'd been her friend at *schul*.

A car came into view—one he judged to be traveling faster than the speed limit. He stiffened when it pulled up in front of Rachel Ann, worried it might hit her. But it stopped, and he realized she knew the driver for she opened the door and jumped inside. She glanced back at her house and then must have sensed him staring at her, for her eyes met his for just a moment.

And then the car took off at a greater speed than it had approached, peeling away from the curb with a squeal of tires. It zoomed down the road. Abram felt his heart leap into his throat as he realized he waited to hear a crash as it sped down the road and vanished from sight.

The door opened at Rachel Ann's house, and her mother stuck her head out. She looked down the drive, then just as she turned back she glanced in his direction. "*Guder mariye*, Abram."

"*Guder mariye.*"

"What was that racket I heard?"

He hesitated for only a moment. "Just a car. Someone wanting to leave rubber on the road instead of their tires."

She shook her head. "Makes no sense."

Then her hand flew to her throat. "It wasn't Rachel Ann's van driver, was it?"

"*Nee.*" It wasn't a lie, he told himself. It hadn't been the van driver...

Her hand fell to her side. "Of course it wasn't." She brightened. "Come for supper, Abram. While Sam naps this afternoon, I'm making pumpkin pie from those pumpkins you brought me."

"*Danki*, I'll do that."

She walked back inside and shut the door. Abram stood there for a moment wondering if he should have told her what he'd seen. He took a sip of coffee and found it had grown cold and bitter. Grimacing, he tossed the contents over the porch railing and went inside.

His mother glanced up and smiled at him as she stood at the stove. "Ready for some breakfast?"

He nodded and walked over to the percolator to pour himself another cup of coffee. "Why don't you let me cook?"

"I like to cook for you."

Abram leaned down and kissed her cheek. "And I don't mind admitting I like you cooking for me. But you don't look like you slept well. Why didn't you stay in bed?"

She made a *tsk*ing noise and shook her head at him. "If you're wanting me to be lazy, you've got the wrong woman."

"Not wanting you to be lazy. Just don't want you to overdo."

"The physical therapist said I'm doing so well I can cut down to one visit a week for the next few weeks."

"Well, that's terrific. I guess pretty soon you'll be turning somersaults." He snatched a piece of bacon and with the ease of years of such behavior escaped a rap on the knuckles with her spatula.

"Very funny. Sit down and get those big feet out of my way."

He did as she ordered and watched her flip a pancake onto a plate piled with them. She brought it to the table along with the plate of bacon, and while she probably thought his attention was on the food, he was noticing her limp had become barely noticeable.

One of the worst moments of his life had been when he got the call she'd fallen and been taken to the hospital. His father had died the year before from a heart attack, so he'd been terrified he'd lose another parent. The doctor had come into the waiting room and told him she'd broken her leg in three places. A broken leg. He'd sighed in relief. He could handle a broken leg. The doctor operated, and his mother had emerged from the hospital with a leg she joked had more metal in it than one of those *Englisch* robots.

The reality was the fall had cost her so much. Abram knew how independent she'd always been, but he'd convinced her to move into the *dawdi haus* here so he could make sure she was taken care of. She'd only agreed because it made it easier for him during the harvest.

Abram constructed a pile of pancakes on his plate, layering four of them with several strips of bacon between. He spread a layer of butter on the pancakes, a puddle of syrup, then cut into the stack. The first bite tasted like heaven after hours of chores. He chewed and watched his mother put one pancake on her plate and pour just a trickle of syrup on it.

His mother shook her head as she watched him eat. "You've been doing that since you were a boy."

"My best invention." He took another bite.

"I love you, but you're in a rut," she told him.

"Am not."

"Are, too."

"Why change something that works?" he asked her as he swallowed another bite.

"I'm worried about you."

He paused, his fork halfway to his mouth. "Worried about me? Why?"

"I looked out the window before you came in. I saw you standing there watching Rachel Ann again. When are you going to say something to her?"

"Gotta go," he said, picking up his plate and carrying it to the sink. "See you later."

"We'll talk later!"

He grinned as he grabbed his hat and left the house.

2

*R*achel Ann plucked the clothespins from the sheets hanging on the clothesline and dropped them into the pin basket. The brisk wind flapped the sheets at her face, and she breathed in the fresh scent of sun-warmed cotton. Laundry day was long and hard, but there was nothing better than sleeping in sheets dried outdoors. Sheets dried with a scented paper sheet of fabric softener she heard *Englischers* used just couldn't be as good.

Sam ran through piles of leaves, shrieking and scooping up handfuls of them and throwing them over his head. When he ran toward her she stepped in front of her laundry basket. "Stop right there! You're not getting my clean laundry dirty."

He just laughed at her and grabbed at the little crib quilt she'd folded and laid on top of the basket. "Mine."

"That's not to play with in the yard, Sam! Give it back!" He ran from her, leading her on a merry chase around the yard.

"You come back, you little monster! I have to get supper started!" She wanted to make something special for dessert. Her *daed* always loved it when she baked.

Giggling, he ran, his pudgy little legs pumping. She caught him near the fence by the road and swung him up in her arms. "You're not supposed to be over on this side of the yard! Now give me that and go play over by the house."

She set him on his feet and tried to snatch the little quilt before he got away, but he was too fast for her. He ran in the direction of the family dog. Brownie jumped up and ran for the front porch. Poor dog, thought Rachel Ann.

A car horn honked and she glanced over to see Michael pulling his car up in front of the house. He waved for her to walk over. She checked to see if Sam sat on the porch playing with Brownie.

"How about a ride?" Michael asked, throwing his arm across the seat. "I put the top down just for you."

Rachel Ann bit her lip. "I can't. I have to get the laundry in and supper started."

"Just a short drive," he urged. "All work and no play makes Jill a dull girl."

"Who's Jill?"

"You, silly."

"I can't right now," she said, backing away from temptation. "Maybe later."

Michael frowned. "I might be busy later." He gunned the engine. "See you."

He accelerated from the curb, taking off with such speed the rear end fishtailed—swaying from side to side. Rachel Ann watched the car spew up a trail of dust before it stopped, did a U-turn, and came roaring back up the road toward her.

Behind her she heard Sam yelling, and then suddenly he was dashing into the street, right into the path of the car.

"Sam! *Nee*!" Rachel Ann screamed and waved her hands and ran after him.

Michael slammed on his brakes and swerved, but the bumper caught Sam and the impact tossed him into the air like a rag doll. He landed in a heap in the middle of the road and lay there, unmoving.

Sobbing, Rachel Ann knelt on the road and tears dripped down onto Sam's face as she bent over him. "Sam? Wake up, Sam. Please?"

She slid her hands under his little body to lift him and felt a hand on her shoulder.

"No! You can't move him!" Abram said sharply. "You might hurt him worse."

A car door slammed and Michael appeared. "I didn't mean to hit him! I couldn't stop."

Abram looked up. "Call 911."

Michael backed away. "I have to go. I can't—"

"Stop right there!" Abram told him, and he stood up. "We Amish forgive, but your *Englisch* police would charge you with hit-and-run. Now call 911, and let's get Sam the help he needs. Rachel Ann and I will both tell the police it was an accident."

Michael ran a shaking hand through his hair and nodded. He pulled out a cell phone and made the call. "We need an ambulance," he shouted into the phone. "There's been an accident."

Rachel Ann took the quilt Sam still clutched in one hand and gently eased it from his fingers. She covered him with it and smoothed his hair back from his forehead. "Wake up, Sam. Please wake up."

Abram's mother rushed up with a blanket. "Here, cover him with this. Keep him warm."

"*Danki.*" Rachel Ann tucked the blanket around Sam.

"I'll pray for Sam and all of you," Lovina said. She patted Rachel Ann on the shoulder.

Rachel Ann glanced down the road as she heard a siren. "Sam, wake up. You love fire engines. Don't you want to see the fire engine? And you get to ride in an ambulance and have the siren make lots of noise."

There was no holding back the sobs as he lay still, even as the vehicles came to a stop just a few feet away.

She looked at Abram. "Oh, Abram, he's not waking up."

"Here, we need to let them help Sam," he said, pulling her to her feet and moving her out of the way of the paramedics hurrying toward them.

"Are you the mother?"

Rachel Ann stared at the paramedic in front of her. "What? Oh, no, he's my brother. My *mamm* isn't home. I was watching him."

Rachel Ann answered one paramedic's questions, while she watched the others check Sam over, then carefully move him onto a gurney. He looked even smaller and more fragile. They loaded him into an ambulance and looked toward her.

Abram pushed her toward the ambulance. "Go. I'll find your parents and send them to the hospital."

One of the paramedics helped her climb into the back of the vehicle, and she sat down on the metal bench. Just before the doors were shut, she looked out and saw Abram standing there holding Sam's little quilt in one hand, his mother's blanket in the other.

She looked down at the skirt of her dress marked with two little handprints from when Sam had clutched at it. Adorable, annoying little Sam. All she wanted was for him to be alright.

&

"I understand you were a witness?"

Abram turned from staring after the ambulance to see a police officer looking at him expectantly.

"Yes, I was. Sam—the little boy—ran out into the road and the driver couldn't stop."

The officer wrote down what he said, and Abram stood there feeling frustrated when he wanted to go get Rachel Ann's parents. But he'd promised Michael he would say Sam had been hit by accident.

Michael stood to the side of the road looking white and shaken. Abram couldn't help feeling a little sorry for him. As soon as the officer finished with his questions, he took the front steps two at a time and ran into the house. The door slammed behind him, sounding like a gunshot.

He hit speed dial on his cell and called a driver and asked if he could come right away. He was in luck—the driver was in between runs and said he'd be there in twenty minutes.

Abram disconnected the call and looked at his mother. "We'll pick up Martha in town at the grocery store and Leroy at the furniture store." He reached for his jacket and checked his pockets for money.

"Here," his mother said. She pulled some bills from her change purse and held them out to him.

"*Danki*. I'll pay you back."

"Don't be silly. I hope Sam is *allrecht*."

"Me, too. Pray for him. I'll see you later."

Alfred, a driver Abram used occasionally, arrived a few minutes later. They stopped off at the grocery store since it was closest.

He found Martha, Rachel Ann's mother, working as a cashier in the front of the store. Her smile quickly faded when she saw him stride toward her.

"What's wrong?"

There was no easy way to say it. "Sam got hit by a car. He's already on his way to the hospital. Go get your things and I'll talk to your boss."

"*Mein Gott*!" She went pale, but she did as he said and hurried off toward the back of the store.

Abram knew her boss wouldn't be happy to lose an employee in the busiest time of the day, but he couldn't refuse. He muttered his hope that Sam would be okay and to let him know if she needed the next day off.

Then they were off to get Rachel Ann's father at the furniture store. Martha brushed the tears from her cheeks and insisted she could tell her *mann* the bad news. She returned with him a few minutes later.

"We appreciate your coming to get us," Leroy said gruffly. "You could have just called."

"I thought this was the fastest way to get both of you to the hospital," Abram said, shrugging off the thanks.

"It was kind," Martha said, shaking her head. "How bad is he, do you have any idea? Was he—" she broke off, struggling for composure. "Was he awake when they put him in the ambulance?"

Again, the truth was hard—but unavoidable. "*Nee*," he had to say. "But the paramedics were there so quickly. He couldn't have gotten treatment faster."

They lapsed into silence as they rode to the hospital. Abram paid the driver while Martha and Leroy almost leaped out of the van the minute it pulled up in front of the hospital's emergency entrance. When Abram joined them he found Rachel Ann sobbing in her mother's arms.

"I'm so sorry! It's all my fault Sam got hurt!" she cried.

"It was an accident," Abram inserted. "He ran out so quickly the driver couldn't stop."

"Are you the parents?" a nurse asked them. "The doctor wants to talk to you."

She led them away, leaving Abram standing there with Rachel Ann. He pulled out a handkerchief and gave it to her. "Why don't we go take a walk while they talk? Maybe get some coffee. "

"Look at me," she said, staring at her dress. It was smudged with dirt and bore bloodstains from poor Sam's head. "I can't go anywhere looking like this."

"Nobody's going to care," he said. "Everyone has their own problems in a hospital, Rachel Ann. *Kumm*, it'll be good to get some coffee and sit down."

Rachel Ann glanced in the direction her parents had gone.

Abram touched her elbow. "They're here now. Let them see to Sam."

Finally, she nodded. They walked to the cafeteria and got coffee. Rachel Ann shook her head when he tried to get her to choose something to eat so he put a chicken salad sandwich for her and a roast beef sandwich for himself on his tray.

They found a quiet corner away from other diners and sat down.

"Eat," he said as he placed her sandwich in front of her. She frowned at him.

"You always were so bossy," she complained. But she picked up half of the sandwich and began eating.

"Thank you for getting my parents."

He shrugged. "It was the least I could do."

She met his gaze. "No, it was so wonderful you thought to do it. Not everyone would have."

Something passed between them. Abram felt like Rachel Ann was looking at him—really looking at him—for maybe the first time since they'd known each other. The noise of other diners, of the cafeteria staff, faded away. Time passed as they stared at each other.

The screech of a chair being dragged across the floor jarred them back to reality.

Abram glanced over and saw another couple taking up residence at the next table. Their quiet corner was no more.

Rachel Ann pulled her gaze away and began eating again. Abram picked up his sandwich and bit into it and wondered what had just happened. Had Rachel Ann looked at him the way he'd thought?

"I hope Michael didn't get into trouble," she said after a long moment.

Abram shook his head. "I told the officer it was an accident."

He noticed she kept glancing at the nearby clock and was eating quickly. She was obviously eager to get back upstairs.

"I'm going to go get some coffee to take to your parents."

They found her parents in the waiting room. Both of them looked pale, and her mother wept quietly into a handkerchief.

"Sam has a concussion and a broken leg," Leroy said. "They've taken him into surgery to fix the leg."

"Did he wake up before they took him up?" Rachel Ann asked.

Martha shook her head. "They did a CAT scan before they took him to surgery and said he has a concussion. They don't know when he'll wake up." She wiped her eyes with her handkerchief.

Abram handed her and Leroy their coffee, and he and Rachel Ann sat on the sofa opposite them. No one spoke and Abram couldn't think of anything else to do. A nurse poked her head in about two hours later and said the doctor would be out soon to talk to them.

"How is Sam doing?" Rachel Ann spoke up, but the nurse was already gone.

Another hour passed before the doctor came to talk to them.

"Sam came through the surgery well. He's going to have a cast and have to be on bed rest for a while, but children are still growing so they heal faster than adults. He'll be out of recovery soon and you can see him. "

"When will he wake up?" Leroy asked.

"I'm sorry, we just don't know."

"Thank you, Doctor," Martha said in a subdued tone.

An hour later, Abram followed Leroy, Martha, and Rachel Ann up to the pediatric unit and waited outside while they sat with him. Rachel Ann emerged a few minutes later with reddened eyes and tear-stained cheeks.

"*Mamm* and *Daed* said for me to go on home," she told Abram in a dull voice. "They must hate me for what happened to Sam."

"They don't hate you," he said quickly. "Come on, let's get you home. Here, sit down and I'll call the driver."

"I don't blame them," he heard her saying as he pulled out his cell phone. "I should have watched Sam better."

He made the call and turned back to Rachel Ann. But she wouldn't talk to him, wouldn't look at him, all the way home.

"I'll take you to the hospital in the morning," he said when they got out in front of their homes.

She nodded, but he wasn't sure she heard him. He watched her walk away, her shoulders slumped.

❧

Rachel Ann walked into her home and shut and locked the door behind her. The sound of the lock echoed in the quiet.

It didn't feel like home for a minute. There were no delicious smells coming from the kitchen, no sounds of Sam running through the house. No *Daed* sitting in his favorite chair reading *The Budget* at this time of the evening.

And it was all her fault.

Her feet dragged as she climbed the stairs to her room, hung up her jacket, and set her purse on her dresser. It was tempting to throw herself on her bed and cry herself to sleep, but she felt she'd cried herself out.

She was wrong. As she walked past Sam's room, she made the mistake of glancing inside. The youth bed their father had made for him stood in a corner of the room. His teddy bear and favorite bedtime story book lay on the sheets. Rachel Ann felt tears burn against the backs of her eyelids again as she remembered how gleefully he'd run around the yard with his quilt this afternoon.

She forced herself to walk past the room, past her parents' empty bedroom, and descend the stairs to the kitchen. For a moment she just stood there, wondering why she'd come to this room. Then she saw the kettle on the stove. Might as well make a cup of tea.

While the water boiled, she remembered how she'd never gotten to make supper and the cornbread her father loved. Maybe they'd get to come home tonight. Maybe they'd be hungry. She knew she was just dreaming, but thinking about making supper might keep her from thinking about where her family was right now.

She scrubbed potatoes and put them in the oven, then got a big bowl out of the cupboard, made cornbread, and slid the pan into the oven. Pork chops went into an iron skillet on top of the stove. Green beans canned at summer's end completed the meal.

While she was waiting, she made a cup of tea and sat drinking it. Delicious smells started wafting through the room, but they didn't make the room feel less lonely since she sat at the big kitchen table by herself.

Her mother had assured her she'd call if Sam's condition worsened. So she supposed no news was good news. She grimaced. She'd always hated that expression. It suddenly occurred to her she needed to call Leah and tell her she couldn't come to work the next morning. It was too late to call her at home, so she called the shop and left a message on the machine.

The food was finally done, but her parents didn't arrive. She put everything into containers and set them into the refrigerator, hoping the family would be home to enjoy the meal tomorrow.

With a sigh, she turned off the kitchen light and climbed the stairs again. She stopped at Sam's room and got his teddy bear and took it to her room. After she changed into her nightgown, she took it to bed with her, clutching it to her chest and wetting it with tears.

3

$\mathcal{R}$achel Ann woke to banging on the front door. She shot up straight in her bed and then realized it was morning. Groaning— she'd only fallen asleep as dawn's light crept in the window—she got out of bed and went downstairs to answer the door.

Abram stood on the doorstep holding a shopping bag. He grinned at her. "Your sleeping buddy?"

She blinked sleepily at him. "What?"

"What's his name?"

She glanced down as he gestured at her arm. Color flooded her face as she realized she clutched Sam's teddy bear under her arm— and she was standing in the doorway dressed in her nightgown. She quickly ducked behind the door and frowned at Abram as he laughed.

"Alfred is going to be here in twenty minutes," he said. "Better get a move on if you want to go see Sam."

"Be right back!" She shut the door and raced up the stairs to get dressed. She was back in ten, dressed, and carrying her jacket, purse, and the teddy bear.

"I'm taking it to Sam," she said when Abram glanced at it again.

"Never doubted it," he said. He lifted the shopping bag in his hand. "I've got another surprise in here for him."

Before she could ask what it was, the van pulled into the drive.

Abram's mother stuck her head out the front door. "Tell your *mamm* and *daed* I'm praying for Sam. I'll let everyone I see today know."

"She'll get word out on the Amish grapevine," Abram said with a grin as he opened the van door and waited for Rachel Ann to climb inside.

"This was nice, but you didn't have to go to the hospital again."

"I want to see how the little guy is doing."

Rachel Ann knew Sam followed Abram everywhere; he practically idolized him. Abram was the youngest in his family and never seemed to mind his little shadow.

Martha and Leroy looked haggard when Rachel Ann and Abram walked into Sam's room. Rachel Ann's heart ached when she saw his little head swathed in bandages and his leg engulfed in a big cast. He looked so tiny and defenseless.

"Here, put this on him," said Abram. He reached into the paper bag he'd carried and pulled out Sam's quilt—all washed and dried and none the worse from yesterday.

She held it to her chest for a moment—so surprised at his thoughtfulness—and then walked over to tuck it around his little body. His teddy bear went under one arm, and then she tucked the quilt over him, too. Maybe it was her imagination . . . she thought she felt the barest movement . . . but when she looked at Sam's face his eyelashes remained as still as his little body.

Abram looked at Leroy and Martha. "My *mamm* sent her breakfast sandwiches and coffee. We thought you might like a break from the room."

"I don't want to leave him," Martha said.

"I can stay with him," Rachel Ann spoke up. "I already had breakfast and I'd like to sit with him." She hadn't eaten breakfast—food was the last thing she wanted. She just wanted to see Sam.

Her mother hesitated a moment.

"Please?"

Leroy stood and held out his hand to his *fraa*. "Might do us good to stretch our legs a bit, get some coffee. Rachel Ann'll let us know if Sam wakes."

Martha nodded. "We'll be in the waiting room."

Rachel Ann pulled a chair up beside Sam's bed and sat. "C'mon, sleepyhead, wake up. I brought your bear and your storybook."

A nurse came in to check Sam's temperature and blood pressure. She smiled at the bear. "I see we have another patient."

"He loves that bear."

"Beautiful quilt," the nurse said, admiring it as she folded up the blood pressure cuff.

She smiled. "I made it when my mother told me she was having a baby. I'm not good at sewing, but I wanted to make something for her to put in the crib."

"Well, I think it's beautiful. I could never do something like this."

"You could if you took a quilting class at the shop where I work," Rachel Ann told her. "Naomi is a great teacher. She makes it look easy, and the students have fun." She dug in her purse, found one of the cards Leah kept on the front counter in the shop, and handed it to the nurse.

"I'll think about it." She smoothed the quilt over Sam's shoulders.

"When's Sam going to wake up?" Rachel Ann blurted out.

The nurse's smile faded. "I'm sorry, I don't know. Sometimes the brain gets such a shock it just needs time to recover. It could be today or days from now. He's in good hands. His doctor is the best in the area."

She looked at Rachel Ann. "And remember he's in the best hands. He's in God's hands."

Rachel Ann nodded. But God had taken little Daniel Zook home last year. What if He took Sam? She didn't want Him to have

Sam. She wanted Sam to stay here and wake up and be the little brother she loved.

Surely God wouldn't punish her for not being a good sister and take him, would He?

The nurse paused at the door. "Talk to him. He can hear you even if he doesn't react."

She turned her attention back to Sam. "You heard her. She says you can hear me. So I want you to wake up, you hear? I will get you anything you want, if you wake up. You've scared *Mamm* and *Daed* and me long enough. Nobody's mad at you. But we'd like it if you woke up and talked to us, *allrecht*?"

But although she watched his face carefully, his lashes lay still on his cheeks and the rise and fall of his little chest was the only movement he made.

She started when there was a quiet knock on the door. Her eyes widened when she saw Michael stick his head in.

"Is it okay if I come in for a few minutes?" he asked, glancing around the room.

She stood and clasped her hands in front of her. "Sure."

"Where are your parents?"

"They're having breakfast with Abram, my next-door neighbor."

He pulled on a string in his hand and several brightly colored balloons followed him into the room and bobbed around his head.

"Is it safe for me to be here? I mean, are your parents mad at me?"

Rachel Ann shook her head. "They know it was an accident."

He tied the balloon strings to the footboard of the bed. "I was hoping the little guy would be awake to see these."

Her lips trembled. "He hasn't woken up yet."

"You mean yet today."

She shook her head. "No. Not since the accident."

"Oh man, I'm so sorry!"

She began crying, and he stepped forward and put his arms around her. "I'm so scared!"

"It's going to be alright," he said, patting her back.

Dimly she heard the door open. "Rachel Ann!" her father thundered.

❧

Abram was as shocked as Rachel Ann's *daed* when he opened the door to Sam's hospital room.

Rachel Ann stood in the arms of Michael—the *Englisch* man whose car had hit Sam!

She jumped back, looking so guilty Abram couldn't help wondering if they'd been kissing. A shaft of jealousy shot through him.

"Michael was just giving me a hug," she said, wiping tears from her cheeks with her hands. "We weren't doing anything bad."

"There is no touching for any reason," Leroy told Michael sternly.

"Yes, sir, I mean no, sir," Michael said. "I'm sorry. It won't happen again."

He extended a shaky hand to Leroy. "I'm Michael Lansing. I'm so sorry I wasn't able to keep from hitting your son. He darted out into the road so fast—"

"Abram told us," Martha said. She glanced at the balloons that bobbed in the breeze from the air conditioner vent. "Sam loves balloons."

Michael rubbed the palms of his hands on his jeans. "I didn't just come to bring the balloons. I wanted to tell you all the bills for Sam's treatment will be taken care of."

Martha's hand flew to her mouth. "Oh my," she said, and she stumbled toward a nearby chair and sat down.

"Maybe you should talk to your parents before you undertake such a responsibility," Leroy said.

Michael stood straighter and met his gaze. "I did and we talked to my insurance company. They'll probably cancel me after this year and who knows what the premiums are going to be someplace else. But since it was my car that hit him, it's only fair. I'm just grateful the police saw it as an accident or things could have been worse for me."

He shrugged and turned to look at Sam. "Just hope the little guy comes out of this okay."

"They're running some more tests today," Martha spoke up. "A CAT scan, an MRI, I don't quite understand what it all means."

"They're tests that can see inside the head and body. They tell the doctors a lot. My brother's pre-med, so I've heard a lot about them." He glanced at the clock on the wall. "Well, I have to get to my job. Nice meeting you folks."

Leroy shook hands with him again and stroked his beard as he watched Michael leave the room. "Well, if it works out it will surely save our community from raising the money."

Martha sat quietly weeping. Leroy patted her shoulder.

Rachel Ann stood looking awkward and unsure of what to say. "Do you want me to stay so you both can go home and get some rest?"

Her father shook his head. "Doc's supposed to be coming in soon. What did Leah say when you called her?"

"I left a message on the machine at the shop."

"Well, your *mamm* and I will be here, so you can go on in. It's likely we'll be needing the money if we have to be away from our jobs to be here with Sam for some time."

Abram saw how she tried to hide her feelings, but he saw her shoulders slump, saw how she swallowed several times and tried to school her expression.

"I'll go on then," she said quietly. "Maybe after I can bring up the supper I made."

Her father nodded and went to stand and stare at Sam. Her mother searched for something in her purse. "Here," she said, holding out some bills. "For the driver."

"She doesn't need it," Abram said. "I can drop her off. I have some errands in town. She can ride with me and save the money."

Martha smiled at him. "Thanks, Abram." She stood and went to join her husband at Sam's bed.

Abram cast a quick look at Rachel Ann and saw how hurt she looked. He knew the couple was upset, but she was forced to walk out of the room without even a good-bye. Then he reminded himself it wasn't his place to judge. Troubled, he followed her out the door.

"I have a breakfast sandwich for you," he told her when they got outside. "Some coffee, too."

"Thanks, but I'm not hungry."

She sounded listless, not herself.

"You won't make it through the morning without eating."

"Abram, you sound like a parent."

"I'm a friend who cares about you."

"*Danki,* but I'll be *allrecht.*"

They sat on a bench outside the hospital, and Abram called the driver. Rachel Ann lapsed into a moody silence, and he decided to leave her alone.

She got out at Stitches in Time and turned to Abram. "*Danki* for everything, Abram. I appreciate it."

"Have a *gut* day!" he called after her.

"You, too," she said without enthusiasm. She disappeared into the shop.

"How's her kid brother doing?" the driver asked him. "She looked so upset I didn't want to ask her."

"He has a concussion and a broken leg. He still hasn't woken up."

"The wife and I will say a prayer for him tonight."

"Thank you."

The driver checked traffic and pulled out onto the road. "Okay, hardware store up next."

Leah glanced up from the cash register as Rachel Ann walked into the shop.

"Rachel Ann! I wasn't expecting to see you today. Does this mean Sam is doing much better?"

She shook her head. "My parents said I might as well be at work." She kept walking toward the back of the shop to put her things up. Her purse went into a cupboard and her jacket went on a peg. When she turned around, she found Leah standing in the doorway watching her and looking concerned.

"Where's your lunch?"

"I didn't pack one."

"What about breakfast?"

"I didn't pack one." Confused, she stared at Leah.

Leah walked into the room, pulled out a chair, and gestured for Rachel Ann to sit.

So she sat.

"What's wrong?"

"You know what's wrong. Sam got hit by a car. He's in the hospital."

"But that's not all, is it?"

Rachel Ann shook her head as the tears began to fall. "They blame me. Oh, they won't say anything, but they blame me. They wouldn't let me stay at the hospital last night and today they said I should go on to work because they wanted to talk to the doctor and if Sam was going to be in a long time and they had to stay with him then we might need the money so—" her breath hitched, and she couldn't go on.

Leah handed her a box of tissues, then filled the teakettle and set it on the stove. "They sound like they're so worried they don't know what they're saying."

"They hate me."

"*Nee, kind,* they don't hate you. They're just in a state of shock. It'll get better." The kettle whistled. "In the meantime, have a cup of tea and a pecan roll before you start working. You look like a ghost and I don't want you frightening the customers. And Rachel Ann, I can give you ten more hours a week since we're getting busier with the holidays."

Rachel Ann tried to smile. She did feel a little better after she ate and drank a cup of tea.

It felt good to be back in familiar surroundings in the shop, too. She'd been too miserable when she walked in to notice Mary Katherine working steadily at her loom at the other side of the shop. Naomi sat with some quilting students, and when she looked up and saw her, she waved. Anna wasn't in the shop. It must be her day to work at home. Emma stood at the fabric cutting table sorting through a box of fabric scraps for her rag baskets.

Leah asked her to take care of walk-ins while she worked on some orders, so Rachel Ann found herself busy helping customers find fabric and thread and yarn and such. Conversations about the right fabric, how much yardage to get, and whether cotton or nylon thread was better for a particular project kept her focused and her mind off worrying about Sam.

A steady stream of customers poured through the store. Whether they were Amish or *Englisch,* the shoppers were buying—and buying a lot, saying they were making their gifts for Christmas.

The list of projects was endless: a quilt for a grandson's college dorm room, a sweater for a granddaughter, booties, and a Christmas tablecloth . . . and that was just one customer's list.

"So what are you making?" Mary Ruth leaned on the fabric cutting table and asked. Then she straightened and put a hand over her mouth and looked embarrassed. "Oh, I'm so sorry. I guess you don't have much time with Sam in the hospital." She paused. "I guess it was lucky you were close by when the car hit him."

"What do you mean?" Rachel Ann paused in the cutting of the fabric.

"Well, if you hadn't been near he might have laid there hurt for a long time before he got help."

And if I'd been paying attention he might never have been hurt at all, Rachel Ann couldn't help thinking. Tears threatened and her hand shook on the scissors but she blinked back the tears and finished her job. She wrote the amount of fabric and price on a slip of paper and pinned it to the edge before handing it to Mary Ruth.

"Can I help you with anything else?" she asked with forced brightness.

"I think this is it for me today. It'll get me started with my main presents. See you at the wedding Thursday."

"Wedding?" She stared at Mary Ruth for a long moment. "Oh, *ya*, of course."

Mary Ruth took her purchases to the front counter for Leah to ring them up. Rachel Ann stood there staring around her at all the people, all the gaiety, all the color, and never felt so hollow inside— so empty and alone. Life seemed to be going on without her.

Naomi rushed up. "Rachel Ann, could you do me a favor? I forgot to bring the cookies I made for the quilting class. Could you walk down to the bakery and get some for me? I'd go, but I'm helping a student who came in early."

"*Schur.*"

It felt good to get out of the store and walk in the brisk fall air to the bakery. There was no need to put on the mask she felt she'd been wearing at the shop, no need to talk to anyone. She didn't pass anyone she knew, and the few tourists she passed only gave her curious glances.

Cinnamon, sugar, nutmeg, and other delicious scents hit her the moment she opened the door to the bakery. The aromas and the glass cases filled with dozens of different pastries didn't tempt Rachel Ann's appetite at all.

"Rachel Ann! How is your *bruder* doing?" Linda asked as she looked up from behind the counter.

"The same."

Linda's eyes showed compassion. "I'll keep praying. You look tired. Do you have time to sit and have a cup of tea?"

"*Nee.* I came to get two dozen cookies for Naomi's class."

A timer dinged. "I have some just coming out of the oven," Linda said. "Give me a second."

She headed to the back of the bakery and returned with a pan of raisin cookies. "I'm a little behind. Lost my part-timer two weeks before Christmas—my busiest time of the year." She jerked her head toward the Help Wanted sign tacked on the wall nearby as she took her place behind a glass case.

"Now, what kind?"

"Naomi said mix them up."

Into the box went Snickerdoodles, peanut butter, oatmeal raisin, chocolate chip, and butter cookies. "Want one on the house to eat now?"

"*Nee, danki*, I'm not hungry."

Linda closed the box, set it on top of the counter, and took the money from Rachel Ann. "Things will get better. Just keep trusting God."

Rachel Ann opened her mouth to say it was hard and then she shut it. Linda needed a part-time baker, and she needed to bring some more money into the house while her parents stayed at the hospital with Sam.

"Linda, you know I love to bake."

"*Ya,* and you're a fine baker." Linda lifted her brows.

"Tell me about the part-time job. What are the hours?"

A few minutes later, Rachel Ann walked out of the bakery, a box of cookies in her hands and a new job starting early the next morning. Linda had even said her driver could pick her up on the way.

Linda had said to trust God. Who knew He'd provide what she needed so quickly.

Now if He'd just heal Sam.

4

$\mathcal{A}$bram woke when he heard a van pull into the driveway of Rachel Ann's house. He got out of bed and looked out the window, wondering if her parents were coming home late from the hospital.

The door to the van opened, and he recognized Linda from the bakery in the lit interior. Rachel Ann stepped inside, the door shut, and the van drove away.

This had been going on for a week. How on earth was Rachel Ann going to manage working a nearly full-time as well as a part-time job?

He went back to bed—he didn't get up for another hour or so as a rule—but instead of sleeping found himself thinking about her.

Leroy and Martha had come home last night while he'd been outside, and he'd talked with them for a few minutes. Rachel Ann had nodded to him but walked inside as he checked on Sam's progress. She had looked pale and quiet.

Whenever a member of his community ended up in the hospital and accumulated big medical bills everyone rallied to help pay them. Abram decided he'd go visit the bishop and see what was being done for the family to help with Sam's expenses. Yes, Michael had said he and his father had talked to their insurance company about paying the hospital bills, but who knew if it could be depended upon. And it didn't pay for the wages Martha and Leroy were missing as they sat with their son at the hospital.

In the end he got up, his mind too abuzz with his thoughts. Might as well get started with the chores. He had Leroy's horses to feed and care for as well as his own. Then he could hitch up the buggy and go on into town.

He dressed and tried to be quiet as he went downstairs for coffee, but a few minutes later his mother padded into the kitchen bundled up in her warm robe.

"You're up early," she said as she took a seat at the table.

She nodded when he held up the percolator, and he poured her a cup and set it before her.

"I heard the van picking up Rachel Ann." He sat and added sugar to his coffee. "Why are Leroy and Martha allowing her to work herself to death?"

"It's not for us to judge," she said quietly. "I know you care about her but so do her parents. There must be some reason she wants to do it. Maybe she's trying to bring in some extra money since Leroy and Martha aren't working right now."

He frowned into his cup. "But you know our community will be helping." He rubbed his forehead. "So much changed so quickly. And is still changing. I can't imagine what will happen if Sam doesn't recover. It's all so sad. So unnecessary. Why does a little boy have to be hurt and his family devastated like this?"

"Are you questioning me—or God?"

Abram looked up at her. "I find it hard to figure out why something like this happened—why it *had* to happen. How is this God's plan? I know it's His will. He made it happen. But how does this figure into His plan?"

"It's not our job to try to tell God what to do or how to do it. We have to trust, Abram. We have to take some things on faith. One thing I know: God isn't punishing their family."

"I wish I felt as sure. I know Rachel Ann, and I know she's probably punishing herself for Sam being hurt."

"You'll be there for her as a friend." She got to her feet. "Now why don't you go take care of chores and I'll start breakfast."

"You should go back to bed and get some more rest. I can see you're in pain."

"I can do it later. How about *dippy* eggs and sausage and biscuits?"

"Sounds good. I'll be back in no time."

She laughed. "I thought you would."

❧

Rachel Ann had been cooking and baking since she was a little girl. But she'd never baked such huge amounts of cookies and pastries at one time.

Linda had set up her bakery to look like the inside of an Amish kitchen since the tourists liked to buy "the real thing" as they called the authentic cookies, whoopie pies, and other goodies. There were no big stainless steel mixers, so Rachel Ann felt her arms were getting a real workout as she used a big wooden spoon to mix up a batch of pumpkin whoopie pie batter in an enormous red pottery bowl.

"How are you doing back here?" Linda came back to ask. "Here, let's get a little cool air in here. You're looking a little warm." She opened a window, and a welcome gust of cool fall air drifted in.

It was warm wearing a big white apron over her dress, but Rachel Ann didn't mind. She was enjoying filling the big baking sheets with scoops of cookie dough and putting them in the giant ovens roaring with heat. She slid the last sheet of the current batch into the oven, set the timer, and stretched her sore back muscles.

Next, she was trying Linda's recipe for red velvet whoopie pies, a tourist favorite. She glanced at the clock. Another hour and she had to switch gears and go to her other job.

Linda came back with two steaming mugs of coffee. "Sit, you have time for a break before that batch comes out."

Rachel Ann perched nervously on a stool. Linda had a reputation for being a stern taskmaster—fair but expecting a lot out of her workers. So far Rachel Ann thought she'd done pretty well—she'd only burned one batch of cookies.

"I've known you since you were born so I had no doubt you'd be a hard worker," Linda told her.

Relieved, Rachel Ann smiled. "*Danki.*"

"I do think you're pushing yourself just a bit, though," she said. "You're doing nearly twice as much as my last part-timer. I don't want you to wear yourself into the ground."

She glanced over at the oven as the timer went off. "What have you got in there right now?"

"Gingerbread cookies. I think I have time to do a batch of red velvet whoopie pies before I leave."

"*Gut.* People love those. Just watch your time. I don't want to make you late to Leah's."

Rachel Ann nodded and slid from her stool. She grabbed potholders, pulled out the cookie sheets, and laid them on a wooden table to cool. "I thought I'd take a gingerbread boy to the hospital for Sam." She used a spatula to slide two of the cookies onto the table to decorate.

"I didn't realize he'd woken up. How wonderful!"

Her face fell. "He hasn't, but I'm hoping."

Linda patted her hand. "All in God's timing, dear one."

Rachel Ann looked into Linda's kind eyes and bit back the words she wanted to blurt out. Why did God have to be so slow? She wanted Sam awake and okay *now*.

She decorated the gingerbread boys with raisin eyes, a cocky white icing grin, and a jacket of red icing and green gumdrop buttons. They went into a bakery box lined with several layers of scrunched up tissue to protect them.

"See you tomorrow," she told Linda when she walked into the front of the bakery.

"Have a *gut* day and tell your parents I'm praying for Sam," Linda said. "Oh, here's your paycheck. There's a little something extra in it for your efforts."

"*Danki*," she managed, a little overwhelmed with Linda's kindness.

Earlier she'd wished God's timing was faster, and it was no different when she did her shift at Stitches in Time. She just wanted the day to be over so she could visit Sam. It had been a week since the accident—a long week. Time for Sam to wake up.

Leah smiled when Rachel Ann approached her at the front counter at the close of the business day and asked if there was anything else she needed to do.

"*Nee, kind*, it's time for all of us to be done with work and be with our families," she said with a smile. She reached into the cash drawer and handed Rachel Ann her paycheck then glanced at the front window. "There's your ride now."

Rachel Ann clutched her paycheck to her chest. It was going to feel so good to hand over not one but two paychecks to her parents tonight.

"See you Sunday!" she called and hurried outside. The van door opened, and to her surprise Abram stepped out.

She stopped in her tracks. "What are you doing here?" A horrible thought struck her. "Nothing's wrong with Sam?"

"*Nee*, I'm just catching the same ride as you," he assured her quickly. "I had to be in town and, if you don't mind, I'm going to stop by and see Sam with you."

"No, I don't mind." She climbed into the van, said hello to the driver and other passengers, and settled into her seat.

Abram climbed inside and shut the door then took the seat next to her. It was a little disconcerting—she'd never sat quite so close to him. He glanced at the bakery box she held carefully on her lap.

Rachel Ann caught his glance of curiosity and hid her smile. Abram had quite a sweet tooth. She just bet he was wondering what was inside the box. And she had no doubt he'd be trying to get a bite of one of the cookies if she let him.

Her parents were just leaving to get some coffee in the cafeteria when they arrived. "Our driver will be here in forty-five minutes to take us home," Leroy told them as they left.

"Sam, Abram and I are here to see you," Rachel Ann announced as they entered the room.

"Hi, Sam," Abram said before he took one of the chairs beside the bed.

Rachel Ann moved quickly to the bed and set the bakery box on the end of it. She leaned down, gave him a quick kiss on his chubby little cheek, and then took a seat. Reaching into her tote, she pulled out a book and opened it.

"Sam, the nurse told me people can hear when they're unconscious so I'm going to talk to you about Christmas," she told Sam. "It's coming up soon, Sam, and you're going to want to be out of here and home so you can hear *Daed* read the story about Jesus and get your presents."

She glanced at Abram who'd quietly taken a seat on the other side of the bed.

"I brought your story about the gingerbread boy, Sam." She read the story, turning the pages and glancing at him occasionally to see if there was any change in his expression.

"And that's the story of the gingerbread boy," she said, sighing as she finished and closed the book. "I brought you a surprise, Sam. Maybe you'd like to wake up and see it."

She opened the bakery box and lifted a cookie out of it. "Ah, Sam, you should see Abram looking at your cookie. It's a gingerbread boy I baked just for you." She waved it under his nose. "Smell it? It's all sugar and spice and raisin eyes and gumdrop buttons. Yummy, Sam."

When there was no reaction, Rachel Ann turned to Abram and held out the cookie. "What do you think, Abram? Doesn't it look like a delicious cookie? Bet you'd like to eat it. But it's Sam's cookie."

Then she realized Abram's attention was focused totally on her. "You smell so good," he said. "All sugar and spice."

"It's from working in the bakery," she said, a little disconcerted. Abram had never looked at her quite like this.

She drew in a deep breath to steady herself and caught the scent of wood on him. It was a familiar scent—her father worked as a furniture maker and often smelled the same.

But as they continued to stare at each other, he didn't remind her of her father at all.

"I—uh, do you want a cookie? I have more in the box." She drew back and gestured at it.

"Would love one. *Danki.*"

She gave him the one in her hand just as her mother walked into the room.

"What's going on?" she asked, her gaze moving from the two of them sitting close to the box on Sam's bed.

"I just made some cookies and was telling Sam about them."

Martha moved closer. "There's sugar on his cheek. You didn't try to feed him any, did you? He could choke."

"*Nee,* of course not! I just waved it under his nose. The nurse said people who are unconscious can hear so I talked to him about Christmas."

"Yes, well, I don't know I agree with her theory," Martha said with a frown. She brushed at his cheek and straightened. "It's time to go home."

Feeling chastened, Rachel Ann closed the bakery box and stood. "Bye, Sam. I'll see you after work tomorrow." She leaned down and kissed him, and several grains of sugar stuck to her lips. As she walked out of the room, salty tears mixed with the sugar on her tongue.

The trip home was silent.

Rachel Ann and her parents looked exhausted as they climbed into the van, so Abram didn't attempt to carry on a conversation with them. Other passengers seemed just as tired and didn't talk much.

Halfway home Rachel Ann's head slid down to rest on her mother's shoulder, and it appeared she fell asleep. Martha pulled back a little and murmured something Abram couldn't hear, but Rachel Ann straightened and put a little distance between herself and her mother on the seat and didn't nod off again.

Abram ached for Rachel Ann. His mother had said her parents weren't unloving, just a little preoccupied and, like many Plain folk, didn't often show affection in public, and Martha had always seemed a little stern since she was a former teacher. But most of the passengers in the van were Amish and wouldn't have thought anything of Rachel Ann asleep on her *mamm*'s shoulder. He'd seen other people nap on the ride to and from work. Work days were often long and hard, and travel to and from work added to them.

He'd been up since before dawn and put in a long work day making furniture, but strangely, he felt energized. Part of it was because he didn't often go into town and he'd never worked in the furniture shop. He'd enjoyed doing something different and the company of other men engaged in the same work.

They arrived home, and Abram's mother came out onto the porch and waved to them. "There's a nice supper waiting for you. Enjoy!"

"*Danki*, Lovina," Martha called.

"I better do chores first," Leroy said.

Abram clapped him on the back. "*Nee*, you won't. You go on in and eat supper, and I'll take care of them."

He went into the barn and began feeding and watering the horses. Betty leaned over her stall and greeted him. Abram stopped to stroke her side. He'd swear she batted her eyelashes at him before rubbing the side of her face against his arm.

"You two flirting again?"

Abram turned to grin at Rachel Ann.

"Here, I figured you'd want to have a treat for your special girl." She held out a small apple.

He laughed as the horse nudged him to take the apple. "Is she like this with your *daed*?"

"*Nee*, just you. She knows she can charm you."

He found himself wishing he could charm her as easily as her father's horse. "You didn't have to bring this out here. You should be inside eating your supper."

"I'm not hungry."

"Did you eat too many Christmas cookies at the bakery?"

She shook her head. "You don't tend to do that when you're preparing food. Not only is it unhygienic, you just lose interest in eating it when you're exposed all day."

"It *was* one good gingerbread man."

He watched her smile bloom. "I'm glad you liked it. Wish Sam would have woken up and taken a bite of it."

"Soon," he said. "Soon."

Her lips trembled. "You can't promise that." She sighed. "Well, thank you for doing *Daed's* chores so he can rest."

"I'm happy to help."

She smiled. "*Gut* Abram."

Then she turned and left him, moving with her quiet grace.

He gave the apple to Betty, walked out of the barn, and came to a stop when he saw Rachel Ann standing at the foot of the driveway talking to someone in a car. Michael. It was that Michael guy who had hit Sam with his car. He said something to Rachel Ann, and she turned and walked back to her house, went in for a minute, then came out again and got into Michael's car.

Abram shut the barn door with a thump. He crossed the yard and climbed the steps to his house, suddenly feeling tired.

"There you are," his mother said, looking up from setting a plate on the table for him.

"I was doing Leroy's chores."

"You're a *gut* man."

"*Ya, gut* for me." He washed his hands and took his seat at the table.

"You don't sound happy, *sohn*. What's the matter?"

He gave her a rueful glance. "Rachel Ann just called me *Gut* Abram."

"I gather it's not what you'd like her to call you."

He snorted as he split a roll open and slathered butter on it. "*Nee.*"

She poured a cup of coffee for both of them and joined him at the table. "You can't make someone see you for what you are. They recognize something special in you or they don't. If she doesn't, she's not the woman God set aside for you."

"I know." He picked up his fork and stirred the mashed potatoes on his plate. "She just went off with the *Englisch* guy again."

His mother reached across the table and patted his hand. "I don't see it going anywhere. Rachel Ann just needs to grow up a little. She's experimenting a bit during her *rumschpringe* with a look at *Englisch* life. It's just a rebellion against her parents because they're so strict. But Abram, she's not going to leave her family and her church."

He shrugged and used his fork to stab a piece of chicken on his plate.

"I hope you're right. But it still doesn't mean she'll look my way when she's done with Michael and her *rumschpringe*."

"She might not, but I think she's a smart young woman. Time will tell." She covered her yawn with her hand. "Well, it's bed for me. *Gut nacht*."

With that, she got up, set her cup in the sink, and left him to eat his supper.

5

$\mathcal{A}$ car pulled up into the drive and honked.

Rachel Ann found herself smiling when she saw Michael behind the wheel.

He leaned out the window. "Hey, pretty lady, wanna go for a drive?"

She bit her lip. "I don't know, I just got home . . ."

"If you're hungry we can grab a hamburger."

"*Nee*, I mean no, I'm not hungry. Give me a minute. I need to tell my parents."

"Don't be late," was all her mother said when she told her she was going for a drive.

She got into the car and fastened her seat belt. "I can't be out late."

"It's Friday."

"I'm tired. I've had some long days the past couple weeks. I've been working at the bakery in the mornings, you know, the one near the shop. Then I go to see Sam."

"How's the little guy doing?"

"There's been no change."

He bent his head, then looked at her. "That's rough. Maybe a nice ride will help."

They drove through an *Englisch* neighborhood where Christmas lights were beginning to twinkle on. Rachel Ann's eyes widened as she looked at the colorful light displays. So many lights. So many colors. It looked like so much work. So much money. Christmas decorations were so simple in her community and definitely didn't use electricity.

"What must the bills be for some of these displays?" she asked him.

He shrugged. "Pretty high. But it's just once a year. How do Amish people decorate for Christmas? I mean, since you don't use electricity?"

"We put evergreen boughs on the mantel, candles, that sort of thing. My *mamm* likes to put pots of poinsettias around. No Christmas trees . . ." She trailed off. Unless Sam improved dramatically—and soon—she doubted they'd be decorating or celebrating Christmas.

Michael left the *Englisch* neighborhood and headed out of town.

"Listen, I know where there's a party."

"Sorry, I can't tonight. I'm just too tired. I'll understand if you want to drop me off back home and go yourself."

"Nah, it's okay." He shot her an easy grin. "We'll have our own party. I have something to celebrate."

He pulled into a convenience store parking lot. "What kind of snacks do you like?"

"Thanks, but I told you, I'm not hungry."

"Tostitos and salsa it is. Back in a minute."

When Michael returned to the car a few minutes later she realized she'd almost fallen asleep. He set a grocery bag on her lap and started the car.

"So what do you have to celebrate?" she asked him.

"School's over for the semester," he said as he drove. "Now I get to take a break. The parents are even talking like they might give me the money to go to Florida for the break."

The drive relaxed Rachel Ann—maybe a little too much. She was finding it hard to stay awake even though Michael entertained her with stories of finishing up his final exam.

"Now I'm off until after the first of the year," he said. "Even pulled up my GPA so my dad is happy."

"GPA?"

"My grades." He pulled down a deserted road and shut off the car.

Rachel Ann felt a little uneasy. She hadn't ever parked with a man before. That was what the *Englisch* called it—parking. And when you parked you made out. She knew what it meant. Her heart jumped into her throat. She wasn't ready.

He reached for her and she jumped back and her head hit the car window.

"Hey, easy! I'm not going to attack you." He took the bag from her, pulled out a six-pack of beer, and handed one to her.

"I don't drink much," she said. What a thing to say. She didn't drink at all. She started to hand it back to him, but he'd already popped the top on his own.

"It'll relax you," he told her. "And it's just one. For me, too. Not taking a chance on a DUI."

He turned and set the rest of the six-pack on the floor of the back seat. "Aren't you going to drink your beer? Don't tell me it's your first beer."

"Of course not," she lied. She didn't know why she lied. It just felt a little weird admitting she was twenty-one and had never tasted a beer.

She took a sip and scrunched her nose. It tasted a little bitter, a little yeasty. She didn't like it much, so she took small sips. Michael didn't notice. He unscrewed the jar of salsa, ripped open the bag of Tostitos, and began shoveling chips loaded with salsa into his mouth.

"Hungry, huh? Didn't you have supper yet?"

"Hmm?" He popped another chip in his mouth. "Yeah, I had supper. You sure you don't want some?"

"No, thanks."

"Want another beer? You're not driving."

"No, this is plenty." She took another sip and watched him work his way through the bag of chips.

She looked up through the sunroof. It was a star roof tonight. They seemed to be moving. Getting blurry. She blinked. Must have been her imagination. She took another sip of the beer and felt a warm glow in her tummy, a fizz in her bloodstream. This must be why people drank . . .

Michael reached across her to grab some paper napkins from the glove compartment. He wiped his fingers off and grinned at her. "That filled me to half empty." He fingered the ribbon on her *kapp*. "I've never seen you with your hair down."

She brushed his hand away. "It's nothing special."

"Why don't you let me be the judge of that?" He tugged at the ribbon and she yelped. "Sorry."

"It's held on with pins," she said. She took another sip of the beer and realized she'd drained the can. Hmm. No wonder she was feeling so relaxed. She looked at Michael and sighed. Maybe she was being silly. He just wanted to see her hair.

She began pulling the covering pins from the *kapp*. Then she dropped it into her lap and reached to undo the bun at the nape of her neck. She loosened the strands of hair and ran her fingers through it.

"Wow, I had no idea it was this long," he said as her hair tumbled free and fell to her waist.

"I've never cut it."

He touched it. "Soft." He leaned closer. "Smells good. Like flowers."

She sighed again. He was such a nice man. She leaned back in her seat and looked up at the sunroof again. The stars wheeled and turned.

෨

Rachel Ann woke at the knock on her door. "Rachel Ann? Rachel Ann?"

She winced at the sound of her mother's voice. Her head pounded, and she found she was lying in bed fully dressed. To her utter horror, Rachel Ann saw she'd thrown up on her lap.

"Rachel Ann?"

"I'm fine!"

"You sounded like you were throwing up."

"No, I was just coughing. I think I'm coming down with a cold. If you don't mind, I'm going to stay in bed for a little while."

"Your *dat* and I will be going to the hospital. You'll have to stay away from Sam until you're well."

Rachel Ann flopped back on her pillow, muttering under her breath. It's what she got for lying. She sat up and began unpinning the bodice of her dress and carefully pulled it off. If she hadn't felt sick to her stomach before, she certainly felt it now as she looked at the skirt of the dress. Ugh!

She balled up the dress and wondered what to do with it. Her mother would ask questions if she put it in with the laundry. She couldn't throw it away—she didn't own enough dresses—so for now all she could think to do was shove it under her bed and try to wash it while her mother wasn't home. Moving around made her stomach roil. Climbing back into bed, she wrapped her arms around herself and took several deep breaths. Eventually, the nausea passed and she slept.

The next time she woke the room was filled with sunlight, sending shafts of pain into her skull. Squeezing her eyes shut, she groaned and turned to face the wall. Her hair fell in her face as she moved. She frowned. Usually she braided it before she fell asleep. Well, it was obvious the one beer on an empty stomach had affected her more than she'd thought. She supposed she should be grateful she hadn't run into either of her parents when she came home.

Then her eyes shot open, and she bolted up straight in bed. She pushed back her hair and stared down at herself. Michael had persuaded her to take down her hair last night and he'd touched it. She couldn't remember anything afterward. Had he persuaded her to do anything else? She pressed her hands to her temples and tried to remember, but everything was a blank.

Nausea swept over her again. She swung her legs over the side of the bed and barely made it to the bathroom in time. After she finished retching, she sank to the cold floor and began crying. What a mess she was, she thought as she wiped at the tears on her cheeks.

Finally, the chill from the floor forced her to get up and shower. She dressed, grabbed her soiled dress, and went downstairs. She washed her dress in the sink. Wrung it out the best she could and carried it upstairs to hang in her bathtub.

Deciding some fresh air might help her headache, she slipped on her jacket and took a cup of coffee out and sat in a chair on the porch to drink it. It was a little cool today, but she figured being outside might help her feel better.

"*Guder mariye*, neighbor!" Abram called from his porch.

She glanced over and waved and regretted the gesture when he took it as an invitation to walk over. She didn't feel up to conversation.

"You didn't go to the hospital with your *mamm* and *dat*," he said as he settled his lanky frame into a chair next to hers.

"No, I thought I was coming down with something when I woke up."

"Yeah?" He gave her a close look. "What?"

She closed her eyes and rested her head against the back of the chair. "Stupidity," she whispered.

"What?"

She opened her eyes and looked at him. "I just woke up feeling awful, and *Mamm* didn't want me to give Sam anything contagious. But it's just a bad headache."

"So you'll live?"

She stuck out her tongue at him. He laughed.

"What is it with you?" she asked him a little crossly. "You just seem to sail through life. Never in a bad mood."

"Oh, I get them. I just don't take them out on other people." He gestured at her cup. "Is there more in the kitchen? I could use a cup."

"Help yourself." She knew she should apologize, but she just wasn't ready to yet.

"Want me to refill your cup?"

She nodded and held it out to him. "*Danki.*" Here he was being nice even after she was cranky with him.

He came out with two cups and handed one to her. For several minutes the only sound was the creaking of his rocking chair and the occasional car passing on the road.

"I know you're going through a lot, Rachel Ann," he said quietly. "It's a difficult, confusing time, and I apologize if I've seemed to look like I have all the answers. I sure don't."

"I didn't have to bite your head off," she told him.

He grinned. "I'll survive. Headache better?"

"Some."

"How much longer are you working at the bakery?"

"Just through Christmas."

"*Gut.* It's been a lot for you to work two jobs."

She shrugged. "It's the least I could do. It's bringing in some extra money. And you know, I enjoy baking so it's not been a hardship."

"Rachel Ann, everything is going to work out. You'll see." He finished his coffee and set the cup on the table between them. "Did you have a nice time last night? I saw you go with Michael."

"It was *allrecht*," she lied. "We just went for a drive." She didn't like the way he was looking at her, waiting for her to say more. "What about you? Did you ever date an *Englisch* girl during your *rumschpringe*?"

He shook his head. "I'm not like you. I've never been interested in exploring the *Englisch* world."

Right now Rachel Ann was remembering the phrase about curiosity killed the cat.

"I will admit I went to an *Englisch* party or two."

"You did?" Shocked, she stared at him. He'd never shown any indication of that sort of behavior.

He reddened. "Don't you dare share that with anyone."

"Who would I share it with?" She studied him. "Was it because you weren't interested in the *Englisch* world—or because you had to help your *dat* with the farm the last few years he was alive?"

"It wasn't a sacrifice to help with the farm. I always loved growing things. *Daed* helped me discover how much I loved growing things. It was a gift worth far more than the land he left to me after he died."

A brisk wind sent some leaves skittering down the drive. Rachel Ann shivered.

"Cold?"

"A little."

"You should go inside before you do get sick."

"There you go again, thinking you know what's best for me."

"Tell you what—if you're feeling *allrecht* and your *mamm*'s okay with it, I'll take you to see Sam at the hospital tomorrow. I haven't seen the little guy in a couple days."

"That would be nice." She debated apologizing again for being cranky with him earlier, but he was already getting to his feet.

"Oh, here, I saw this in your driveway earlier this morning," he said and dropped her *kapp* in her lap. "See you tomorrow."

⊱⊰

Abram saw what little color Rachel Ann had in her face drain, leaving her as white as the *kapp* he dropped in her lap.

"I found it before your parents came outside. I picked it up and saved it for you."

She closed her eyes, and when she opened them she didn't look at him. "*Danki.*"

He left her then. It wasn't his business how the *kapp* had come to be in the drive instead of on her head . . . he'd speculated, of course. He couldn't help it. Amish girls and women were never seen without them. Once, he'd even seen a toddler cry when her *kapp* slipped off her head.

If the wind had caught it and snatched it from her head, surely she'd have tried to catch it. Maybe she'd accidentally knocked it off getting into the car—no, that couldn't have happened. Women used covering pins to secure their *kapps* to their hair. Had she taken it off once she was in the car with Michael?

The last question plagued him most of all.

This Michael . . . he didn't know anything about him since he was *Englisch*. What kind of man was he? Some *Englisch* guys liked to date Amish girls because they were so innocent, so much less assertive and more eager to please than *Englisch* girls. They thought they could talk the Amish girls into doing what they wanted.

Oh, he wasn't saying all Amish guys were perfect gentlemen. There were weddings conducted outside of the usual wedding season, and births occurred less than nine months after some ceremonies. But he couldn't help worrying about Rachel Ann seeing Michael.

He went into his house and tried to distract himself by doing some work on his books. The farm was in good shape financially. His father had been one of the first in the area to grow organic produce, and Abram had followed in his footsteps. People were more conscious of what they ate these days and willing to pay a little more for organic.

The pile of seed catalogs caught his eye. Winter was the time when farmers got a break and had a chance to plan their crops, order their seed, do basic maintenance. He decided in addition to potatoes, zucchini, squash, and corn, he'd add some rows of a new variety of squash this year.

"Abram?" His mother stuck her head in the doorway of his den. "Marlon is here."

"*Danki.*" He walked outside to meet him.

"Got that desk ready?" Marlon, the owner of the furniture store Abram built furniture for in his spare time, sat in his buggy.

"It's in the barn. Pull into the drive and we'll load it."

Marlon looked impressed when he entered the barn with Abram. He ran a hand over the satiny surface. "*Gut* work. I'm glad you could finish it in time. We have an *Englisch* customer who ordered it for his daughter for Christmas."

They lifted it and carried it outside and loaded it into Marlon's wagon. Marlon tied it down so it wouldn't tip over on the ride into town.

"We could use a few more of the keepsake boxes if you have the time."

"I'll see what I can do."

"*Danki.* See you Monday."

"I'll be there."

Abram walked back to shut the barn door but instead found himself wandering inside. He had some time to work on another small project and looked over his stash of wood. He pulled out the pattern he used for the little boxes Amish women used to store the pins for their *kapps* and keepsakes and, from what he heard, *Englisch* women used for jewelry.

Kapps. It reminded him of Rachel Ann's *kapp* he'd returned to her earlier. Amish men never saw an Amish woman's hair uncovered unless they were married or their fiancées let them see it.

Once again he found himself wondering how Rachel Ann came to lose her *kapp*. An unaccustomed surge of jealousy swept over him as the thought struck him Michael might have gotten to see her hair down.

Disgusted with himself, he set the pattern down and left the barn. Restless, he went for a walk in his fields, his favorite place to think and reflect. They were barren now, resting for the season. Maybe it was time for him to stop looking in Rachel Ann's direction. He believed God set aside a woman for a man, and because he'd fallen in love with her he'd decided she had been chosen for him.

But it was evident from Rachel Ann choosing to date Michael and to be interested in *Englisch* life she was not only not in love with him—she wasn't even looking at the man who lived next door.

He kicked at a root protruding from the earth. When a crop didn't grow, you changed plans and planted something different. He was twenty-one now, and his farm was doing well. Other women had let him know they were interested, but he'd never pursued them because of how he felt about Rachel Ann. If he wanted a wife and a family, it was time to do something different.

He stood there in the middle of his fields, hands on his hips, and stared out at the road. Cars and buggies shared the road, all going somewhere on this Saturday afternoon. Tomorrow was Sunday—a church Sunday. If he remembered correctly, there would be a singing in the evening. He couldn't remember the last time he'd attended one. This time of year he didn't have the excuse of too much work to do on the farm . . .

And he no longer had on the blinders that made him see only Rachel Ann.

6

Rachel Ann chewed on her fingernails all the way to the hospital. She kept worrying over the night she went for a drive with Michael and didn't know how to stop herself from obsessing over it. It had kept her from being able to eat all day and made her so distracted at both jobs several people had asked if she was okay.

Then she walked into Sam's hospital room and her knees went weak.

The bed was empty.

She stumbled to a chair and sank into it. She couldn't breathe. Sam couldn't be . . . he couldn't be . . . she couldn't even think the word.

A nurse started to walk past the room, glanced inside, and stopped. "Something wrong?"

Rachel Ann waved at the bed. Tried to talk but she couldn't.

"Sam's just having another CAT scan downstairs," the woman said. She walked in and bent to give Rachel Ann a hug. "Breathe, honey. Sam's still with us."

She concentrated on forcing air into her lungs, but all she managed to do was hyperventilate.

"Calm down, he'll be back up here in just a few minutes. I'll go get you a cup of water."

"Thank you." Rachel Ann watched her hurry out of the room and shook her head. Seeing the empty bed had been as bad as seeing Sam hit by Michael's car.

"You're shaking," the nurse said when she returned with the water.

She took a sip of water and shrugged. "I shouldn't have jumped to such a conclusion."

"It happens more than you think."

She left, and Rachel Ann sat and watched the clock. Ten of the longest minutes she'd ever experienced ticked past before Sam was returned to his room. He looked so small in the bed. So still. She knelt by the bed, put her head down, and wept.

"Rachel Ann? What are you doing?" Her mother stood in the doorway looking stern. "Are you sick? I didn't want you to visit—"

"I'm not sick," she said, lifting her head. "I got scared to death walking in and finding Sam gone. They took him for a test and I didn't know. I thought he was dead." She heard her voice rising, becoming shrill, but she couldn't stop herself. "I thought he was dead!"

She burst into tears—great big hiccupping sobs she couldn't stop.

Her mother put her arms around her and patted her back, but it just made Rachel Ann cry harder. "Rachel Ann, you must stop! You'll make yourself sick!"

"What's going on?" she heard a familiar voice ask.

"She can't stop crying."

"Rachel Ann? You're not feeling any better?" the nurse asked her. She looked up at Martha. "Looks like anxiety to me. I'll be right back."

The nurse returned with a wheelchair and helped Rachel Ann into it.

"I'm not sick," Rachel Ann managed to say. She clutched her chest. It hurt to breathe. "Where are we going?"

"ER."

"I'll go with her," she heard her mother say as the nurse pushed the chair out of the room and into the hall. "Leroy, you stay here with Sam."

The ER bustled with activity, but the nurse got her right into a small exam room. "Anxiety attack," she said tersely to another nurse. "She's having some chest pain and difficulty breathing."

They helped her onto a gurney, stripped off her dress, and got a hospital gown on her, all the while taking her personal information. The oxygen they hooked up immediately began to relieve the tightness in her chest and make it easier to breathe.

She felt embarrassed they were making a big fuss over her when she felt she should have been able to calm herself down. Her misery must have shown because the nurse who'd brought her down patted her arm.

"It's nothing to be ashamed of, dear," she said. "This has been a stressful time for all of you. I have to go back upstairs, but you have them call me if there's anything I can do for you."

Rachel Ann nodded. "Thank you."

"I have a few more questions for you, and then the doctor will be in to see you," said a nurse who pulled her laptop computer on a rolling cart closer. "Are you single? Married?"

"Single."

"Are you pregnant?"

She froze, and her gaze shot to her mother who was reading a chart on the wall. "No," she said quickly.

The nurse paused and her fingers went still on the keyboard. Her eyes narrowed as she glanced at Rachel Ann's mother, then she asked a few more questions about her symptoms.

A man came in pushing a cart. "I'm here to draw some blood," he said cheerfully.

"I'll go see what's holding up the doctor," the nurse said. "Mrs. Miller, would you mind stepping outside for a few minutes while Ben here does his job? The room's a bit small."

Her mother nodded and left the room, closing the door behind her.

The nurse looked at Rachel Ann with kind eyes. "I sent her out so you can have some privacy. It's vital you're honest with us about whether you could be pregnant. We don't want to give you anything that could harm your baby if you're pregnant."

"I don't know if I am," Rachel Ann said miserably.

"When was your last period?"

"Three weeks ago."

The woman frowned. "So you think you got pregnant recently?"

Rachel Ann blushed. "I don't know. I was with my boyfriend last week . . . I was stupid, I had a beer and . . ."

"I see." Her face cleared. She patted Rachel Ann's hand. "It's too early for a pregnancy test, so I'll make a note for the doctor not to give you anything that could affect a baby just in case, okay? Think about purchasing a pregnancy test to use in a week or so if you miss your period. Then, if it's positive, make an appointment with your doctor, okay?"

She nodded and tried not to wince as her blood was drawn. Her mother returned to the room after the technician left, and then the doctor came in. She examined Rachel Ann and ended up diagnosing her with an anxiety attack just as the nurse had said.

"Sometimes our bodies just can't handle any more stress and this happens," she said, looping her stethoscope around her neck. "It's nothing to be ashamed of. I'm going to give you something for it, and you'll be fine."

She turned to Rachel Ann's mother. "How are you and your husband holding up?"

"We're fine," Martha said. She sat primly, her hands folded in her lap, her shoulders held stiff and straight. Rachel looked away from the disapproval on her face. *Mamm* didn't approve of being emotional in public.

"Well, if you need anything, please don't hesitate to reach out to us," the doctor said.

Rachel Ann took the pill a nurse brought in and swallowed it with some water. It was the last thing she remembered until the nurse shook her shoulder and woke her and told her they were discharging her.

Their driver was waiting in the ER parking lot. Rachel Ann's parents helped her into the van, and she slept all the way home.

❧

"I haven't seen you at a singing in a long time, Abram."

He turned from helping himself to a brownie during the break and found himself looking down at Sarah Zook.

"*Gut-n-owed*," he said. "I've been busy."

She pushed her wire-rimmed glasses up her nose and glanced around. "Is Rachel Ann here? Did you bring her?"

"No, why do you ask?"

She shrugged. "You're neighbors."

He couldn't help feeling relieved. There was no way he wanted anyone to think he'd harbored a secret crush on Rachel Ann for years.

"I miss seeing her. She was at church, but she and her parents rushed off right away afterward. And she's been working so much."

Abram heard the wistfulness in her voice. "Keep trying to see her. I think she'd appreciate it. She could use a friend right now. It's been tough on her with her brother in the hospital."

"I will." She smiled at him. "You're a good friend to her."

"We've lived next to each other all our lives."

"That's not it. I heard what you've been doing for her and her family."

He shrugged. "It's our way. I haven't done anything special."

"If you say so. I see you like my brownies," she said as he picked up another one.

"They're great."

"I'll make you some more and bring them by your house next time I stop by to visit Rachel Ann."

He studied her, wondering if she was talking to him because she was interested in him or if she was just making conversation. Singings were one of the activities where couples paired off—one of the reasons why he hadn't attended many. He didn't need to go looking for a woman because he'd always only had eyes for one— Rachel Ann.

But the more he talked to Sarah, the more he came to think she was just a nice young woman who wanted to talk to him. She'd been a year behind him and Rachel Ann in *schul* and so shy she barely spoke. While some of the other *maedels* wore dresses in brighter colors, she always wore browns and grays and reminded him of a quiet little mouse.

Others were drifting away from the refreshments and looking like they were about to start singing again. Abram had enjoyed singing the hymns, but tonight he was enjoying it even more talking to Sarah.

"Sarah, would you like to go for a drive?"

Her cheeks pinked and her eyes sparkled behind her lenses. "It would be nice. I came with my brother. Let me go tell him I'm getting a ride with you."

Sarah might have seemed shy, but once they were in the buggy and it was just the two of them traveling the dark roads in the buggy, she talked about everything from working with her parents on their farm to the upcoming holiday, to how David Zook had gotten a broken leg from being kicked by his horse.

The conversation turned to Rachel Ann.

"I never had any desire to experiment with the *Englisch* world like Rachel Ann," she said as she stared out the window of the buggy. "I know you probably think it's because I was too chicken, but I just wasn't interested in life outside our community."

"Why would I think it was because you were chicken?"

She turned to him and laughed self-deprecatingly. "Most of the time people don't know I'm in the room. I've always been like that."

"I knew you were in the room."

She shot him a quiet smile. "You're just being nice. You've always been like that."

"*Nice* sounds boring. And I'll take quiet over being around someone like . . . well, I won't say who or I'll lose my nice label."

She laughed. "I know who you mean. I saw her talking to you several times this evening."

"Sarah, did you come over to rescue me?"

"I might have."

They were traveling down a stretch of road unlit by streetlamps, but he could hear the smile in her voice. He grinned. She might be shy, but she had a sense of humor. He wondered why other men hadn't taken the time to look past her shyness and see there was something special about her.

He was truly sorry to have the evening end. "We'll have to do this again."

"That'd be nice. *Gut-n-owed*, Abram."

"*Gut-n-owed*, Sarah."

As he pulled into his drive, he realized he'd had a good time. He unhitched the buggy, led his horse into its stall, and watered it. When he stepped outside, he saw Rachel Ann and her parents were coming home.

He frowned. Something was wrong. Leroy and Martha were helping Rachel Ann from the van. She seemed unsteady on her feet. He wondered if she was sick. She'd seemed fine earlier when he had seen her.

"Do you need some help?" he called over, but Leroy shook his head.

Abram went inside and found his mother sitting at the kitchen table drinking tea.

He lifted his brows. "You weren't waiting up for me?" he asked incredulously.

She laughed and shook her head. "*Nee.* I just felt like a cup of tea before bed. The water is still hot if you want one."

He preferred coffee but didn't feel like firing up the percolator or settling for instant. So he poured a mug of hot water and sat at the table dunking a tea bag in it until the liquid was nearly black.

"Oh, for the days when caffeine didn't keep me awake," Lovina said. "There are some peanut butter cookies in the jar if you want."

"I had two big brownies at the singing," he said. "They were almost as good as yours."

She gave him an arch look. "Who makes brownies almost as good as mine?"

"Sarah Zook."

"Nice girl."

Abram nodded. "*Ya.* We went for a drive afterward." He drank half the tea and made a face. He just didn't care much for tea.

He yawned, then got to his feet. "Going to bed. See you in the morning." He bit back a smile at her look of disappointment when he bent to kiss her cheek. He knew her so well—she wanted to talk more about Sarah. Maybe he shouldn't tease her like this . . . but he couldn't resist.

At the doorway he turned. "We'll talk more in the morning."

She grinned and tossed a dishcloth at him.

❧

"I'm so glad we could come together today," Sarah whispered to Rachel Ann as they climbed the stairs to the Zook house.

"I can't stay long," Rachel Ann told her. Amish weddings went on all day, and there was no way she could bear sitting here trying to look like she was having a good time. "I want to go visit Sam."

"Just stay as long as you can." She sighed. "It's so good to see you again. I've missed you."

"I've missed you," Rachel Ann told her and meant it. All she'd done since Sam's accident had been work, visit Sam, sleep, and start the whole process all over again.

She watched with Sarah as Emma and Isaac said their vows before their friends and family. Sam's accident had meant she had to tell Emma she couldn't be one of her *newhockers*, her attendants.

Rachel Ann remembered how Isaac had been a little wild during his *rumschpringe*, cutting his hair in an *Englisch* style, driving around in his buggy with a sound system blaring hard rock. Emma had confided she was beginning to believe she and Isaac wanted different paths.

And then something had changed. His best friend had fallen off a roof they were working on, and it changed Isaac. It made him think about things, he'd told them. He joined the church, and now he and Emma were being married

Emma had never looked happier, and Isaac beamed as he sat beside her at the *eck*, the corner of the wedding table, and the wedding meal was served.

Rachel Ann turned to Sarah. "I need to go now."

"Can't you just have something to eat first?"

"I'm not hungry."

"You look like you've lost weight. Just eat a little something. Then maybe—" she hesitated. "Do you think I could go with you and see Sam?"

"You know he's not awake."

Sarah touched her hand. "I know. I'd like to go and just be there for you, Rachel Ann. You look like you're about to fall apart."

Rachel Ann sighed. "I already did."

"What?"

"I'll tell you about it later. *Allrecht*, I'll eat something, and then I'd love it if you come with me. I've missed seeing you, too."

She forced down some of the baked chicken and *roasht* and some of her favorite creamed celery. One bite of cake was all she could manage—the frosting was so sweet it was sickening to her.

"Well, look who's here! How did you manage to drag her here, Sarah?"

Rachel Ann looked up and saw Abram smiling down at her. No, he was smiling down at Sarah. Hmm, she thought. Interesting development.

"I could only come for a little while. We're about to leave. Sarah's going to the hospital with me to see Sam."

"I'd like to give you a ride, but I promised to drive several people home."

"It's *allrecht*," Rachel Ann said. "I already called the driver."

As it turned out, it was a good thing Abram didn't drive them. The minute they were in the van and on their way Sarah turned to her. "So what did you mean you'd already fallen apart?" she asked quietly.

Rachel Ann told her about the anxiety attack, carefully leaving out the part about the pregnancy scare.

"Oh my," Sarah said. She leaned over and impulsively gave Rachel Ann a hug. "I'm so sorry."

It felt good to have someone comfort her. Rachel Ann returned the hug and felt grateful Sarah had reached out to her.

"So, how is Michael? Are you still seeing him?"

"I haven't seen him for a few days," Rachel Ann said. "He's on break from his classes, so I imagine he's been having some fun with his friends."

"But you're still seeing him?"

"*Ya*, why?"

"Are you thinking of marrying him?"

"I'm just dating him. The whole purpose of *rumschpringe* is giving us a chance to look at what we want. It's all I'm doing."

"I don't think you can just say that," Sarah said, leaning forward and looking at her earnestly. "You're taking such a big risk."

"Risk?"

"If you get serious about him, you know what it means. Everything about your life changes. You lose your family, your friends. Your church."

Rachel Ann knew all that. She pressed a hand to her stomach. What Sarah didn't know was just how much she'd already risked.

7

Rachel Ann was glad to return to work on Monday. When she was working she didn't think about all her problems.

Her arm and shoulder muscles ached a bit after her morning mixing cookies and kneading bread and lifting heavy pans. She had to concentrate so she didn't get burned when she pulled the pans from the hot ovens. There was no question it was the most strenuous work she'd ever done, but she still enjoyed it.

Customers kept her on her toes at Stitches in Time. It was important to recognize regular customers and call them by name. She spent a lot of time familiarizing herself with the stock. She'd never felt skilled at quilting or knitting, so she worked hard to be better informed so she could answer her customers' questions. She'd learned not to let her attention stray after making a mistake cutting yardage for a customer.

All of it kept her mind off whether she'd suffer consequences from her drive with Michael. And worrying about Sam.

Elizabeth, her best friend and her cousin Saul's wife, showed up at noon. She hugged Rachel Ann. "Come to lunch with me."

"I brought my lunch."

"You can leave it in the refrigerator and eat it tomorrow. C'mon, it's my treat."

"Go, Rachel Ann, it'll be good for you to get out," Leah urged.

Anna walked over. "*Ya*, go."

"I'm outnumbered," Rachel Ann pretended to complain.

But there was something about Elizabeth. Her eyes sparkled and her foot tapped as she waited for Rachel Ann to agree. Something was clearly up.

So she went for her jacket and purse and followed Elizabeth out of the shop. They went to a nearby restaurant to save time and ordered.

"I wanted to see how you were doing," Elizabeth began. "Saul and I went by to see Sam yesterday. I know this has been incredibly hard on all of you. We've been praying."

"*Danki.*"

Their lunch came, and Elizabeth happily dug into the open-faced roast beef sandwich and mashed potatoes dripping with gravy. Rachel Ann picked up half of the ham and cheese sandwich she'd ordered and chewed with little enthusiasm.

She glanced up and found Elizabeth watching her.

"I'm not hungry," she said with a shrug

"You have to eat to have the energy to work," Elizabeth said. "I know you're working two jobs."

"You sound like a *mamm*." Then she stopped and stared, open-mouthed, at Elizabeth.

There was something different about her . . . a kind of excitement. A glow.

"Elizabeth?"

"*Ya?*" She smiled and then laughed and nodded. "*Ya*, Saul and I are going to have a *boppli*."

Rachel Ann jumped up and hugged her. "I'm so happy for you! Is everything *allrecht*?"

Elizabeth nodded. "The doctor said my having a miscarriage doesn't mean I'll have any problems, but he'll be monitoring me carefully."

She sat back down and listened to Elizabeth chatter and tried not to think about what her own reaction would be to a diagnosis of pregnancy.

"How soon did you find out?" she asked her. "I mean, how long after you missed your period did it take to know you were pregnant?"

"I did a pregnancy test ten days after I missed my period. Why? Rachel Ann, you're not—"

"No, no, of course not!" she said quickly. "I have a friend who's concerned she might be pregnant."

She didn't need to worry about being cross-examined— Elizabeth must have believed her because she was picking up the dessert menu propped on the table and looking it over. When Rachel Ann glanced over, she saw Elizabeth had polished off the large sandwich and mashed potatoes.

Elizabeth looked up. "Are you going to have dessert? No? Well, I'm having the apple crumb pie." When their server returned to the table, she ordered the pie and another roast beef sandwich.

Rachel Ann gasped.

"Oh, silly!" Elizabeth said with a laugh. "The sandwich is for Saul, not for me." She looked at the server. "I was about to say make the sandwich to go, please."

The server grinned and nodded. "Would you like a slice of pie for him as well?"

"Good idea. Thank you."

"So what else is going on in your life besides visiting Sam every day and working two jobs?"

"When is there time for anything else?"

"Are you still seeing the *Englisch* guy? What's his name?"

"Michael. *Ya.*"

She studied Elizabeth. "Did you ever date an *Englisch* man when you were in your *rumschpringe*?"

Elizabeth shook her head. "I just wanted to get away from being stuck in the house taking care of all my *bruders* and *schwesders* and left Goshen. I got on the bus to come here, met Saul, and that was it. Who knew God planned for me to meet the man he set aside for me on a Greyhound bus? Or that we'd be working at a store together every day and having a *boppli* later this summer?"

Elizabeth ate her pie with relish all the while chattering about the shop she and Saul owned. "I have been so hungry," she said. "I can't eat like this every day or I'll be big as a house."

Rachel Ann just smiled at her, glad to see her friend so happy.

Elizabeth set her fork down and sighed. "This has been nice. Let's not let so much time pass without seeing each other."

The server brought a bag with Elizabeth's takeout and the check. Rachel Ann tried to pay for her sandwich, but Elizabeth reminded her firmly it was on her.

They walked back to the shop and hugged before parting ways. Rachel Ann realized the break had indeed done her good when she put her things away and went back on the floor.

Leah was talking on the store telephone, and Rachel Ann felt her heart beat faster when she saw her frown. She hung up and looked at Rachel Ann.

"It was your *mamm*. She wants you to come to the hospital."

"Right now?"

"Right now." Leah picked up the phone and began dialing. "I'll call for a ride for you. Go get your things."

Rachel Ann felt anxiety roll over her just as it had the day she'd walked into Sam's hospital room and saw his empty bed. She felt herself hyperventilating, her heart beating faster, her chest becoming tight just like that day. She forced herself to take a couple of slow, calming breaths.

"Take a breath," Leah said, laying a hand on her arm. "She didn't say it was bad news. She just sounded rushed and wanted you there right away."

"Is it *allrecht* if I leave? We've been busy," she stammered.

"Rachel Ann, you're going. We'll be fine."

She went to the back room for her things, and when she returned her ride was already pulling up. The ride was mercifully short, and soon she found herself walking down the hallway to Sam's room.

Her hand shook as she opened the door. Her heart pounded and she felt a little faint. Then the door swung open, and she stood frozen, staring in shock.

☙

"Sam!"

Her little brother was sitting up in bed looking pale and tired, but he was awake!

Rachel Ann rushed to kneel by his bed. "Sam! You finally decided to wake up! Hello, baby *bruder*!" She leaned forward to gently hug him.

"Wachel Ann!" His little arms wrapped around her neck.

Sitting back on her heels, she glanced over to see her mother wiping her streaming eyes. Her father stood in a corner of the room obviously overcome by emotion.

"Leg hurts," he said, pointing to his left leg encased in a bulky cast. He pushed back the fringe of blond hair falling in his face.

"We were watching the doctor examining Sam, and when he pricked the bottom of his foot, we saw a reaction," her mother told her. "His eyelids moved. I saw it and nearly jumped out of my chair. Not a minute later he woke up. I called your father and then you."

"Doctor hurt·my foot. He woked me up." Sam frowned.

Rachel Ann kissed her fingertips and lightly pressed them to his foot. Sam grinned.

"They'll be running some more tests—"

"Tests?" Sam asked, giving his mother a suspicious look. "I don't want hurt."

"But then the doctor said you could go home tomorrow."

"Home." Sam gave them a big grin.

Rachel Ann got to her feet and sank into a nearby chair. She couldn't get over it. Sam awake . . . it felt like nothing short of a miracle, something she'd been praying for and praying for. Emotion welled up in her and she burst into tears.

"Don't cry, Wachel Ann." Sam patted her arm.

She dug into her purse for a tissue and wiped her eyes. "They're happy tears, Sam. I'm just happy you're awake. You've been asleep for a long time."

"Hungry."

Her mother began laughing. "Now we know Sam's back to normal. He's already had macaroni and cheese and Jell-O."

"Still hungry."

"What do you want, Sam?" Rachel Ann asked him. She was prepared to go to the hospital cafeteria and buy him whatever it was if she had to.

"Mac and cheese and Jell-O."

"Again?" Martha shook her head in disbelief. "I'll go ask the nurse if you can have something."

Her father laid a hand on her shoulder. "You stay and talk to Rachel Ann. Let me do something."

Sam got his macaroni and cheese and Jell-O, but halfway through the meal he began nodding off.

"Tired, Sam?"

"*Nee*," he said, straightening up and shoveling another bite into his mouth.

Typical four-year-old, thought Rachel Ann. He would never admit he was tired.

A minute later, his head bent and the fork clattered to the plate. The noise woke him, and he picked up the fork and speared a few more macaroni. His eyelids began fluttering closed, but when his mother tried to remove the fork, his eyes sprang open.

"Not tired," he said firmly.

Finally his eyelids drifted closed, and he couldn't hold sleep off any longer. He slumped back against his pillow. Rachel Ann leaned over and pulled the fork from his unresisting fingers as her mother quietly pushed his tray away.

"He's never tired," Rachel Ann said fondly. "Hasn't wanted to take a nap since he was one. I can't wait for him to come home and run us ragged again."

Emotion welled up again and she burst into tears. "I'm sorry, I'm so sorry."

"What for, Rachel Ann?"

"This," she said, gesturing at her brother and then the room. "This was all my fault! If I'd been watching him better he wouldn't have run into the road and gotten hit!"

"It was an accident," her mother told her. "We don't blame you."

"It was God's will," her father said.

Her mother got up and walked over to her. "Here," she said, handing Rachel Ann some tissues from a box on Sam's hospital tray. "Stop blaming yourself," she said firmly. "Your *daed* and I don't blame you."

She wiped her tears and blew her nose. It was hard to believe they didn't blame her.

"Now, I think Sam's probably going to sleep for a while," Martha said. "He doesn't need all of us to watch him sleep. Why don't the two of you go back to work and come back later?"

Rachel Ann bit her lip. "It's okay he fell asleep? I mean . . . he'll wake up again?"

"Of course he will," her mother said. "Now, go, both of you."

"I'll be back after work," her father told her mother. He looked at Rachel Ann. "Ready to go?"

She nodded, and they walked to the elevator together. They got in and rode in silence for several moments.

"I had no idea you blamed yourself," he said suddenly. "Your *mamm* and I both know how much you love Sam. We know you'd never deliberately do anything to cause him harm."

"*Danki, Daed.*"

"And we might not have told you how much it helped you've been working a second job to bring in more money."

"I'm glad I could help," she said simply.

"Turns out Abram went into the furniture store and took care of my orders and told the boss to pay me for them."

She stared at him. "Abram did that?" She remembered now how one day he'd been in town and gotten a ride home in the van. He'd smelled of wood and sawdust and she'd vaguely wondered why.

"I wasn't supposed to tell you," her father added. "He didn't want anyone to know."

The elevator stopped at the main floor and they got out. "Have you seen Michael lately?"

She shook her head. "He's on Christmas break."

"I wondered since . . ." he trailed off.

"What is it, *Daed*?" Neither of her parents had ever asked about him.

"I hope he hasn't changed his mind about having his insurance pay for Sam's hospital bill."

Her stomach lurched. "He didn't say anything last time I saw him. He seemed so sincere about it, *Daed*. I can't think he wouldn't honor what he said." She hoped.

Her father nodded.

"I'll ask him as soon as I see him."

He patted her shoulder. "*Danki*." He used his cell phone to call their driver, and when he arrived they rode in silence to their jobs.

Rachel Ann knew her parents were thrilled Sam was going to be okay, but she hoped they wouldn't be burdened with the hospital bills.

"Was it bad news?" Leah asked the minute Rachel Ann walked into the shop. She pressed a hand to her throat.

"What? Oh, no, it was good news!" Rachel Ann said quickly. "Sam woke up!"

"*Wunderbaar!*" Leah exclaimed. "Naomi, Anna, Sam woke up!"

They rushed over and pressed Rachel Ann for more information. For the next few minutes they engaged in excited chatter.

Leah waved her hands. "It is indeed a miracle," she said. "I think it's time to thank God for healing Sam, don't you?"

Each of them nodded, and Leah led them in a prayer of thanks for the gift He'd given them of the life of this precious child.

Rachel Ann felt her heart would burst. "*Danki*, God," she whispered. "*Danki* for Sam."

✍

Abram dropped Sarah off at her house and headed home, feeling content after lunch and a drive with her.

His sense of contentment vanished the minute he turned his buggy into his drive and saw Rachel Ann sitting on the porch of her house.

She glanced in his direction and returned his wave, but it seemed to him to him it was half-hearted and she didn't look happy.

He made quick work of unhitching his horse and putting him up in his stall. Then he walked next door, climbed the steps, and leaned against the porch railing. "*Gut-n-owed*."

"*Gut-n-owed*."

"You're home early tonight. Everything *allrecht*?"

Her face cleared, and it felt like the sun came out. "You haven't heard?"

"Heard what?"

"Sam woke up today. He may get to come home tomorrow."

Abram stared at her. "Really? That's amazing news." He sat in the chair next to her. "When did this happen?"

"Around lunchtime. *Mamm* called me to the hospital and I saw for myself. It's why I'm not there now. I decided to come home and straighten up the house instead of going to the hospital again."

He nodded. "I'll take care of your *daed*'s chores in a minute." He tapped his fingers on his knee. "There's something I don't understand, though. When I pulled into my drive you didn't look happy at all."

"*Daed* told me the hospital bills haven't been paid. Michael had said his insurance would pay them. I'm worried he's changed his mind."

"So ask him."

"I haven't seen him for a few days."

"What's wrong, Rachel Ann?"

"I'm worried about how my parents are going to pay those bills."

"Something else is wrong. What happened? Did you and Michael break up?"

"*Nee*," she said quickly.

Too quickly. Was it his imagination that she paled? He wasn't sure, but what he did know was she didn't meet his eyes.

"He's just on Christmas break right now. He said he might be going on a trip with his friends." She stared at her hands folded in her lap.

Something definitely was wrong.

A cool breeze swept across the porch. The ribbons of her *kapp* fluttered, stirring a memory.

He remembered finding her *kapp* in the driveway after she'd gone for a drive with Michael. When he'd returned it to her, she'd looked so upset . . .

"Rachel Ann? Rachel Ann?"

She blinked. "What?"

"If something's bothering you I'd like to help. We're friends. We should be able to talk to each other."

"Nothing's wrong. I'm just worried about what I said—about the hospital bills."

"If Michael's insurance doesn't pay, you know our community will pitch in the way it always has."

She got to her feet. "I need to go inside and get some things done."

"*Allrecht*," he said as he stood. "I need to do those chores."

"Oh, I forgot to say thank you for what you did for my *daed* at the furniture store. Doing his work and seeing he got paid for it, I mean."

"No one was supposed to know about it."

"That's just like you. Always doing good and not looking for a thank-you," she said quietly.

"Anyone would have done it."

She shook her head. "You were already doing his daily chores and you took on even more. *Danki.*"

"No thanks are necessary. I'd do anything for you and your family, Rachel Ann. Anything."

Silence stretched between them—a tenuous thread he was afraid to break by saying anything else. The picture of the *kapp* came to his mind again. If she was in trouble, he hoped she understood what he was offering.

If he was wrong and voiced his concern, he would be saying something about her personal life and he'd appear judgmental and he didn't want to. Some things were best left unsaid.

"Tell your parents how happy I am about Sam."

"I will. *Gut-n-owed.*"

He walked down the stairs and went around the back of the house to the barn, grateful for his chores to take his mind off the path it had traveled.

8

Rachel Ann put a casserole into the oven for supper and looked around for something to do.

She and her parents had spent so much time away from home, the house had stayed relatively clean. There was some laundry to be done, but it was too late to start it. Feeling restless, she decided to go for a walk.

A block from home she heard a vehicle behind her. Its engine sounded louder than most cars, so she moved further right on the shoulder for safety. A glance back had her eyes widening in shock.

Michael!

She heard a screech of brakes as he apparently recognized her. He pulled over onto the grass and waited for her to walk back to the car.

"Hi!" he said, giving her a grin. "I wasn't sure it was you at first."

"You're back from your trip."

"Yeah. It was great. Get in."

She hesitated, remembering the last drive. But they needed to talk. "Can we go back to my house and sit in the drive and talk? I have a casserole in the oven I need to take out in half an hour."

"Sure."

She got in and fastened her seat belt.

Michael checked traffic, did a U-turn, and headed back in the direction of her house. "You look tired."

"Just what a girl likes to hear," she muttered.

He pulled into the drive of her house, shut off the engine, and slung one arm along the back of the seat. His fingers toyed with one of the strings of her *kapp.* She brushed his hand away.

"Michael, we have to talk."

"Sounds serious."

She turned in her seat to look at him. "It is." She hesitated, twisting her hands in her lap as she debated which topic she should bring up first.

"What's up?" he prodded.

"*Daed* said there hasn't been any payment on Sam's hospital bill. You'd said your insurance company was going to pay it."

"These things take time." He pulled out his cell phone and spent a few minutes texting. "There," he said when his fingers stopped flying across the keyboard of his phone. "I just sent a message to my insurance agent and copied my dad. He'll make sure this is taken care of."

He ran his hands over the steering wheel. "Did you think I wouldn't honor what I said?"

"I didn't know what to think."

"Have a little faith."

She jerked her head up and looked at him, wondering if he was joking. Sure enough, a smile played around his lips. She forced herself to look away from his too-attractive mouth.

He leaned closer. "How about a welcome-back kiss?"

She drew back so quickly she smacked the back of her head on the passenger window.

"That's how we got into this mess," she muttered.

"What?"

A van pulled into the drive behind them. Rachel Ann turned and watched her parents get out. Then her mother reached into the vehicle, and when she emerged she held Sam in her arms.

"Oh, my gosh, Sam!" she cried and couldn't get out of the car fast enough.

"Sam?" she heard Michael saying behind her.

Rachel Ann rushed up to her mother and hugged Sam. "Welcome home, baby *bruder*!"

"Cast," he said, pointing to his leg. "Don't want cast." He gave her an imploring look that just about broke her heart.

"Sam, you have to wear it for a while," his mother said with the weary air of someone tired of repeating herself. "You heard the doctor."

He frowned, then turned to his mother. "Ice cream?" he asked, flashing her a charming grin.

"Yes, you can have ice cream after supper."

Rachel Ann bit back a smile. Under normal circumstances, her mother found it hard to deny Sam anything. Now she had a feeling it was going to be hard for *Mamm* to say no to anything her *sohn* wanted.

Michael walked up. "Well, this is a surprise. Hello, Sam. It's so good to see how well you're doing. Rachel Ann didn't tell me you'd woken up."

"You didn't?" her mother asked. "Why not?"

"He just got here," she said quickly. "I didn't have a chance yet."

Michael turned to her father and held out his cell phone. "Sir, Rachel Ann asked me about the insurance. I texted my insurance agent, and I just heard back from him. You don't need to worry. He said they're taking care of the hospital bill. Things just take longer than we'd like."

Her father looked relieved. "It's good to know. Thank you."

"Let's get Sam inside," her mother said, starting for the house.

"I have to be going," Michael told Rachel Ann. "I'll give you a call tomorrow."

She wanted desperately to talk to him, but now wasn't the time. She wanted to go inside with her family, and besides, they would wonder why she was outside talking to Michael.

"Talk to you tomorrow," she told him, and she forced a smile.

She followed her parents into the house.

"Something smells like it's burning," her father said.

"That would be supper," Rachel Ann told him. She rushed into the kitchen to pull the casserole out of the oven. "Well, we can't eat this," she announced as she dumped the blackened mess into the garbage.

"Why are you smiling?" her mother wanted to know.

"This is just too good a day to be upset about something like this," she told them as she grinned at Sam. "What should we have, scrambled eggs or pancakes?"

"Pancakes!" Sam squealed and clapped his hands.

"Pancakes it is."

Abram was feeding a carrot to Brownie when Leroy walked into the barn.

"*Gut-n-owed.* You're home early tonight."

"I got off work early so we could bring Sam home."

The carrot fell from his hand. Brownie neatly caught it before it hit the straw-lined floor.

"Sam's home?" He slapped Leroy's back. "What *gut* news."

Leroy nodded. Although he looked tired, his face had lost some of its tension from the past weeks. "When can I see him?"

"Right now if you like. Rachel Ann's making him supper."

He started for the house, not even glancing behind him to see if Leroy followed. When he stepped into the kitchen he saw Rachel Ann standing at the stove. Sam sat at the kitchen table happily stuffing his mouth with a big bite of pancake.

"Abram!" Sam cried and clapped his hands.

"Sam! It's good to see you!" He slipped into the chair next to Sam's and gave him a hug.

"Be careful of sticky fingers," Rachel Ann cautioned.

But Sam was already patting Abram's cheeks. Abram looked startled for a moment and then laughed.

Rachel Ann rushed to dampen a dishcloth and hand it to him. "Maybe you'd rather Sarah kiss those sweet cheeks," she teased and laughed when he reddened.

"Aren't you in a good mood," he muttered.

"Sam's home," she said simply.

"And what about the other . . . issue worrying you?"

She stared at him, not comprehending.

He glanced around. "Where's your mother?"

"Out in the phone shanty. Why?"

"Now's not the time to talk when someone could walk in," he said as he wiped the syrup off his face. "But anytime you want to talk just let me know."

Martha walked into the room. "Hello, Abram. I didn't know you were here. Rachel Ann, how many pancakes has Sam eaten?"

"Three."

"I want more," Sam told her. He banged his fork on the table.

"Then you can't have ice cream."

He pushed his empty plate away. "Ice cream."

"Please."

"Please," he added, giving his mother a charming smile.

Rachel Ann got the ice cream and a bowl and served Sam two scoops. "*Mamm*? Abram? Can I get you some ice cream?"

Her mother shook her head. "Too full from the pancakes. Unlike somebody we know," she said, watching Sam shovel ice cream into his mouth.

"My mother said I've always been a bottomless pit when it came to eating," Abram said as he stood. "No ice cream, thanks. I need to get home for my supper." He bent and kissed the top of Sam's head. "Welcome home, Sam."

He straightened and looked at Rachel Ann. "Talk to you later."

Was it his imagination he saw confusion in her eyes?

"I was wondering what was taking you so long," his mother said when he walked into the kitchen at his house.

"Sam just came home," he told her. "I was visiting with him,"

She clasped her hands and looked heavenward. "*Danki,*" she whispered. "I wonder if Martha would mind if I paid a quick visit?"

"I don't think she'd mind at all."

She nodded. "I'm going to run over there for just a minute. Go ahead and eat without me."

Abram washed his hands at the sink, picked up his bowl, and served himself the stew he found simmering on the stove. His mother had already sliced bread and set it and butter on the table along with glasses of ice water. A pumpkin pie sat cooling on a rack on the counter.

He measured coffee and water into the percolator and set it on a back burner on the gas stove.

He sat down, said a prayer of thanks for the meal, and dug in as the percolator bubbled and the scent of coffee filled the room. As he ate, he found himself thinking about how lucky he was. Not only did he have a comfortable home, he had someone who cooked for him so he didn't have to rely on his limited cooking skills. He'd been forced to rely on them when his mother had been in the hospital and before she recovered enough to return to the cooking she loved to do.

Two helpings of stew later, he poured himself a mug of coffee and cut himself a large piece of the pie. He added a scoop of vanilla ice cream and grinned as he remembered Sam's happiness eating pancakes for supper and ice cream for dessert.

His mother came in beaming a few minutes later. She chattered as she served herself stew and sat at the table. After she prayed, she dipped her spoon into her stew. "It was so *gut* to see Sam home. And Leroy and Martha already look better. They were looking so strained."

"What about Rachel Ann?" he asked casually.

Lovina frowned. "She doesn't look herself. Maybe it's because she's so tired from working two jobs. Let's hope she doesn't have to do it much longer."

He nodded. "Pie's really good."

"How about the stew?"

Abram grinned. "Fishing for a compliment?" he teased. Before she could respond, he told her he'd had two servings. "I'd have a second slice of pie, but then you'd have to roll me from the table."

"So, what kind of cook is Sarah?"

The sip of coffee he'd just taken went down the wrong way. He coughed and sputtered.

"Are you *allrecht*?"

He drank some water. "*Ya*. Where did that come from?"

"Just wondered, since you're seeing her."

"Being a good cook isn't necessary to see someone," he said carefully.

"No, but if you're courting her . . ."

"I'm not 'courting' her as you put it. I've just taken her out a few times. And how did you know this?" He stopped. "Why do I ask such a thing? The Amish grapevine is faster than the Internet."

"A man who likes to eat as much as you will want a wife who is a good cook," she said a bit defensively.

"True."

"So is she?"

"Her brownies are amazing."

"Man can't live on brownies after he's worked all day in the field."

He laughed. "You just have to have the last word. Tell you what, I'll find out if we get serious, *allrecht*?"

"I suppose I could teach her if she doesn't know," Lovina said as she cut herself a piece of pie. "But sometimes young brides can be touchy about that sort of thing."

Abram noticed she limped a bit as she returned to the table, so he got up and poured her a cup of coffee and set it before her.

"*Danki,*" she said, and she patted his hand. "You're a good *sohn*. I don't want to meddle, but I don't want you to get so used to taking care of your old mother you don't look into finding a wife."

"You're not old," he told her. She wasn't—she was only in her fifties, but he knew her injury had slowed her down a lot and probably made her feel older. "And I'm grateful for you living here."

He reached over with his fork and swiped a bite of her pie. "So tell me, how long do you think his cast is going to keep Sam from being the terror he's always been?"

❧

Rachel Ann cleaned up the kitchen and climbed the stairs to her bedroom. Hours later she was still lying awake and worrying.

God had been so good to heal Sam and let them bring him home. It was truly a miracle, and she was thankful. Now, if He would just assure her she hadn't gotten pregnant. She closed her eyes and prayed and prayed. Her Bible lay on her nightstand. She reached for it and a bookmark someone had given her fell out. The phrase from Hebrews 13:5 printed on it was one that had always soothed her: "Never will I leave you; never will I forsake you." Finally, she fell asleep.

Michael didn't call the next day or the day after. Rachel Ann forced herself to concentrate on work, but she burned her hand at the bakery because she wasn't paying enough attention when she went to get something out of the oven.

Her boss found her holding her hand under the tap, tears running down her cheeks. She fussed over Rachel Ann and bustled around getting ice from the refrigerator.

"How bad does it hurt, *kind*?" she asked as she made Rachel Ann sit down and hold the plastic bag of ice on the burn. "Do you want to go to the emergency room?"

She shook her head. "It's not so bad. I'm just mad at myself for not being careful enough."

Linda made a *tsk*ing noise. "These things happen. I can't tell you how many times I've gotten burned. It's part of the job."

She bustled around, taking pans of cookies out of the oven when the timer buzzed, fixed Rachel Ann a cup of tea, and went back to the front of the bakery when the bell over the door jangled, announcing a customer's arrival.

Rachel Ann took the ice off the burn, applied some ointment Linda brought her, and went back to work.

A rainstorm swept through midday, so there were few customers at Stitches in Time. Leah asked Rachel Ann to straighten the storeroom, a task she welcomed. It meant she could be by herself and not keep a smiling mask on her face.

"Hey there!"

She looked up from straightening several bolts of fabric and saw Mary Katherine standing in the doorway.

"I'm supposed to help you."

"Great," Rachel Ann said and tried to sound enthusiastic.

"You okay? I saw you burned your hand."

"It's not too bad. I just wasn't paying enough attention."

"You seem distracted. I'm a good listener if you want to talk. I promise I won't offer advice unless you ask for it."

"*Danki*, but I'm fine."

"I remember my *rumschpringe*," Mary Katherine said as she rewrapped a bolt of fabric to neaten it. "It was a difficult time. I didn't know what world I belonged in—Amish or *Englisch*. I struggled. One of the reasons I struggled was because I didn't feel loved. I was constantly trying to please my father."

She stopped and shook her head. "I'm sorry, I said I could be a listener if you needed one and here I am telling you about what I went through. But sometimes your parents—especially your *mamm*—reminds me of my *dat*. She always seems so stern." She bit her lip. "If I've offended you, I apologize."

Rachel Ann shook her head. "It's *allrecht*. I know I've probably seemed moody. I appreciate your caring."

They worked silently until Leah called them back into the store twenty minutes later. The storm had passed, the sun came out, and customers came out in droves like mushrooms after a good rain.

Rachel Ann walked out of the shop exhausted and eager to get home. It had been a long day.

Abram was sitting on the porch talking with her father when she arrived home. Just as Rachel Ann was about to step onto the first stair, her mother poked her head out the door.

"Leroy, Sam's asking for you."

Her father went inside and Abram stood. "How was your day?"

"Not so good." She held up her hand. "I even managed to burn my hand."

"How bad is it?"

"Not too bad now. How was your day?"

He shrugged. "Sorry to say it was pretty good. You know it's a slow time of year for me."

She nodded and searched for an excuse so she could go inside.

"Rachel Ann, let's go for a ride."

"A ride?"

"*Ya*. I need to talk to you about something. It's important."

Torn, she hesitated. They'd been friends for years—not just next-door neighbors. They'd shared confidences and problems and secrets.

"Now?"

He nodded. "Now. Please?"

Rachel Ann nodded slowly. "Let me tell *Mamm* I'm leaving."

9

Rachel Ann got into Abram's buggy when he pulled it in front
of her house.

She waited for him to tell her what he wanted to talk about, but
he remained silent as the buggy traveled along. Finally, she turned
to him. "Where are we going?"

"No place in particular. Just for a ride."

"*Allrecht.* So what's bothering you?"

"You."

"Me?" Surprised, she stared at him.

"I've been worried about you. Something's been bothering you
and I've been concerned."

She realized she hadn't been good at hiding her feelings since
this was the second time in one day she'd had someone concerned
about her.

"It's been a difficult time with Sam in the hospital," she said.
"You know that."

He glanced at her, and even though the light was fading, she
saw the doubt on his face. "I don't think that's the only thing that's
bothering you. We've been friends for a long time, Rachel Ann. I
know you."

"I know I haven't been my usual self," she told him. "I'm exhausted working two jobs, but it'll be over soon."

Abram pulled the buggy off the road and turned to her. "I think whatever's worrying you has to do with this guy you're seeing. The *Englisch* one."

"Michael?"

He nodded.

"I was worried when *Daed* said the insurance hadn't paid Sam's hospital bill. Michael had said it would, and I was concerned he'd changed his mind. Can you imagine what it would have done to us? Even if the community helped, it was scary to think about."

"I saw he was here the other day. Did you talk to him about it?"

"*Ya*. He contacted the insurance company, and they said they're taking care of it."

"*Gut*. So why do I sense that you're still troubled?"

"I don't know." She smoothed her skirt, and her burned hand twinged. She thought about using it as an excuse to ask to be taken home.

He pulled his gaze from her and stared through the windshield. "Remember Naomi Stoltzfus?"

"Of course. She left our community several years ago."

"Do you remember why?"

"She decided not to join the church."

She glanced at him. He was still staring straight ahead, not at her.

"It's what she told everyone. But I heard she left because she dated an *Englisch* man and got pregnant."

She jerked her head and stared at him. "I didn't hear that."

"A friend of mine ran into her not long after she left."

"Did—did he marry her?"

"*Nee*."

Silence stretched between them. "Abram, why are you telling me this?" she asked slowly.

"I'm afraid the same thing could happen to you." He turned to her. "Maybe *has* happened to you."

She went cold. There was no way he could have suspected.

"I've worried since I found your *kapp* in the drive. If Michael might have talked you into taking off more than a *kapp*."

"Well," she said, and she had to bite her lip to stop it trembling. "You're blunt."

He sighed. "I'm not trying to pry," he said. "I'm concerned. Rachel Ann, are you pregnant?"

She couldn't have been more shocked. Speechless, she stared at him. "I don't know," she whispered.

"Have you talked to Michael about it?"

"Not yet."

He turned to look at her again, and his gaze was intense. "If you are, if he doesn't do the right thing and marry you, I want to do it. I care about you, Rachel Ann. You know that."

"Enough to take on another man's child? I'm not saying I'm—" she couldn't say the word.

"*Ya*. If you are."

Emotion welled up in her. Marriage was forever in the Amish community. He was making a huge commitment to her in offering. He'd been her best friend all her life, but could friendship extend to doing this for her? "If I am, I couldn't do that to you. What about Sarah?"

"She's a friend. You're more."

"I am?"

"You have been for some time. I've done my best to hide it since I saw you were interested in Michael."

"I didn't know." She'd been too wrapped up in everything that had been happening to notice. Years ago, she'd harbored a secret crush on him, but when it seemed he just wanted to stay friends, she'd forced herself to think of him as just a good friend and confidante . . .

"I was stupid one night and had a beer . . . and later I couldn't remember anything," she confessed. "I can't talk about it. It's just too humiliating." She closed her eyes and shook her head.

"Some *Englisch* guys date Amish girls because they're innocent about such things."

"Not all Amish guys are saints with the women they date," she said tartly. "You and I both know couples who've had to get married."

"True."

A car passed them driving way too fast, and the wind made the buggy sway a little.

"It's not safe to stay here," he told her. He checked for traffic and pulled back onto the road, then made a U-turn and headed back in the direction they'd come.

"When will you know?" he asked.

"It's too soon. Maybe in a couple weeks."

"Long time for this kind of worry."

"*Ya*," she agreed, feeling miserable. "*Ya*."

"What do you want to do?"

She didn't understand him at first. "About your proposal? I need to talk to Michael first. And even if—if I find out that I'm pregnant and Michael doesn't want to marry me, I don't think you and I should rush into anything. *If* I let you do such a thing, I mean."

"So you'll let me know? You won't do anything foolish like leave the community without coming to talk to me?"

"*Nee*," she said and met his gaze. "*Danki*, Abram. You are such a good man. And such a good friend." She leaned forward impulsively and kissed his cheek.

His hand touched his cheek, and she could tell she'd surprised him.

They rode home in silence.

Abram had shocked Rachel Ann with his proposal. But it couldn't be helped. He cared about her too much not to talk to her as bluntly as he had and offer to help her.

Neither of them had talked on the way home.

He dropped her off in front of her house and then went on home and put up his horse and the buggy.

The door to the *dawdi haus* was closed. Light showed under her door, so his mother must be reading or sewing. As much as he loved her, he felt relieved he didn't have to talk to her tonight. He just wanted to be alone after his talk with Rachel Ann.

He lay on top of his bed and thought about their conversation. He'd done more than bring up a difficult topic and offer his support—he'd bared his soul and told her how he felt about her. It hadn't been easy, but he'd felt he had to do it.

Had he just made a fool of himself? Had he been too impulsive?

He'd told her what he felt about her and offered to marry her. She'd called him a good man and a good friend. Well, where had it gotten him? He'd been a good man and a good friend and she'd chosen to date Michael. Would she turn to him only if Michael didn't step up and marry her if she was pregnant? How was he going to feel then?

He sat up. It wasn't good to think this way. He cared about Rachel Ann and he wanted to help her. This was more important than his feeling second to another man . . .

Well, there was no point in thinking about it anymore tonight. She'd said she wouldn't know for maybe a couple of weeks. And she might not even be pregnant. He didn't know a whole lot about it, but women didn't get pregnant every time they were intimate with men.

A good man and a good friend . . .

He wanted to be more to her.

Sleep was elusive. He was finally drifting off when he heard the van picking up Rachel Ann in the morning. He forced himself to stay in bed and not get up and look out as he did sometimes.

She'd looked so tired the night before—she had for some time now. He wished there was some way she didn't have to work her second job. Well, he had no control over it, he told himself. He couldn't go in and work the job for her the way he'd done for her *dat*. Christmas wasn't far away.

Abram spent the next day working on the small keepsake boxes for the furniture store. They were popular Christmas gifts, and the store owner would take as many as he could supply. He didn't need the money, but he enjoyed working with the wood and he had the time as the fields slept during the winter season.

A few days later he had enough to take to the store. And an excuse to stop by and see Rachel Ann.

He surprised her when he walked into Stitches in Time.

"What are you doing here?" she asked him after she finished helping another customer. Then she paled. "Is anything wrong?"

He winced. She was obviously remembering how he'd gone to get her parents the day Sam had been hurt. "*Nee*," he said quickly. "I was just in town making a delivery and thought I'd shop for a Christmas present for *Mamm*. Usually I make something for her, but I thought maybe I'd do something different this year. I don't suppose I could take you to lunch while I'm here?"

Rachel Ann hesitated. She hadn't seen him since the night he'd made his incredible suggestion. It was so generous of him . . . and it had changed things between them. "I go to lunch at noon."

He checked the time. Half an hour. "I'll go visit the bookstore and come back."

He wandered the aisles and couldn't find anything at the bookstore. A new cookbook? A book about quilting? Then a display of gift cards caught his eye. He decided she might like to pick out her own reading material and made his purchase.

When he returned to the shop, Rachel Ann was ready to go. They walked to a nearby restaurant and had to wait a few minutes for a table so they sat on a bench and watched the comings and goings.

"It's a busy time of the year," she told him. "How did the Christmas shopping go? You didn't find anything?"

He pulled the gift card from the inside pocket of his jacket. "I'd still like to do something else. Maybe you can give me some ideas?"

"I like the gift certificate idea. Your mother quilts and knits, but with her injury we haven't seen her in the store much. If you gave her a gift certificate for Stitches in Time she could buy a lot of fabric and yarn ahead of when she might need it."

"She already has enough fabric and yarn to stock her own shop."

"You can never have enough fabric and yarn," she told him. "It's for all the UFOs."

"Alien spaceships?"

She laughed and shook her head. "Unfinished fabric objects."

The hostess came to escort them to a table. Abram watched Rachel Ann look everywhere but into his eyes. He waited until they'd gotten their drinks and ordered. "Rachel Ann?"

"*Ya?*"

Still she didn't look on him. "You haven't looked at me once."

"I'm sorry." She looked up from studying her glass of iced tea, met his gaze, and then glanced away.

"I embarrassed you talking about . . . what we did last time we saw each other."

"*Ya — nee.*" She sighed and shook her head. "But I do appreciate how you cared enough to make me talk about it."

He watched her lift her eyes and meet his directly. "I meant what I said."

"When are you going to talk to Michael?" He stopped and held up a hand. "Maybe you don't want to talk about it here."

"Probably not a good idea. I did leave him a voicemail."

They ate their lunch. Well, he ate his chicken and dumplings, but he noticed she only ate half of her tuna salad sandwich.

"Not hungry?"

She shook her head. "I'm sorry."

He felt like he should apologize for his healthy appetite.

"Did you save room for dessert?" their server asked.

Abram didn't feel right about having dessert when Rachel Ann sat there eating so little because of her tension. But she insisted he get some dessert, so he ordered a piece of apple pie.

While he ate, they talked some more about what else he could get for his mother for Christmas. They rejected a jacket and a new purse. Rachel Ann said women liked to pick their own clothing and accessories like purses.

They walked back to the shop. Rachel Ann carried a to-go box with half of her sandwich, in case she got hungry later.

"You could come inside and look around," she said when they reached Stitches in Time. He shook his head. "I think your idea of the gift certificate so she can stock up on fabric and yarn or whatever is a *gut* idea."

"It's not because you don't want to browse in the store?" she teased. "Some men won't be seen in a shop like this."

"I did go in earlier, and I'll be going into it to get the gift certificate."

"You're right," she said and opened the door and invited him inside.

❧

Rachel Ann saw Michael sitting in his car in front of her house when she arrived home in the afternoon.

"You said we needed to talk," he said when she got into the car. "What's up?"

She took a deep breath. "I'm scared I could be pregnant."

Now it was his turn to jerk away. "What?"

"You heard me." She glanced around, concerned her parents could arrive in the midst of their discussion.

"Rachel Ann, if you're pregnant, it's not mine."

Appalled, she stared at him. "I haven't been with anyone else."

"Well, you haven't been with me."

"What are you talking about? What about the drive we took? I had too much to drink."

He stared at her incredulously. "You had one beer."

She felt heat rush into her cheeks. "I hadn't eaten much of anything that day. It really affected me."

"Rachel Ann, Mary is the only woman who ever had an immaculate conception."

"Mary?"

"As in the mother of Jesus."

"This isn't funny!"

"I'm not trying to be." He ran a hand through his hair, causing it to stand up in spikes. "Don't you remember what happened?"

Her face flamed. "I remember feeling woozy from the beer. I took my *kapp* off and let down my hair and you were kissing me."

"And then?"

"I can't remember," she wailed. "Do you have any idea how worried I am?"

"Well, you can relax," he told her. "Your *kapp* is the only thing that came off then. You fell asleep right after you took it off. I can't tell you how it made me feel. Girl can't stay awake while you're kissing her."

Intense relief washed over her, and she slumped back in her seat. "I feel like such a fool."

"You're not a fool. But I wouldn't advise drinking beer again on an empty stomach."

"I don't intend to ever do it again," she said fervently. "Besides, I hated the taste of the stuff."

"It isn't the best tasting," he agreed. "But it gives you a buzz for cheap."

He tapped his fingers on the steering wheel, looking restless to go.

"Listen, if that's it I need to go. I have something I have to do."

"Sure. I need to get inside anyway. Chores."

He nodded.

She got out of the car and walked up the drive, aware of the squeal of tires as Michael apparently couldn't get away fast enough.

He hadn't even asked about Sam. He hadn't said anything about when she'd see him again. Or Christmas. Couples always planned something for the holidays, didn't they? Even if they didn't have the same traditions.

"Rachel Ann!" Sam shrieked when she opened the front door.

He came hobbling toward her, not letting his cast slow him down much, and threw his arms around her knees. "You're home!"

Her disappointment with Michael, all her tension and tiredness, melted away. "Sam! You're home!"

"I been home, you silly Wachel Ann," he said.

"What did you do today?" she asked, dropping her purse onto a nearby table and picking him up. She gave him a big smacking kiss on his cheek and he giggled.

"Ran his *grossmudder* ragged," her mother told her. "Your *dat* just took her home."

Rachel Ann lowered him into his chair at the kitchen table and got a pad of paper and crayons from a nearby cabinet. "Here, why don't you color us a picture while I fix supper?"

"I can fix supper," her mother said.

"I don't mind. What should we have?"

"Pancakes!" Sam cried.

"I was asking *Mamm*, silly Sam."

He shrugged and went back to coloring.

"Not pancakes," their mother said, pouring herself a cup of coffee and sitting down at the table. "I was going to make spaghetti. There's a pound of hamburger in the refrigerator and a jar of tomato sauce we canned—"

"Spizgetti!" Sam said, looking up with a big grin.

"Spaghetti it is," Rachel Ann said. "And meatballs."

"Meatballs," Sam approved.

"How was your day?" her mother asked.

"*Gut,*" she said as she washed her hands and dried them, careful of the one she'd burned. "Yours?"

"*Gut.* Rachel Ann, how is your hand?"

She shrugged. "Better. Doesn't hurt."

"Do you want some ointment for it?"

"I have some. Linda gave it to me."

"I'll be glad when your job is over. It's been too much for you."

She shrugged. "I was happy to help. And I've enjoyed it. Say, Sam, I brought a surprise home for you."

"What is it?"

"It's for after supper. And if I tell you now, it won't be a surprise. If you eat all your supper you can have it."

"We're having spizgetti and meatballs. When hasn't Sam finished all his supper when we've had that?"

"Or anything?" She filled a pan with water for spaghetti and set it on a burner.

She thought about the two surprises she'd had today—first Abram coming into the shop and asking her to lunch.

And finding out she wasn't pregnant. She hadn't had time to absorb it yet.

Or thank God for answered prayer. She closed her eyes and sent up a silent thank-you until she could do a better job later.

"Rachel Ann! What are you doing?"

Her eyes snapped open. She was standing before the stove. If she didn't want another burn, she'd better pay attention.

"Rachel Ann! Look what I colored!" He held up the drawing he'd made of a gingerbread man, woman, and children smiling merrily. "A gingerbread fam'ly. Fam'ly like us," he said and went back to work putting candy canes in their hands.

"*Ya*, family like us," Rachel Ann said, and she smiled at her mother who sat quietly dabbing at her eyes with a tissue.

10

*A*bram decided to make one more stop before going home after he had lunch with Rachel Ann.

He knew it had been too long since he'd paid a visit to his friend, Saul, at his store, Miller's, when the man greeted him with an expression of surprise on his face.

"Abram! What brings you here?"

They shook hands, and Abram glanced around the store. It had a pleasant, creative feel, full of goods handmade by the Amish for the home. The display window featured a number of items for the Christmas season. Abram forced his attention away from the hand-made cribs and baby furniture in one corner.

"I came into town to do a delivery and a little Christmas shopping. Thought I'd stop in and say hello."

"Hello's *gut*. Buying something's even better," Saul joked. "Who's on your list?"

"I'm finished. I just got gifts for my mother. I didn't have a big list, and I'd have made something for her like usual, but I've been busy lately."

"I heard you've been helping Leroy and Martha."

Abram shrugged. "They're friends as well as neighbors."

He wandered the aisles looking over the merchandise. "Amos does fine work," he said, picking up a carved wooden owl.

"So do you."

"Nothing as creative like this. I mostly build furniture."

"The carving on your small keepsake boxes is fine. Whenever you have some extra time and want to make some pieces for the store, I'll be happy to have them."

Abram stopped before a beautifully carved cradle. Amos was known for them. It made him remember telling Rachel Ann he'd marry her if she found out she was pregnant.

He hadn't been thinking only of helping her. There was a time in a man's life when his thoughts turned to settling down with a *fraa* and having *kinner*. He stood there gazing at the cradle for long moments until he realized Saul stood by his side, probably wondering why he was spending so much time looking at it. Then he realized Saul was staring at the cradle with a bemused expression. "Saul?"

He tore his gaze from the cradle. "*Ya?*"

"Anything wrong?"

Saul shook his head and grinned. "*Nee*, everything's great. Elizabeth and I have some news."

Abram turned to him. He'd been friends with Saul for years, but he'd never seen him as happy as he looked now.

"We're going to have a *boppli*."

"How wonderful!" Abram said and slapped Saul on the back.

He looked up and saw Elizabeth walking toward them. He'd never seen her look so happy, either.

"I'm guessing Saul's sharing our good news," she said, gazing at her husband adoringly.

Abram wondered what it felt like to have someone look at you like that. Saul was returning her look. He wondered if they even remembered he stood there.

"I'm so happy for you. Such wonderful news—especially at this time of year."

"We decided to tell a few close friends and our parents but that's all for now," Saul said.

"Well, then, I'm honored."

Several customers walked in, and Saul and Elizabeth excused themselves to help them. Abram wandered around, enjoying the clever displays—something he was sure Elizabeth was responsible for, because they hadn't looked as creative before she'd started working here.

Although their community didn't put up Christmas trees, many shop owners used them at the holidays for the *Englisch* customers. One stood in the display window, hung with little quilted patchwork ornaments.

Little carved wooden birds lined one shelf. Some were realistic interpretations and others were whimsical little creatures. He picked up one of them and found himself smiling. It looked like the kind of thing to cheer Rachel Ann up.

"I love these birds," Elizabeth told him. "I bought several of the little sparrows when I first started working here. They reminded me if God provides for the sparrow, He'd provide for me. I was on my own for the first time and not sure I'd be able to take care for myself."

She touched her finger to the funny little frog Abram held. "This would make a great gift."

"That's what I was thinking."

She grinned at him. "Who will you be giving it to?" she asked him as they walked around the store.

"I think I'll keep it a secret," he told her.

"I had lunch with Rachel Ann recently," Elizabeth said. "It was before Sam came home. Such a miracle. God is *gut*."

Had she guessed the frog was for Rachel Ann? Well, he wouldn't tell her even though she was Saul's cousin. He studied Elizabeth as she straightened a display. Had Rachel Ann told her she was worried about being pregnant? They were *gut* friends . . .

"Something wrong?"

He realized she'd turned and found him staring at her. "*Nee*, I was just thinking I should get Sam a couple of those wooden puzzles."

"I agree."

Saul walked up, finished with his customer. Elizabeth handed him the puzzles to ring up.

"Well, it was *gut* to see you and we thank you for the business," Saul said with a chuckle.

"I'm glad I stopped by," Abram told him.

There was a lot of traffic on the road home. Impatient drivers passed his buggy several times, once entirely too close, but they didn't affect Abram's mood. He'd had a good day taking Rachel Ann to lunch and shopping for presents. The news Saul and Elizabeth were going to be parents had cheered him up as well. *Kinner* were gifts from God—even when they might come unexpectedly, like if Rachel Ann were pregnant.

He'd always celebrated the spiritual side of Christmas, but he'd never made so much of an effort to find gifts as he had today. He was actually looking forward to Christmas Day. It was entirely possible he and Rachel Ann would be announcing an upcoming wedding at Christmas. He found himself grinning at the thought.

☙

"Your gingerbread people are going fast," Linda told Rachel Ann. "I think we should skip making more of the Snickerdoodles and do a few dozen more of the people."

Rachel Ann grinned as she started a new batch of gingerbread cookie dough. "*Allrecht*. I got the idea for the people from Sam." She glanced at his drawing she'd tacked up on the bakery refrigerator.

"So glad he's home. I told you not to worry. You know, it's nice to see a smile on your face. I haven't seen it for a long time."

"*Danki.*" Linda didn't know Sam wasn't the only reason she was smiling today.

Linda took the latest batch of cookies to a nearby worktable to wrap them in batches of a dozen each in cellophane and big, bright ribbons.

Rachel Ann used a big wooden spoon to cream the butter and sugar. The ginger, cinnamon, nutmeg, and cloves smelled so Christmasy . . . time seemed to be coming faster and faster these days. The holiday would be here soon. She hadn't thought about it much with all the worrying about Sam and being pregnant.

Heat flooded into her face as she thought about how she needed to talk to Abram—how foolish she felt she'd worried for nothing. She knew Michael thought she was naïve. Abram would probably think so, too, but he knew Amish girls were sheltered and innocent compared to the *Englisch* ones Michael knew. Abram deserved to know he wouldn't need to make good on his offer to marry her.

She still couldn't believe he had been so generous—and selfless. Even if he had feelings for her as he said he did, he knew she'd been dating someone else and not looking in his direction.

"Shall I open a window?" Linda asked. "You look a little warm."

"*Nee*, I'm fine," she said quickly. She sifted the flour and dry ingredients and stirred, grateful when Linda turned back to wrapping up the packages of cookies.

"I'm putting some of the gingerbread families in the display window along with these," she said. When Rachel Ann walked into the front of the bakery with another tray of them a little while later she couldn't help feeling a little twinge of pride when she saw people peering in the window and pointing at the gingerbread cookies. Some came in and bought a whole "family" to take home.

Before she knew it, her shift was over and it was time for the one at Stitches in Time. She found herself glancing in the two windows. Crafts created by everyone in the shop were displayed in the window—everyone but her. Leah had been generous in encouraging her to try a craft with an eye to selling it in the shop as Mary Katherine, Naomi, Anna, and Emma did, but Rachel Ann didn't feel qualified to do anything in this area. She'd never been good at any of the sewing or quilting like so many Amish women. It was baking she enjoyed and seemed to have a talent for.

It was, at least, easier to work in the shop since Sam was home now. She'd liked the bakery job better during the time when customers who knew he'd been hurt made her feel guilty. Well, on reflection, they hadn't made her feel guilty. She had done that job herself. It didn't matter if her mother had told her she and her *dat* didn't blame her. She suspected she would always blame herself.

Leah greeted her warmly when she stepped inside. Mary Katherine and Naomi were happy to see her, too, although she suspected it had a lot to do with the bakery box she carried.

"What did you bring us?" Mary Katherine asked. "Here, let me take it so you can put your things up."

Rachel Ann bit back a smile.

"Mary Katherine, you didn't even say hello!" Naomi chided her cousin. "*Guder mariye*, Rachel Ann," she said. "What did you bring us?" She tried to take the box from her cousin.

She laughed. "Sticky buns with pecans."

"My favorite!" Mary Katherine cried.

"I thought cinnamon rolls were your favorite."

"Anything she bakes is your favorite," Naomi scoffed. "Coffee or tea, Rachel Ann?"

She glanced at the clock. They had fifteen minutes before the shop opened. "Tea, please."

Mary Katherine put a bun on a plate, fixed a cup of tea, and set both of them on a small tray. She carried it out to Leah and then joined Naomi and Rachel Ann at the table.

"Promise us you'll bring baked goodies in after you quit working at the bakery," Mary Katherine said as she picked up a bun and took a bite.

"Promise."

"Maybe you should think about baking at home and supplying the bakery after the part-time job ends. It would be easier on you than going into the bakery early five mornings a week," Mary Katherine suggested.

"What an interesting idea," Rachel Ann said. "I'll have to think about talking to Linda about it."

"So, how's Sam?"

"*Gut*. Still complaining about his cast, but he gets around just as though he's not wearing one. Our *grossmudder* says he runs her ragged every day when she watches him."

"Are you still seeing Michael?" Naomi wanted to know.

"I don't think so," she said slowly, surprising herself. "What I mean is, I don't think I want to anymore. I think I was interested in him because I was so curious about the *Englisch*. But he's not the man I thought he was."

She stared into her cup. Michael had only visited Sam once in the hospital. It was nice he'd seen to it the hospital bill was paid, but then again it was his insurance. She hadn't felt he was sensitive about the way he'd responded to her anxiety about being pregnant. Okay, so she was naïve . . . but did he have to make her feel that way?

She reminded herself he couldn't make her feel naïve unless she let him, any more than she had to feel inferior to other Amish women, because she wasn't skilled at quilting or sewing.

Suddenly aware of silence, she looked up. Mary Katherine and Naomi were watching her with sympathy.

"Sometimes you have to date someone to know they're not right for you," Naomi said. "I dated the wrong man before I married Nick. It was pretty unpleasant at the end."

She shivered, then shook her head. "The man was from another Amish community so I didn't know him well. Nick was *Englisch* then, but I'd known him for years and I think it makes a difference."

"Maybe it's one reason why our marriages work," Mary Katherine said, looking thoughtful. "We usually know the man we marry for a long time. We grow up with them, become friends before we find ourselves falling in love."

Rachel Ann thought about what Abram had said to her about how his feelings had changed, had grown for her.

She knew he was the best friend she'd ever had, and she cared deeply about him as well. Had she taken him for granted and thought there was something—some*one*—better out there and missed out?

There was silence again.

"Where'd you go this time?" Naomi asked, her eyes twinkling. "What's on your mind? Or should I say who?"

Mary Katherine poked her with her elbow. "Stop teasing."

"I'm only asking what you want to know," Naomi retorted.

"You're being as nosy as Anna."

"I'm telling her you said so."

"She knows she's nosy."

Rachel Ann laughed and stood up. The three acted more like sisters than cousins. Sometimes when she was around them she found herself wishing she'd had a sister.

"Ready to open up?" Leah asked as she walked in and set her plate in the sink. "I have a feeling it's going to be a busy day."

"They're the best kind," Naomi said. "Those and a day when I have a quilting class."

Rachel Ann took a sip of her tea and thought a busy day would help the time go quickly. And she wouldn't have time to think about talking to Abram . . .

Rachel Ann rehearsed what she was going to say to Abram all the way home.

What a stupid mess had come from one small act—drinking a beer. So much had changed so quickly . . . too many hours of worry. It was much like how in a blink of an eye Sam had been hurt and they'd endured so much anguish.

She still felt nearly giddy whenever she remembered she no longer had to worry about being pregnant. When she started her *rumschpringe*, she'd looked at whether she wanted to join the church. She didn't struggle as much with religious issues as some Amish youth did. Nothing bad had ever happened to her to make her upset with God—even Sam's accident hadn't done that, because she'd blamed herself for it happening.

Her parents hadn't objected to her dating Michael like she'd thought they might, but they hadn't seemed happy about it. However, they had insisted she keep attending church as long as she lived under their roof. She'd agreed, and they had looked relieved she hadn't argued.

There was just this curiosity about the *Englisch* world . . . and guys she hadn't grown up with.

Well, this morning, when she'd been talking with Mary Katherine and Naomi, she realized she just didn't feel the same about Michael. Or exploring the *Englisch* world.

Sometimes she was so tired after her long days at work she fell asleep on the ride home. Tonight she felt wide awake and was looking forward to talking to Abram.

Now she just had to find a time and place to talk to him.

When she arrived home, she found a note on the kitchen table saying her parents had gone to visit her *grossmudder* with Sam and would be home around eight. There was homemade vegetable soup and the makings for sandwiches in the refrigerator for her supper.

Rachel Ann set her purse and lunch tote down. This time of the day Abram could usually be found in the barn taking care of his horses or working on some projects for the furniture store.

She saw the glow of a battery-run lantern as she walked over to the barn. "Abram?"

"*Kumm!*" he called.

She pushed open the door and walked inside, careful to close it behind her to keep in the warmth. Abram sat at a worktable carving a rose design into the top of a dark wooden keepsake box.

His face lit up when he saw her. "*Gut-n-owed.*" He got up and brought her the chair he'd been sitting on. "How are you doing? Feeling *allrecht*?"

Rachel Ann nodded, basking in the warmth of his smile. She sank into the chair, grateful for the chance to sit down after being on her feet all day.

He pulled over a bale of hay and sat near her, so close their knees nearly touched.

"I have something to tell you," she said slowly.

"You found out already?"

"You could say so." She hesitated. Michael had made her feel almost stupid she hadn't remembered.

Abram reached over and took one of her hands. "There's nothing to worry about. I told you I'd marry you."

She stared at him. It had been growing dark the other night when he had shocked her with his proposal. Now, in the light of the lantern, she saw how sincere, how caring he was.

"I don't have to worry about being pregnant," she told him.

"You went to the doctor?" he asked, and then he reddened. "Sorry, maybe you found out another way."

She shook her head. "I had a talk with Michael." She closed her eyes in remembered embarrassment.

He released her hand. "I see. So he wants to marry you."

"*Nee.*" She clutched her hands in her lap. "This is hard to tell you."

"What is it? Oh, Rachel Ann, don't tell me you're getting an abortion."

Shocked, she shook her head. "Abram, I feel like such a fool. I told you I had a beer that night on an empty stomach. He said I fell asleep and nothing happened. I couldn't remember anything, so I thought the worst."

She got to her feet and paced. "After he dropped me off at home, I managed to walk inside and crawled into bed, and when I woke up, my *kapp* was gone and my hair was down and I panicked."

"Rachel Ann, calm down. It's understandable. You're a young, innocent *maedel.*"

"He made me feel stupid." She sank down into the chair again.

"You're not stupid."

Silence stretched between them. The horses munched their feed. Allie, the barn cat who divided her time between the two barns, woke and strolled over to wind herself between Abram's legs. He scratched her head absently and seemed lost in thought.

"What are you thinking?" she asked him at last.

"I have to admit I'm kind of disappointed."

"Disappointed?"

He lifted his head and looked at her. "I wouldn't have minded marrying you. Raising a *kind* together."

Emotion welled up in her. She shook her head. "I'm not sure I could have allowed you to make such a sacrifice."

"Don't call it a sacrifice," he said brusquely.

Her eyes widened.

"You're a woman any man would want for a *fraa.* If I hadn't dragged my feet maybe I'd have—" he broke off.

"You'd have what?"

"I'd have asked to date you. But then you met Michael."

She absorbed what he'd said. What would have happened if she hadn't just seen him as a friend and she'd traveled down a different path?

"Is it too late?" she found herself asking.

He looked at her. "Too late?"

"To see if we can be more than really good friends."

"But what about—"

"I'm not seeing him anymore," she said definitely. "I haven't talked to him yet, but it's over."

Abram raised his eyebrows. "When did you decide this?"

Rachel Ann shrugged. "Today. It's taken me some time, but I think I'm seeing more clearly lately. So what do you say?"

"Are you asking me if I want to date you?"

She bit back a smile. "*Ya.*"

"How soon can we start?"

She laughed and stood. "Why don't we go out to supper tomorrow night?"

"It's a date."

11

Rachel Ann eyed the scraps of dough left after she cut out another batch of gingerbread people. There wasn't enough left to cut out more cookies, but she had an idea.

She found some parchment paper and scissors and cut out a smaller gingerbread shape. Then she rolled out the scraps and cut out the smaller cookie with a knife. She placed them on a baking sheet and kept a careful eye on the time since the cookies were so small. After they were done and cooled, she decorated them and put them into a box.

Later, when she got to Stitches in Time, she found Naomi and presented her with the box. "I brought something for the display window."

Naomi opened the box, looked inside, and gave her a delighted smile. "For the tea party!"

Rachel Ann watched as Naomi placed the little gingerbread cookies on a child-sized table set with teacups and plates. Amish dolls made by Leah sat around the table in one corner of the display window. Naomi had sewn a quilt in Christmas greens and reds with fat white snowflakes. Tote bags woven by Mary Katherine sat stuffed with presents wrapped in brightly colored paper. Several teddy bears wore Anna's popular knitted baby caps, cardigan sweaters, and mittens made in festive holiday colors and patterns.

Hers was a small contribution to the window but a cute touch. Naomi made a little sign proclaiming the cookies were from the bakery and propped it on the table.

"Now there's something from all of us in the window," Naomi said.

Rachel Ann found an idea forming as she stared at the cookies. She put her purse and lunch tote up. There was a lull in customers— many tourists took the time for a leisurely lunch at one of the local Amish restaurants—so she hurried to the bolts of fabric to select one of brown felt.

The bolt made a clunking noise as she unfolded it on the cutting table. A couple of yards should do it, she decided as she cut what she needed. Then she picked up one of the woven shopping baskets and walked over to the notions aisle. She chose white rickrack, buttons in several colors, and fabric braid. A package of foam pillow stuffing completed her purchases.

She cut a gingerbread man shape about a foot and a half tall and a foot wide during a break, and after she ate a quick sandwich at lunch, she sewed it up on one of the shop's sewing machines. Turning the material inside out she stuffed it and basted the small opening shut. It was fun to decorate the pillow with rickrack to look like a jacket and cute colored ball buttons to resemble gumdrop buttons, the same way she decorated gingerbread cookies.

"Why Rachel Ann, this is quite clever," Leah said. "I had no idea you did this sort of thing."

Startled, Rachel Ann looked up. She'd been so absorbed in sewing on shiny black buttons for eyes she hadn't heard the older woman approach.

"I'm making it for Sam for Christmas."

"I'd like to see you make some for the shop. They'd sell well right now, but you're working so much . . . where would you get the time?"

"You mean it?"

Leah regarded her with kind eyes. "About liking it?"

"*Ya.*"

"I think it's clever the way you combined your talent for baking with sewing. And I do think we could sell some. It's just a shame, but I don't think you have time to make any with the shop busy and you working two jobs."

Rachel Ann nodded. "Maybe I can make a few on my day off."

Leah patted her shoulder. "Just don't wear yourself out. When you're not working two jobs you could make them for next Christmas."

"True."

"You could think of other shapes, too. Maybe other storybook characters or shapes like cupcakes or something."

Her mind whirled. "*Danki* for the encouragement. And the ideas."

Leah nodded and smiled. "You have more in you than you think, *kind*." A customer hailed her, and she hurried to help her.

Rachel Ann stared after her. What did she mean?

She had to set the pillow aside as customers began streaming in after their midday meals, full of Amish food and Christmas cheer. They left with shopping bags full of gifts and craft kits.

The cramps hit just before the shop closed. Rachel Ann kept what she needed in her purse during the last week or two of the month when she expected her period, so she wasn't caught unaware. In a shop full of women, though, she knew there were emergency supplies in a cupboard in the back room.

She slipped into the bathroom with her purse and then went into the back room to take some aspirin with a glass of water. The cramps were so bad she sank into a chair and wondered if she'd get through the last half hour of work.

"Are you *allrecht*?" Leah asked as she walked into the room.

"*Ya.*" She got to her feet and tried not to wince.

"*Nee*, you're not. What's wrong?"

"It's just cramps. I took something. I'll be fine in a few minutes."

"Sit, I think we could both use a cup of tea," Leah said and set about making it. "Things have slowed down. Rain's coming."

So they sat and drank their tea, and within a few minutes they heard the patter of rain against the window.

Leah sighed. "We had a *gut* day. I wish the rain had held off until we got home. Oh well, God has a reason for it now."

When they walked back into the shop Naomi and Mary Katherine were finishing up with customers. When they left, Leah locked the door. Everyone collected their things and waited by the door for their rides.

As she rode home, miserable with her cramps, Rachel Ann pressed a hand to her abdomen and wished she could be home already. She wanted to crawl into a ball under the quilts on her bed and will the cramps away.

Then she remembered she was supposed to go out to supper with Abram. She sighed. So much for starting the new direction of their relationship this evening.

&

Abram happened to be in the front yard when Rachel Ann came home.

Allrecht, so it wasn't a coincidence. He knew what time she usually arrived home after work.

She saw him and waved, so he walked over.

The minute he got closer, he saw something was wrong. Her face looked pinched and pale, her eyes a little puffy as if she'd been crying.

"Are you *allrecht*?" he asked, mentally kicking himself. Of course she wasn't.

"I'm sorry, Abram, but I'm not feeling well. I can't go out with you this evening."

He tried to hide his disappointment. "No problem. I'm sorry you're not feeling well. Is there anything I can do?"

She shook her head. "*Nee. Danki*," she added. "I just need to take some aspirin and get in bed."

Abram nodded and walked her to her door. "Feel better. See you tomorrow."

"'Night."

He walked back to his house. His mother stood at the sink washing dishes. "Back already? I thought you were going out with Rachel Ann."

"She's not feeling well. I don't know what's wrong. Maybe a headache. Or a stomachache. She had her hand on her waist and looked like she'd been crying."

"Men. So dense," his mother said, shaking her head.

"What?"

"Think about it."

Puzzled, he just stared at her.

"Abram, maybe it's her time of the month."

"Oh," he said slowly, suddenly understanding. He felt his face flush. "Uh, should it be bothering her so much?"

"*Ya*, some *maedels* have a hard time."

"But she'll be *allrecht* tomorrow, right?"

"Maybe, maybe not."

"Oh." He stood there for a moment, wondering what he was going to do with a suddenly free evening. He did not want to spend it the way he always did—doing more work.

Abram walked into the living room, pawed through several issues of a farming magazine, and chose one. He threw himself into the easy chair before the fire. He thought about how his mother had teased him about not guessing why Rachel Ann didn't feel well. Did she think unmarried men knew about such things? Especially when they didn't have a wife or a girlfriend?

He thought about the timing of . . . Rachel Ann's problem. If it had happened a few days earlier it would have relieved her mind so much about her fear she was pregnant. She'd also have avoided what she said had been an embarrassing talk with Michael.

So, both of them had been told they didn't know much about certain things. Boyfriend or mother, it was a little sobering to know you didn't know about such things.

He shrugged and tossed the magazine aside. Oh well, if his mother wasn't teasing him about this it would be about something else because she loved to joke. They had an easy relationship where they could talk about almost anything. She even occasionally prodded him about finding a *fraa*. Many Amish parents kept out of their children's lives when it came to dating. They often didn't know their *sohns* or *dochders* were engaged until the announcement of their pending marriage was made in church.

She'd have been thrilled if she knew he'd proposed he and Rachel Ann get married. He knew his mother loved her like a daughter. And the possibility of having another grandchild? He couldn't think of a word to express the magnitude of how she'd feel about it. She had four from his *bruders* and *schwesders,* but he knew she'd love more. The Amish loved children, and the people he knew who had grandchildren cherished them even more.

For now, it felt like he rattled around in this big house. It's why he didn't mind having her living here, although she spent most of her time in the *dawdi haus* in the rear of it.

Restless, he got up, shrugged into his jacket, and walked out onto the porch. The wind was cool, snaking down the back of his neck. A light snow had fallen all day. He pulled the collar up and wondered if the weather forecast of an unusually cold winter would prove true.

Abram glanced at Rachel Ann's house, finding her bedroom window and noting it was dark. He hoped she was feeling better.

He made a last check of the horses and shut the barn door. Still feeling a little restless, he went back into the house, washed up the percolator and his coffee mug, and set them to drain on the counter. He knew if he didn't do this and his mother happened to come into kitchen later in the night she'd be cleaning up in the middle of the night. The woman was obsessive about cleaning.

Finally, he went to bed and read a novel. He was usually too tired to read more than a few pages before he fell asleep. Tonight, he managed nearly forty pages before the book slipped from his hands and he fell asleep.

He woke when he heard a vehicle pull into the drive of Rachel Ann's house before dawn. She was evidently going to work at the bakery, so he guessed she must feel better. On the other hand, Rachel Ann was a hard worker. It would take a lot to make her stay home.

As he moved through his day doing chores and working on the trinket boxes and driving his mother to a doctor's appointment, he thought about calling Rachel Ann at the shop to find out if she wanted to go out for supper. But he remembered that his mother had said Rachel Ann might not feel well for more than a day. So he decided he would wait for her to let him know when she was ready.

He didn't see her for two more days.

She surprised him with a visit to the barn when she came home from work. He could see she still carried her purse and lunch tote, so she hadn't gone into her house yet.

"Feeling better?" he asked.

She nodded. "*Ya, danki.* Maybe we can go out for supper one evening this week. If you're still interested, I mean."

"Of course I'm interested. If you said let's go now, I'd be hitching up the buggy before you could blink."

"Really?"

He set down the cloth he'd been using to polish a finished keepsake box. "Really."

"I'll take your dare," she said. "Let's go. I'll tell *Mamm* I won't be having supper with the family, and you can hitch up your buggy."

He grinned as she turned on her heel and started toward the barn door.

They went to a little family-style restaurant the locals patronized—Rachel Ann's choice. "They have the best fried chicken. Don't tell my *mamm* it's better than hers."

"I've eaten here," he told her. "It's better than my *mamm*'s, too."

The place was busy for a weekday night, filled with customers who were probably going out to do Christmas shopping after work.

The hostess seated them in a booth, and they ordered fried chicken, mashed potatoes, and biscuits.

"Mmm," Rachel Ann said, and she sighed as she wiped her fingers on a paper napkin.

"You like eating someplace like this more than somewhere fancy?"

She nodded. "I've never been a fancy person."

"But I want to take you someplace nice sometime."

"This is nice."

"You know, the kind of place where we treat ourselves to a special meal and it feels like—" he stopped for words.

"Like a date," she finished for him.

"*Ya.*"

"I know the kind of place you mean and it'll be nice sometime. But this is still a treat after a long day. And it's still our first date."

She met his gaze and smiled, and he found himself smiling back. For a long moment, the sounds of people talking and eating around them faded away, and he felt something shift between them. They were actually making a change in their relationship.

A child wailed at a nearby table and brought them back to the present.

"So how's work going?"

"Baking lots of Christmas cookies at the bakery and selling a lot of Christmas gifts at the shop."

She told him about Leah's reaction to the pillow she was making for Sam for Christmas and how she could sell some at the shop. He heard the surprise in her voice. She not only didn't talk about it with *hochmut*—pride, not encouraged in their community—she seemed a little shy and insecure about the idea of selling a craft at the shop.

"You talk like this was totally unexpected."

"The women at the shop are so talented," she said with a tone of wonder in her voice.

"You're talented," he told her.

"I'm good at baking, but I've never been good at anything to do with sewing."

"Maybe you've just never given yourself a chance."

"You always know just what to say."

Abram was glad the server walked up and asked if they wanted dessert, because he didn't know what to say to her just then.

❧

Rachel Ann filled a glass with water from the tap and swallowed two ibuprofen.

"Are you still having cramps?" her mother asked her.

"*Ya.*" It had been a long week. She sat at the kitchen table wishing she could skip church. She loved church, but the thought of sitting three hours on a hard bench was taking a lot of effort this morning.

Her mother set a plate of toast and a cup of coffee in front of her. "I know you're not fond of coffee, but try some this morning. It always helped me."

"I remember you told me you used to have bad cramps," Rachel Ann said as she stirred some sugar into her coffee.

"Maybe it's time to go see the doctor."

She raised her eyebrows. Doctors were usually a last resort, seen only after homeopathic remedies had been used. But she *had* done everything she could think of to relieve her cramps. She'd come to dread that week of the month.

"You're probably right. But doctors are expensive."

"Make an appointment, Rachel Ann."

She'd nearly had to call in sick one day this week . . . maybe seeing the doctor would prevent it. Suffering the pain was bad enough, but to miss work just wasn't done.

Rachel Ann ate the toast and took several sips of coffee, but she couldn't handle more than that. She just didn't like coffee.

"Where's Sam?"

"He's in the barn with your *dat*." She glanced at the clock. "It's time to leave."

Rachel Ann got up and carried her plate and cup to the sink. The ibuprofen hadn't started working yet, but maybe by the time they reached the Stoltzfus house where services were being held she'd feel better. She reminded herself after the service she and Abram had plans for lunch and a drive.

He had already taken a seat in the men's section of the room and looked up and smiled when she walked in. She smiled in return and took a seat with the women. As she'd expected, it was hard to sit on a hard bench, but Ben Troyer inspired her with his message from the book of Mark, and when the assemblage began singing a favorite hymn, it seemed something in her relaxed and the pain slipped away.

"You're looking pretty," Abram told her quietly after the service. "Blue's my favorite color on you."

It was also the favored color for wedding dresses in her community. She felt color rush into her cheeks. Was he trying to send a message? She glanced up at him but couldn't tell.

"Are you ready to leave?"

She nodded. "What about your *mamm*?"

"She's riding home with your parents."

"*Gut.*"

"Where shall we go?" he asked as they walked toward the front door.

"It's your turn to choose."

They feasted on hot meatball subs and cannoli at an Italian restaurant and then took a drive.

The combination of the rich, heavy food and the gentle motion of the buggy on top of a restless, pain-filled night made Rachel Ann drowsy.

She woke with her cheek resting on Abram's shoulder. He held the reins in his left hand and his right arm held her close. The feeling of contentment, of being cherished was too tempting. She lay still, not wanting to move. But it wasn't proper for two unmarried people to be seen in such close contact.

Reluctantly, she stirred and scooted out from under his arm. "Sorry, I fell asleep."

He shot her a grin. "So I already put you to sleep."

She laughed. "*Nee*, I just didn't sleep well last night. Then we had such a big lunch."

"What did you think of John and Rosemary's announcement?"

"I was surprised," she said carefully. "I didn't know they were dating. I haven't had much time to talk with friends lately. Did you know?"

He shook his head. "I've been working a lot and haven't talked to friends much lately either."

Well, he'd seen Saul and Elizabeth, but he didn't feel he should share their news. Then he glanced at Rachel Ann and wondered if she knew about the baby.

"What?" she asked when she saw he was looking at her.

"I stopped in at Saul and Elizabeth's store when I was in town the day you and I had lunch."

"Oh?"

"They were doing well."

"*Gut.*" She eyed him. Where was he going with this? "I had lunch with her last week."

Their gazes met and she saw humor in his eyes. Then at the same time they said, "You know!" and they laughed.

He reached across the distance between them, and she slipped her hand in his. They sat a respectable distance apart to anyone who passed them. But the connection felt intimate and so strong.

12

Rachel Ann told herself it was time to call Michael and tell him she didn't want to see him any longer.

She wasn't sure she needed to do it. He hadn't stopped by since the day she'd talked to him. But it was the right thing to do. Besides, she didn't want him stopping by and have to deal with it at an unexpected time.

So she went outside to the phone shanty and dialed the number he'd given her.

He sounded surprised when he answered. After all, she never called him.

"Rachel Ann? Is something wrong? You never call me. Did you get a cell phone?"

He'd asked her to do it to make it more convenient for them to stay in contact and reminded her other Amish had cell phones, but he didn't seem to believe her when she said she couldn't afford it.

"No. Listen, Michael, I'm just calling to say I won't be seeing you anymore."

"You're dumping me?"

"I wouldn't call it that, I just—"

"You're dumping *me*?" he demanded.

"I'm not dumping you. This isn't about you. I just don't want to date someone who isn't Amish. Michael, if we had worked out, and you wanted to get married—"

"Whoa, who's talking marriage?"

She almost laughed at the alarm in his voice. "We date to find a marriage partner in my community, Michael," she continued, "If we married, I'd have to leave my church, my family, my community. I don't want to do it."

He sighed. "Oh. Okay."

"It's for the best," she told him. "I enjoyed knowing you and wish you the best."

"Whatever."

"Merry Christmas," she said, but she heard him disconnect the call.

She thought about the conversation as she washed dishes after supper. Part of why she'd begun dating Michael was a curiosity about the *Englisch* world. He was so different from the Amish men she knew. She'd heard the expression "opposites attract."

But what she'd found was that Michael might be intriguing but he wasn't as mature as she'd expected. And in the end, as she'd told him, she wasn't interested in leaving her community. And he certainly wasn't interested in offering marriage.

Just as she was finishing up with the dishes she heard a knock on the back door. "Come in!" she called.

Abram stuck his head in. "I thought I'd see if we could go for a drive."

"Oh, I'm sorry, I can't. I'm watching Sam until he goes to bed. *Mamm* has a headache, and *Daed's* in the barn working on a rush project for the furniture store. You can come in if you want, though."

"Abram!" Sam cried from his seat at the kitchen table. He held out his arms for a hug, and Abram bent to lift him into his arms.

"*Gut* to see you, Sam. Hey, did you draw this?" Abram asked, looking down at the drawing Sam had made with crayons.

"*Ya,*" Sam said, his smile fading.

"Rachel Ann? Did you see this?" Abram looked over at her.

She wiped her hands on a dish towel and walked over to look at the drawing Sam had been making. Sam had drawn a little boy with blond hair and a cast on his leg. The boy had big fat tears sliding down his cheeks.

"Who's this, Sam?" she asked gently, knowing the answer to her question.

"Me," he said, and the corners of his mouth turned down.

"What's wrong, Sam? Why are you feeling so sad?"

He shrugged.

"I think I know what's wrong," Abram told her. "I'll be right back."

When he returned a few minutes later, he plucked her jacket and Sam's from the pegs near the door. "We're going for a drive," he told them. "I asked your *daed* and he said we could. A quick one."

Sam beamed while Abram helped him with his jacket and flung his arms around Abram's neck when he lifted him. Mystified, Rachel Ann slipped on her jacket and followed Abram out the back door.

He put Sam in the back seat of his buggy and tucked a quilt around him. Turning to Rachel Ann, he helped her into the buggy.

"Where are we going?" Sam wanted to know.

"You'll see."

Abram shot her a grin. "I think Sam's getting tired of being cooped up in the house," he told her.

"He is," she agreed. "The doctor said he'll have his cast off soon, though, right, Sam?"

"*Nee,*" he said, and he sounded sulky.

"Sam, he said after Christmas," Rachel Ann reminded him. "It's not long now."

"It is to a four-year-old," Abram said in a low voice.

She sighed. "True."

"Where we goin', Abram?"

"You'll see."

"You said that already."

"You asked me already," he responded. "You'll like where we're going."

A few minutes later Abram pulled into the parking lot of a convenience store. He got out and helped Sam out of the back seat. "We'll be right back," he told Rachel Ann. "Sorry, but just us guys are going in."

Sam chortled. "Just us guys."

She watched them go inside. Abram handed Sam a small shopping basket, and the two of them walked up and down the aisles filling it with she had no idea what. Finally, they emerged carrying plastic shopping bags.

"Did you buy out the store?" she asked as Abram tucked Sam back in his seat.

Sam giggled. "No, we left some stuff for other people." He dug into one of the bags and held out a Drumstick ice cream cone to her.

"Why, *danki*, it's my favorite!" she said, touched that he remembered.

"I know. Abram tole me."

She glanced at him. "Oh?"

"*Ya,*" Sam said. "And I got him—"

"An ice cream sandwich," she finished.

"*Ya!* How'd you know?"

She turned to smile at her brother. "Because I've known Abram for a long, long time. And you got a Fudgsicle." She sat back in her seat and looked at Abram. "Was that a *gut* idea?"

"It shouldn't be a problem. It's not going to melt as quickly as if it was summer."

"Well, we'll see if your theory proves correct," she said dryly.

"It won't take long to get home."

She noticed he signaled to his horse to speed up a moment later.

"What else did you get?" she asked Sam.

The plastic bags rattled as he investigated the contents. "Sparkle glue," he said, holding it up for her to see. "I'm going to make Chrismas cards. Lots o' other stuff, too."

"Sam? Where's your Fudgsicle?"

"On the seat right here," he told her in a cheerful voice.

It was hard to see Abram's face in the dim light but she thought she saw him wince. "The upholstery's washable," he said.

"Sam, eat the Fudgsicle and don't make a mess."

"*Allrecht*," he said cheerfully. "But it's got a little fuzz on it now, Rachel Ann."

"Give it to me and I'll wipe it off," she told him, chuckling at Abram's expression of dismay.

"Here." Sam handed her the ice cream bar.

Rachel Ann stared down at the cold chocolate mess in her hand. Why had she thought he'd hand it to her with the stick end? He was only four. She sneaked a look at Abram and saw him grinning.

She used her free hand to dig in her purse for a tissue, wiped the fuzz from the bar, and handed it back to Sam. "No more ice cream in the buggy," she told Abram sternly.

"Yes, ma'am."

As they rode home, Rachel Ann found herself thinking about how good Abram was with Sam. He'd make a good *dat*, Abram would.

"You're quiet tonight," he said, breaking into her thoughts.

She blushed, glad he couldn't know what she was thinking.

❧

Abram kept finding his thoughts going to the church service of the past weekend.

Most Amish weddings took place in the fall here, with some scheduled in December and few in the month of January. The upcoming marriage of two church members had started him thinking.

Things had been going well between him and Rachel Ann. If only she'd joined the church . . . they could get married now. Instead, they would have to wait until next fall.

He sighed. There was no point in thinking that way. After all, he couldn't change things. He was happy they were dating.

The trouble was, he was a man. He wanted more. He wanted to have her as his *fraa*, in his home, not in the one next door. He wanted to see her first thing in the morning, eat supper with her every evening, and climb the stairs to their room with her at night. He wanted to have *kinner* with her, put down roots.

He shook his head, trying to force his thoughts down a more acceptable path. A walk, some fresh air was what he needed. He left the barn and walked his fields.

Rachel Ann found him there, her smile a warm beacon on a gray, cloudy day. The cool late fall breeze whipped her forest green dress around her body, alternately molding then concealing her slender shape.

"It's *gut* to see you," he said, trying not to think about if they were married he could give her a kiss, hold her hand, suggest—no, he couldn't go there.

She stared at him, looking puzzled. "What?"

He hesitated. "I was just thinking if you'd joined the church, we could be making plans to get married now."

She blushed. "But we just started dating."

"I know how I feel. I've been waiting for you for a long time."

"But . . . I . . ." Overwhelmed, she pressed her fingers against her mouth. "I don't know what to say. I didn't know how you felt, that you wanted more. I just came to the realization for myself recently. In a way, maybe it's a good thing we can't get married right away. Marriage is forever. We need to make sure what we feel will last."

"My feelings aren't going to change," he said quietly. "Do you think yours will?"

"*Nee.* But I think we don't need to be in a rush. We should enjoy the time and get to know each other better." She looked around. "I guess it's kind of like your fields. There's a time for everything."

"You mean like Ecclesiastes? 'There is a time for everything, and a season for every activity under the heavens.' "

She nodded and smiled at him. "You have the patience to tend your crops. The next months will take some patience, but after the harvest . . ."

"I can wait, if I know we'll be together."

Her smile grew brighter. She held out her hand, and he clasped it. They might have stood there longer, but the wind grew cooler and she shivered.

"You should get inside. You don't want to catch cold."

She turned to walk back to her house, and he joined her.

"I forgot. I came out here to ask you if you wanted to eat supper with us tomorrow night. Sam has something he wants to give you."

"Give me?"

"*Ya*, he kind of likes you."

"I kind of like him, too. I think it'd be pretty amazing to have a couple like him." He chuckled. "You're blushing."

"Don't tease."

"*Ya*, a couple little boys and a couple little girls."

"You've done some thinking about this."

"I have. Have you?"

"Some. But it's up to God. He gives us what we should have."

"True."

They'd reached his house. "I'll go tell my mother I'm eating with you and your family."

"The invitation includes her as well."

"She'll be there. She kind of likes Sam as well."

Rachel Ann laughed. "Sam has all of us wrapped around his little finger."

"His sticky little finger."

"Did you get the Fudgsicle out of the upholstery?"

"*Mamm* had the perfect thing to clean it. Says she had great experience cleaning up after another messy little boy. Can't imagine who she's talking about. Must be one of my *bruders*."

"*Schur*. See you tomorrow at six?"

"We'll be there."

He watched her walk to her house and go inside. Turning back to the barn, he made sure his horses were fed and watered and his tools were put away.

The spicy scent of chili and cornbread hit him the minute he walked into the kitchen. "Hungry?"

"Always, especially for your chili." He sat down and sprinkled some shredded cheese on top of his bowl of chili. "We've been invited to supper next door tomorrow. Rachel Ann said the invitation came from Sam."

"How sweet. We were all blessed when Martha had him. I know having a baby so many years after Rachel Ann was a surprise. But what a *wunderbaar* surprise."

Abram remembered the conversation he'd had with Rachel Ann out in the fields. He found himself looking at all the empty chairs around the big wooden table his father had built. Sometimes he missed his two *bruders* and his *schwesder*, but they were older and married and had their own *kinner*; now they sat at this table only at holidays. It was just him and his *mamm* until he married and brought his *fraa* home.

Rachel Ann had said they shouldn't be in a rush, and they should enjoy the time and get to know each other better. There was a time for everything, she'd added.

He looked at his mother. Maybe this was a time to enjoy his time not just with Rachel Ann but with others as well. His mother looked tired tonight, and he thought she moved a little awkwardly as if she was in pain.

"How was your day?" he asked her. "You had a doctor's appointment today, didn't you? What did she say?"

Abram listened while she told him, then at his prompting went on to relate how she and a friend had met for lunch and did some shopping at Stitches in Time. When they finished supper and the apple crisp she'd made for dessert, he insisted he should do the dishes so she could rest after her busy day.

As the sink filled with water he looked over at Rachel Ann's house. He could see the family sitting at the kitchen table. Tomorrow, he and his mother would be joining them. He'd been invited to supper at their house many times, but he found himself a little impatient to be part of that family unit and be close to Rachel Ann.

℞

The drive into work gave Rachel Ann time to think about what Abram had said the night before about her joining the church.

If her parents—especially her mother—hadn't insisted she keep attending church during her *rumschpringe* she might have gone ahead and joined. But because they'd pushed, she'd resisted and dug her feet in. She'd been so curious about *Englisch* life . . . then when she'd met Michael, well, she supposed dating him became her area of rebellion.

Then came the accident and all its trauma. And she'd added hours to her day by hiring on at the bakery. She didn't have time to think now, let alone be studying to join the church.

In a way, she wasn't sorry she hadn't joined the church yet. As much as she cared about Abram, as much as she knew she might be falling in love with him, the idea of suddenly getting married was a little scary.

And shouldn't it be? Who jumped into marriage quickly, when there was no divorce here?

She shivered at the thought.

"Cold?" Linda asked her. "I've got a shawl in my tote bag."

"*Nee*, I'm fine."

"Ladies, do you need me to turn up the heat back there?" the driver called back. He'd evidently overheard their conversation.

"We're fine, thanks."

They hurried from the van to the bakery. Linda unlocked the door and flicked on the lights. No need to turn up the heater. The ovens quickly warmed the place, and the two of them set about working. The early morning hours passed quickly with mixing and baking.

Later in the morning, she was taking a break in the back room of Stitches in Time when Jenny Bontrager walked in looking for coffee.

"Mind if I join you?" she asked Rachel Ann.

"Please do. I was just finishing a letter." She slid it into an envelope, licked a stamp, and affixed it to the corner. There, she'd made her request to the bishop to take the necessary classes to join the church.

She looked up at Jenny. "You took the classes to join the church. Were they hard?"

Jenny shook her head. "They'll be easy for you because you're Amish. Remember, I was *Englisch* before I converted so there was so much to learn about things like the *Ordnung*." She studied Rachel Ann. "So you decided it's time to join?"

Rachel Ann nodded. "I hope I didn't worry my parents too much."

"Parents are going to worry no matter what. You took the time you needed and looked around and came to the decision to stay. It's all that's important. I think it's the right path for you."

"I do too." She studied the simply dressed woman her mother's age who sat opposite her. Once, Jenny Bontrager—maiden name Jenny King—had been famous as a network correspondent roaming the world. Then she'd been injured by a car bomb and come here to recuperate at her Amish grandmother's home. And she'd been reunited with the boy next door she'd loved years before when she visited.

Her relationship with a boy next door had worked out well. She and Matthew Bontrager were happily married and had four *kinner* and two *grosskinner* now.

Leah bustled into the room. "Jenny, I found another skein of yarn with the right dye lot you wanted." She handed it to her.

"Thanks. This'll teach me to buy more than I need next time. I'm knitting a sweater for one of my grandbabies," she told Rachel Ann. "Anna got me hooked on knitting. I'm finally past making mufflers."

She stood. "It was nice to talk to you, Rachel Ann."

"You, too."

"Is there anything else I can get you?" Leah asked her.

"No, I think I'll browse a bit. I might see something for a last-minute Christmas gift."

Leah took the seat Jenny had vacated and studied her. "How are you feeling today, Rachel Ann? I hope your cramps are gone."

"*Ya, danki.* It reminds me, though. *Mamm* thinks I need to go to the doctor. Do you think I could use my lunch hour to go later this week, if I can get an appointment?"

"Of course. I hope she can do something about them for you. It's a shame to see some young women suffer so."

She gestured at the letter sitting on the table in front of Rachel Ann. "Did you want me to put it in the outgoing mail basket?"

Rachel Ann nodded. "*Danki.* I wrote the bishop to tell him I want to start taking classes so I can join the church after New Year's."

"I'm so glad to hear it."

"I'm sure my parents will be happy to hear it, too. And—" she stopped and blushed.

"And a certain young man who lives next door to you?" Leah asked with a twinkle in her eyes.

Rachel Ann was saved from a response when they heard the bell over the front door jangle several times. "Sounds like it's getting busy."

"It's going to be like this all the way to Christmas," Leah said cheerfully. She jumped up with the energy of a woman half her age and hurried out of the room.

Rachel Ann followed her, looking forward to the festive air the shoppers carried with them this time of year.

Hours later, she enjoyed a different kind of time, a quiet one spent with Abram in his kitchen after she'd eaten supper with him and his mother. The night before, supper at her house had been lively with Sam enjoying being the center of attention as he passed out "Chris-mas cards" and regaled everyone with stories as they ate.

Tonight, supper had been quiet with just the three of them in Abram's kitchen. As soon as they were finished, Lovina retired to her room with a cup of peppermint tea, and Rachel Ann and Abram washed and dried the dishes.

Rachel Ann wasn't sure if Lovina needed to go put her feet up as she said, or if it was her way of giving the two of them some time together, but she was grateful. A buggy ride after supper was nice, but the nights grew colder and automobile drivers weren't careful about watching out for slow-moving Amish buggies.

"I sent the bishop a note asking to sign up for classes so I could join the church," she told him as she handed him a plate to dry.

Rachel Ann smiled as he reacted with surprise and nearly bobbled the plate. "*Wunderbaar!*" Then his grin faded. "I hope you didn't think I was pressuring you when we spoke about this the other night."

She shook her head. "It was time. I thought about talking to him about it the last time I saw him at church, but there were so many people who wanted his attention. So I wrote a note on break today."

One more step toward her future, she thought.

They finished drying the dishes and then sat at the big table sipping coffee and talking about everything from the holidays to what he planned to plant in his fields come spring. It had always been easy to talk to him. Elizabeth had told her once she was a good listener, but the fact was, she thought she'd learned how from being around Abram. He'd always listened to her when they sat by the pond and talked—so much more than any family member or friend.

Well, she and Elizabeth were friends now since Elizabeth had moved to Paradise. But her relationship with Abram had always been as good friends. He was one of the few people who gave total attention to you when you talked, but more, she could share her hopes and dreams with him.

"It sounds like you love the work at the bakery so much," he said after she talked about her morning constructing gingerbread houses. "How are you going to feel leaving there after the holidays? I know the work has been hard on you, but whenever you talk about it your face lights up."

She frowned and stared at her hands folded on top of the table. "I knew it was temporary when I started," she said. "I'm going to miss it. At least I feel a little more confident at the shop. Leah likes my work. She saw a gingerbread man pillow I was making for Sam for Christmas and says she wants me to make some to sell at the shop."

"I think your heart is in the bakery," he told her, and he reached over and put his warm, work-roughened hand over hers. "Maybe someday you'll want to open your own bakery."

Her eyes widened. She'd never even thought about it, and yet, he could envision such for her.

"My own bakery?" she whispered, almost afraid to say it aloud.

"Why not?"

She nodded slowly as she looked into his eyes, so warm and encouraging. "Why not?" She loved how he understood her so well. "Mary Katherine said I should think about baking at home so I didn't have to go into the bakery so early. It's a way to continue to bake there. I could take what I made into town when I went into Stitches in Time each day. I might think about it."

"Sounds like a *gut* idea," he said. "And maybe one day you'll want to think about owning a bakery of your own like I said."

She smiled, liking the idea of it. And loving him for being so supportive. "Maybe."

13

Rachel Ann had her hand on the door of Stitches in Time when she heard someone call her name. She turned and saw Emma coming up the walk loaded down with a stack of cardboard boxes in her hands.

"Let me help!" she cried, taking the top box and holding open the door so Emma could stagger inside with her load.

They set them on the closest worktable, and Rachel Ann watched Emma take a deep breath. "What's all this?"

Emma grabbed scissors and slit the lid of the box open. She lifted out woven cloth baskets made of red, white, and green material. By the time she finished opening the boxes she had half a dozen lined up on the worktable.

Leah walked over to inspect them. "Very nice," she approved. "Wrap up some little boxes to look like Christmas presents, put them in a few baskets, and let's get them in the display window. Then let's scatter the rest around the shop with different things in them to give customers ideas how to use them. Oh, and remember we already have advance orders for two of them. You'll have to call the customers so they can come pick them up."

"How did you get so many done in a week?" Rachel Ann asked her.

"Isaac had to work some overtime because one of the other roofers was out sick, so I had some evenings to myself. I got some help from my mother, too. She said she enjoyed it because it reminded her of the rag rugs she used to make."

Rachel Ann felt a little envious. She'd only been able to make two gingerbread pillows. Her *dat* had carried the sewing machine upstairs to her room so she could sew without Sam seeing what she was doing. But she was so tired after her long days—and everything couldn't be about work. Sometimes she spent evenings with Abram . . . God had a plan for everything, and it evidently wasn't the time for her to be creating for the shop.

Marriage obviously agreed with Emma. Watching her relationship with Isaac hit some interesting bumps in the road had taught Rachel Ann not to think everything went smoothly. But it was obvious that God had planned for Emma and Isaac to be together.

Customers kept her hopping and her mind off wishing she could have made some more pillows. By the time lunchtime rolled around, she was ready to take a break. Restless, she decided to take a walk before eating her sandwich. The air was cool but invigorating, and she enjoyed the bustle of others walking on the sidewalks and window shopping.

She couldn't walk past Elizabeth and Saul's store without popping in for a minute. Elizabeth was sitting on a chair supervising Saul who was arranging some carved wooden figurines. She looked up and smiled as Rachel Ann leaned down and hugged her.

"You're looking well," she said. "How are you feeling?"

"*Wunderbaar*! Saul insisted I sit down, so I'm supervising."

Saul grinned. "Hello, Rachel Ann. How's business at the shop?"

"Very busy. The bakery is, too."

"Saul got me two of your cookies yesterday," Elizabeth told her. "A little gingerbread boy and a gingerbread girl. I told him they were too pretty to eat. But, of course, I did," she confessed with a laugh.

Rachel Ann stared at her, her eyes wide. "Two cookies? Does this mean you're going to have *zwillingbopplin*?" she asked.

Elizabeth laughed and shook her head. "*Nee*. Not that it wouldn't be such an amazing gift from God, but I will be grateful for one *boppli*." She looked at Saul. "Imagine taking care of two at once."

Was it her imagination that Saul looked a little pale at the thought? Rachel Ann wondered.

"It would be a lot," Saul admitted. "There, are you happy with this display?"

"Very nice." Elizabeth turned to Rachel Ann. "What do you think?"

One of the carved figurines caught her eye. Was it—yes, it was a frog with a touch of mischief in its eyes. It reminded her of a certain person . . . and one summer day.

"I love it," she said impulsively, picking it up. She turned it over and looked at the price tag.

"Twenty percent discount for friends," Elizabeth told her.

"Sold!"

"Can you stay for a cup of tea?"

Rachel Ann dug in her purse for her wallet. "Maybe next time. I'm just out for a quick walk on my lunch break. I left my sandwich back at the shop."

Saul rang up the sale while Elizabeth wrapped the frog in tissue paper and tucked it into a gift bag.

"I'll stop by day after tomorrow?"

"Sounds *gut*. And I wouldn't mind if you brought some more of those gingerbread cookies," Elizabeth said.

"I don't know, is it me you want to see or my cookies?" Rachel Ann teased.

"Both!"

The door opened, and Elizabeth glanced over and grinned. "Speaking of *zwillingbopplin*," she told Rachel Ann with grin.

Katie and Rosie, the store's part-time helpers, walked in carrying boxes. They set them down on a nearby table.

"There's more in the van outside if you want to help," Katie told Saul, her eyes twinkling. "Rosie and I have been busy."

Saul nodded and headed outside.

"Katie and Rosie, *gut* to see you!" Elizabeth waved a hand at Rachel Ann. "Look who came to visit."

The twins rushed to hug Rachel Ann, chattering about how happy they were to see her. They'd missed church the previous Sunday in order to care for an ailing relative.

Saul came back in with two boxes in his arms and headed for the storeroom.

"We cleared two shelves for your jars," Saul told Katie and Rosie when he returned. "Will it be enough?"

The two women nodded. Rachel Ann studied them as they unloaded little jars of jams, jellies, fruit butters, chow chow, pickles, and relishes. Elizabeth claimed she could distinguish between the two of them, but Rachel Ann had always had trouble doing so. They both had heart-shaped faces, brown eyes, and chestnut hair, and were compact rather than petite. They even enjoyed wearing the same colored dresses most days.

"We brought extra pumpkin butter and cranberry jam because they're so popular this time of year," Rosie—*nee, Katie?*—said, setting some jars on a shelf.

She pulled a jar filled with layers of beans and dried vegetables from the box and handed it to Elizabeth. "We're calling this soup in a jar," she said. "All someone has to do is pour this into a pot of boiling water and simmer it for a couple of hours and they have enough soup for a family."

"Should be popular with the tourists," Elizabeth said.

"I love the way you packaged everything." The twins had made up labels for their products for their Two Peas in a Pod business with a photo of an Amish farm and gingham fabric squares wrapped around the lids with raffia.

Her eyes widened at the jar of bacon-flavored pickles. "I don't believe I've ever tasted bacon-flavored pickles."

"My *grossmudder* Lavina's recipe," one of the twins said. "Here, try a jar on us."

Rachel Ann tried to argue with them, but they wouldn't hear of her paying for the pickles. Glancing at the clock, she tucked the jar in her bag with the frog, said a quick good-bye, and left the store. Time had passed so quickly she was in danger of being late back to the shop.

She swung the little bag by its handles as she walked back to the shop, wondering what Abram would think of such a silly gift. But the frog reminded her of one hot summer day when they were children. She and Abram had packed lunches and met at the pond at the edge of the woods near their houses. She'd been a bit of a tomboy back then, and Abram had been a typical boy and tried to scare her with a frog. She'd turned the tables on him, neatly plucking the frog from his hands and sitting down on a big rock to admire the little creature.

Her mother had been appalled when she returned home, her hair a tangled mess, her *kapp* in her hands, muddy streaks all over her dress. Remembering, Rachel Ann wondered if her mother had ever despaired of her leaving those tomboy years behind.

She and Abram had been friends for years, and now they were dating. Who knew it all started with those days spent at the pond . . . she wondered what Abram would think when he unwrapped his Christmas present.

☙

Abram checked his appearance in the mirror over his dresser. Going into town midweek for lunch with Rachel Ann was a rare treat. Farm work took up much of the time during other seasons. Satisfied he'd done a decent job ironing his shirt—he was a grown man who didn't need his mother tending to all of his needs as he'd reminded her—he left his room.

"Abram, look who's here," his mother said when he walked into the kitchen.

"Sarah, *gut* to see you."

She gave him a shy smile. "Abram."

He had a few minutes before he needed to leave, so he walked over to pour himself a cup of coffee, sat down at the table, and reached for a cookie from a plate piled with them.

"Sarah was telling me her *dat* is on bed rest for an ankle injury."

"He hates it," Sarah told them. "But he has to stay off his feet for a week or two, and it's been hard for *Mamm* and me to make him stay put and not do his chores."

"How can I help?"

She touched her fingers to her trembling lips. "I don't know why I should be surprised. You always help when you hear someone needs something."

Abram shrugged. "Everyone pitches in here in our community."

"None as much as you, Abram."

"I need to make a phone call and then I can drive over."

"*Danki.*" She turned to Lovina. "And thank you for the tea and cookies."

"Let me wrap some up for you to take home."

"*Daed* will love it. *Mamm* and I haven't had much time to bake with doing *Daed*'s chores as well as our own."

Abram walked into his bedroom, pulled out his cell phone, called Stitches in Time, and asked to speak to Rachel Ann.

She came to the phone sounding a little breathless. "Abram? Is everything *allrecht*?"

"*Ya.* I wanted to tell you that I can't come into town and take you to lunch today. I have to go over to help Melvin Zook with some chores."

"Sarah's *dat.*"

"*Ya.* He's on bed rest. I'll see you after work?"

"*Schur.* See you later."

Abram hung up, sorry to hear the disappointment in her voice. He changed back into work clothes, hung up his good ones, and walked back into the kitchen.

"I figured you needed lunch, since you won't be going into town," his mother said as she put a sandwich on a plate and set it on the table.

He'd told her he'd be running some errands in town, but not that he'd be having lunch with Rachel Ann.

She made herself a sandwich and sat at the table opposite him. They said a silent prayer of thanks for the meal and began eating.

"So was Rachel Ann disappointed?"

"What makes you think I was going in to see her?"

"You got dressed up."

"Maybe I was going into town to buy your Christmas present."

"You came home with a lot of packages last time you went into town. I think you got it then."

His eyes narrowed. "You haven't been snooping in my room, have you?"

"*Nee.*" She chuckled and her eyes sparkled with mischief. "Are you forgetting how when you were a *kind* you were always snooping around looking for your presents?"

"You never had proof."

She merely looked at him. "Mothers know."

"I'm leaving now. Try not to go looking for your present."

He grinned as he went to hitch his buggy. She'd never find where he hid her presents. He hadn't been afraid she'd go looking for them—it was simply because he hadn't wanted her to stumble on them when she went into his room with laundry or whatever.

The Zooks were happy to see him. He visited briefly with Melvin who looked pale and in pain as he lay propped up in bed.

His sprained ankle was taking too long to heal, he complained, but his *fraa* reminded him he wasn't being good about staying off it enough. He'd learned he was going to have to stay off it for a while, he said, so he was grateful for Abram's help.

Abram set to work mucking out stalls and doing Melvin's other chores. When he was finished it was nearly suppertime. The scents of roast chicken made his stomach growl when he let himself in the back door.

"Abram! Will you join us for supper?" Sarah asked him as she looked up from the stove where she was stirring something in a pot.

"*Nee*, I have to be getting home," he told her.

"Can I at least get you to have a cup of coffee?" She lifted the pot.

A cup would taste good on the cool day. "*Allrecht, danki*. Mind if I wash up here at the sink?"

"Be my guest."

She poured two cups and joined him at the table. "*Mamm* and I appreciate your help so much."

"I'm happy to help. I'll be back in the morning to take care of the horses. Do you have a piece of paper and pencil? I'll write down my cell phone number to call if you need to."

Sarah fetched the paper and pencil, and after he wrote down the number she looked at it. "I've missed seeing you," she said as she lifted her eyes to meet his.

"I—" he broke off when her mother bustled into the room.

"Abram, can you stay for supper?"

"Not tonight, but *danki*. I just told Sarah I'll be back in the morning. I gave her my number if you need to call me."

He pulled into his drive just as Rachel Ann was being dropped off by her driver.

She walked over and smiled at him, "Hi."

"Hi. If you can give me a few minutes to get cleaned up I'd like to take you out to supper to make up for missing lunch."

"That would be nice. Come over to the house when you're ready."

They went to their favorite local restaurant—Rachel Ann's favorite—and he relaxed against the cushions of the booth.

He asked her about her day and enjoyed seeing her enthusiasm about working at both the bakery and the shop.

"You look tired," he told her as they were served their food.

"*Danki,*" she said wryly. "So do you."

He flexed his shoulders, sore from double chores. "They need the help."

"So, how was Sarah?" she asked casually.

❧

Rachel Ann shivered in the thin paper gown as she sat on the exam table in the doctor's office.

She listened as the nurse explained what the doctor would be doing. She'd never had this exam called a pelvic, but she was willing to endure it if it helped her have less painful periods.

The nurse took Rachel Ann's blood pressure, frowned, said it was a little high, weighed her, and said she was underweight. She seated herself on a stool and proceeded to ask her dozens of questions about her health history. She even wanted to know about Rachel Ann's mother's periods and births. "Some things tend to run in families," she said and went to find the doctor.

Dr. Ramsey, a middle-aged woman with kind eyes, came in the room, shook Rachel Ann's hand, and introduced herself. She looked over the nurse's notes while the nurse helped Rachel Ann scoot down on the table and put her feet into the stirrups.

The doctor was calm and patient and explained what she was doing at each stage of the exam. Rachel Ann tried to relax—something both women told her would make the exam less stressful. But she still flinched a couple of times and felt a twinge of pain.

"You can sit up now," the doctor told her, and the nurse helped her sit up and pull her feet from the stirrups.

They left her to get dressed, then the nurse showed her into the doctor's office. "You have endometriosis," the doctor said. She explained how endometriosis causes painful periods for young women and often causes problems for them when they wanted to get pregnant. Rachel Ann listened earnestly and tried to understand the doctor's explanation of what happened each month during her periods, but she was grateful when the doctor handed her some brochures to read later.

She also gave Rachel Ann a prescription for birth control pills. Rachel Ann gasped and felt herself blushing madly.

The doctor looked up. "I am not assuming you're active sexually. These pills are used to treat the endometriosis. It's important to use them. As I said, this condition can cause infertility."

She hesitated, then took a deep breath. "Rachel Ann, I'm afraid you may already be infertile."

"I'm only twenty-one!" she cried. "I want to have babies."

"I know how important children are to the Amish," the doctor said quickly. "It's why I want to be aggressive with your treatment. I see by your chart, you're single?"

She nodded. "I'm dating someone."

"If you want to have a baby, you need to start as soon as possible."

"We can't get married until the fall."

The doctor stared at her and frowned.

"We only get married in the fall, after harvest," she explained. Well, there rarely were some marriages that quietly took place when a couple anticipated their wedding vows. But the doctor was saying that it was unlikely Rachel Ann could get pregnant, so there would be no early marriage.

"I want to do a simple test called a laparoscopy," the doctor was saying. "It's done in the hospital, but you go home the same day."

"I have no insurance." The community would come together to pay for medical expenses, but she would be too embarrassed to ask for help to pay for something like this.

"Make an appointment to see me in a month and let's talk about it, see how you're doing."

Nodding, feeling numb, Rachel Ann tucked the prescription and brochures into her purse and stumbled out of the office.

∞

"Rachel Ann, back already?" Leah asked her when she walked into the shop. "Are you *allrecht*?"

She'd learned how to pull a mask over her face after Sam's accident so she could get through her day. Now she did it again.

"Everything's fine. I was just told I'm too thin. Guess I'll have to eat more of what I make at the bakery," she joked.

Some customers walked in just then, saving her from having to pretend she wasn't upset about what she'd heard at the doctor's office. She rushed to the back room to put her things away and then returned to the shop to help the customers, aware Leah watched her with concern.

She got through the day and never felt so grateful to get in the van and go home. Sam had gone to his doctor, too, and had come home with a new cast. He pushed the food around on his plate, looking so unhappy he occupied the attention of Rachel Ann's parents, so they didn't notice she was quiet and barely ate.

As much as she'd have liked to talk to her mother about the doctor's visit, tonight wasn't the time. Rachel Ann cleared the table, did the dishes, and escaped to her room.

She threw herself on her bed and once, when she heard footsteps on the stairs, wondered if her mother was coming to tell her Abram was here to see her. But it was only her father with Sam in his arms, come to say *gut nacht*.

An hour later, she heard Abram's buggy pull into the drive and travel back to his barn. She glanced at the small alarm clock on her nightstand. She doubted he'd call now. He'd know her parents would feel it was too late. She sighed, torn between wanting to talk to him and yet not sure what she would say.

Would Abram want to marry her now? She knew he loved *kinner*. Amish families were large. One of the things they had had in common was the wish their families had been larger. And he'd even been willing—eager—to marry her when he thought she might be pregnant.

Rachel Ann sat up as something occurred to her. Was this condition hereditary? Was it why her mother had only had two *kinner*? She fished in her purse for the brochures and began reading.

There was a knock on her door. "*Kumm!*" she called as she swept the brochures back into her purse.

Her mother poked her head in. "Are you *allrecht*?"

She nodded. "Just tired. I thought I'd go to bed early."

"Christmas will be here soon. Then you can stop working two jobs." She hesitated. "Your *dat* and I have appreciated the money you've given us, but if we'd known how hard it would be on you we wouldn't have let you do it."

"I offered," Rachel Ann pointed out. "And I do enjoy working at the bakery."

"Well, as I said, Christmas will be here soon and you'll go back to just the one job." She tilted her head as if she heard something.

"Doesn't sound like Sam's gone to sleep yet. I'm going to go settle him down."

"Do you want me to go?"

"*Nee.* You get some sleep."

Rachel Ann nodded. "*Gut nacht.*" The door closed.

She got ready for bed, but even though she was exhausted she couldn't sleep. Finally, she gave up and got up. She knelt at the window and looked over at Abram's house. A light shone in his bedroom window. He was still up, but there was no way for her to call him without going outside to the phone in the shanty, and it was too cold and too late to do so. What would she tell her parents if they heard her slipping out?

Besides, what was she going to say to him? Would he understand or want to break it off with her? And would she want him to stay if they found out she couldn't have *kinner*? His *dat* had passed the farm on to him, but he'd have no *sohn* to leave it to. She sighed. The past weeks had been so difficult with Sam being hurt and now this . . .

She put her chin on her arms that were folded on the windowsill and stared up at the stars blinking against the black sky. *Why, God? What did I do to deserve this?*

When Sam had run into the road and been hurt she'd blamed herself. But this thing wrong with her. She hadn't made it happen to herself. *Why, God?*

14

Rachel Ann was finishing up the supper dishes the next evening when she heard a knock on the back door.

She turned as she heard the door open. "Abram! I wasn't expecting you."

He frowned. "I'm sorry, I know I haven't seen you for a couple of days. I've been helping the Zooks."

She stood there, biting her tongue, upset with him, and not trusting herself to say something.

"Rachel Ann? Aren't you going to invite me in?"

She let out the breath she hadn't realized she'd been holding. "*Ya.*" She continued washing dishes.

"Maybe we should go for a drive," he said after a moment. "You look upset and your family's still up."

Rachel Ann hesitated and then nodded. "I'll meet you out front."

She dried the few remaining dishes, slipped on her jacket, and her footsteps faltered. Was Abram going to tell her he was seeing Sarah again? He'd spent so much time over there at her house . . . and they had dated for a time a few months ago.

Her mother walked into the kitchen, and her eyebrows went up.

"I'm going to go for a drive with Abram." She buttoned up her jacket.

"I haven't seen him for a few days."

"He's been helping the Zooks."

"You don't sound happy about it."

"I'm not." She sighed. "I guess it makes me selfish."

"I'd say it makes you human."

Rachel Ann's eyes widened. Her mother didn't usually make remarks like that. Her heart warmed.

"Maybe you should talk to Abram."

Abram sat waiting in his buggy in the drive. Rachel Ann climbed inside, and they set off. After a few minutes, she felt him glance at her.

"What's wrong? Are you upset with me?"

She wanted to roll her eyes. Men! "I haven't seen you for days."

"You know I've been helping—"

"I know." She realized she'd sounded sharp. "How long are you going to do this?"

"As long as Melvin needs help."

She sighed and stared out her window at the barren fields they were passing. "Is there no one else who can help?"

He ran his free hand through his hair. "I'm the one they asked."

"Sarah asked."

"Does it matter who asked?" He stared at her. "Rachel Ann, they needed help, and Melvin could hardly come to see me to ask."

"They have a phone," she pointed out, and then she sighed. "I'm unhappy you rushed to help them and I haven't seen you. How long is this going to go on?"

"Just another week."

"You're *schur*?"

"Are you saying you don't want me to help when I see a need?"

"I'm saying you don't have to be the only one. The family shouldn't be leaning on you so much you neglect your own family and your own life."

"So you're saying I've neglected you."

She folded her arms across her chest and stared unseeingly ahead. "*Ya*," she said finally.

"Has it occurred to you your working a second job has taken time away from us seeing each other, too?" he asked quietly.

Rachel Ann turned to stare at him. "Are you serious? I had to do it to earn some extra money to give to my parents. And it's early in the day."

"I know. But often you come home so exhausted we don't see each other. I've tried to understand. It's all I'm asking now, for you to understand I need to help them."

It occurred to her then that Abram had given up countless hours of his time to help her family when Sam was hurt. She wondered why he didn't remind her of it now. Instead, he stared at the road ahead.

Rachel Ann felt petty and grew even more upset. Was it so wrong to want him to put her—their relationship—first? Last night she'd needed to talk to him. Still needed to talk to him. But now, there was this distance between them.

Tell him what the doctor said! a little voice inside her urged. But the fear was too great.

The silence between them grew.

"I'll go over there earlier tomorrow, so I'm finished before you get home."

Surprised, she turned to look at him. He was extending an olive branch. She nodded.

"Is something wrong, Rachel Ann? You seem tense."

"I told you what I was upset about."

"You're sure that's all?"

"*Schur*," she said quickly. It pained her to lie to him. She never lied.

"Then why won't you look at me?"

She turned and met his gaze. "I'm looking."

He reached for her hand and she let him take it. "You're cold."

"I'm fine."

"You'd tell me if something was wrong?"

"Of course."

He squeezed her hand, sighed, and released it. "I guess I should get you back home so you can get some rest."

"*Ya.*" Feeling relieved, she folded her hands in her lap.

Abram checked traffic, then made a U-turn and headed back home. He pulled into his drive and stopped so she could get out. "I'll see you tomorrow when you get home."

She nodded. "Tomorrow. *Gut nacht.*"

"*Gut nacht.*"

Rachel Ann forced herself to take her time walking to her house, not wanting to have him think she just wanted to rush away. Once inside, she was grateful her parents had apparently gone upstairs.

All she wanted was to be alone.

❧

Abram thought about his conversation with Rachel Ann several times the next day.

Something was bothering her no matter how much she denied it. He didn't think it was just because he hadn't seen her for a few days.

Well, he was going to find out when they got together this evening.

"Abram, I thought you might like a cup of coffee. Black, right?"

He looked up from mucking out a stall to see Sarah. "*Ya, danki.*" He set the shovel aside and took the mug from her.

One True Path

She took a seat on a nearby bale of hay and smiled at him. "*Mamm* is making pot roast for supper and said I should see if you can stay."

"*Danki*, but I can't tonight." He took a sip of coffee, winced when he found it too hot to drink, and blew on it to cool it.

"What's your hurry?" she teased.

"I promised—" he stopped, his natural reserve kicking in. "I have to be getting home," he said.

He watched the corners of her mouth turn down and then, with a conscious effort, she brightened and smiled at him. "It's been so nice having you here. It's hard to see you go at the end of the day."

"*Danki*."

"So how is Rachel Ann?" she asked as she smoothed her skirt. "Guess she's happy her little brother is home from the hospital."

Abram nodded, picked up the mug of coffee again, and sipped quickly. He was determined to stay on schedule and keep his promise to see Rachel Ann when she got home.

Sarah got to her feet. "Well, I'm going to hitch the buggy and take *Daed* to his doctor's appointment."

"I'll get the buggy," he told her, and he set the mug down.

As he moved past her, she touched his sleeve and looked up at him. "*Danki,* Abram."

A little disconcerted at the warmth in her gaze, he nodded and walked out of the barn. He hitched the buggy and helped Melvin inside.

"Pray I get good news from the doctor," Melvin said, grunting as he settled into the seat. "I'm tired of lying around while another man does my chores."

"I don't mind helping out," Abram told him sincerely. "Abe Stoltzfus said for me to tell you he's sorry to hear you've been laid up, and he's going to be stopping by to help me do whatever you need starting tomorrow."

Melvin nodded. "*Gut.* I appreciate the help, Abram, but I've been concerned it's too much for one man on top of his own responsibilities."

Abram clasped his shoulder. "It's been no problem, Melvin."

He returned to the barn to continue mucking out the stalls, saying a prayer as Melvin requested. He didn't mind helping, but he knew the older man would be glad to be on his feet again caring for his home and animals.

The time alone in the barn gave him a chance to think again about Rachel Ann. No one in this community looked for an easy life. Hard work, service to others, these were expected in his community. So he'd been surprised she'd been upset about his helping the Zook family last night.

All he could think was she'd been overtiring herself working too hard and enduring such an emotional, frightening time seeing Sam being hit by Michael's car. It's why when she'd been upset with him last night he'd tried to be understanding and not defend himself or argue with her. He'd felt a little gratified she'd missed him, and so it hadn't been a hardship or even a compromise to tell her he'd be home on time tonight, so they could be together.

Still, he wondered as he had last night if there wasn't something more bothering her than she'd admit. . . . He remembered how he'd known there was something on her mind not so long ago and there had been a reason for it—she'd worried she might have made a terrible mistake and become pregnant. Because they were so close he'd known something was wrong, and because he cared so much for her he'd offered to marry her. He'd been happy for her that she wasn't, but for himself there had been more than a moment's regret he wouldn't be making her his *fraa* so quickly.

Well, he didn't always understand the path God led him down, but his insistence on persuading Rachel Ann to confide in him had changed something between them. They were more than friends now, and he was going to do whatever he had to do to make her happy, to feel safe and loved.

He finished up and carried the coffee mug with him to the kitchen.

"Abram, come in," Edna said when she opened the back door. "Would you like a refill on your *kaffe* before you go?"

Abram glanced at the clock. He was doing good on time. "*Ya*, that would be *gut*. Then I'll be heading home."

"Melvin and I appreciate your help so much," she said as she set the filled mug of coffee on the kitchen table.

"He said he was hoping the doctor will tell him he can get back to doing his own chores." Abram sat at the table.

"I hope so, too," she said fervently, sitting down with her own mug of coffee. "He's been having a hard time not being able to do his chores."

"Sam—Rachel Ann's brother—has had a hard time not being able to do what he wants, either." Abram grinned. "I don't guess taking Melvin to the convenience store for ice cream and glitter glue would help put him in a better mood, would it? It probably only works on a four-year-old."

She laughed. "*Nee*. But I'm hoping a good report from the doctor and my pot roast will help. Plus, I'm baking his favorite pie."

Abram grinned. "Sounds like you believe the old saying that the way to a man's heart is through his stomach."

She laughed. "It is with some men. Like my *mann*."

He finished his coffee and glanced at the clock. "I should be going."

"Sarah told me you can't join us for supper tonight. I hope you can sometime soon. She and Melvin and I enjoyed it when you used to come to supper."

"I did, too," he said as he walked to the door. "*Gut nacht*."

Something finally clicked as he got into his buggy. He was so focused on Rachel Ann that he had missed the fact Sarah was still interested in him.

Couples were private about dating in this community, so he hadn't wanted to mention he had plans with Rachel Ann. But if Sarah knew, maybe it would discourage her thinking the two of them might see each other again.

He'd have to find a way to drop the fact into the conversation next time Sarah showed any interest in him.

~

Rachel Ann made extra gingerbread cookies and brought two dozen of them to the shop. Anna was teaching her knitting class this afternoon and asked her to bring cookies since she hadn't had the time to bake any.

"*Danki*, Rachel Ann. I had some special orders to finish for customers."

"I'm happy to help."

"How much do I owe you? And don't you dare say nothing. You did those at the bakery, so I know Linda will expect to be paid for them."

Rachel Ann told her and tucked the payment into her purse to give to Linda at the bakery tomorrow morning. She walked out into the shop as Leah opened for the day.

One of the things Rachel Ann liked about working here was how you never knew who might walk in to shop. Many locals—*Englisch* and Amish—shopped here for their sewing, knitting, and crafting needs and for gifts. Then there were the tourists from far-away states and countries visiting the area who stopped in.

She'd been a little shy when she first started working here but deliberately worked to overcome it because she wanted to get to know people better. Growing up an only child until Sam was born four years ago, she'd missed having *bruders* and *schwesders*. She watched Mary Katherine, Naomi, and Anna, cousins but close as *schwesders,* and wished for that closeness sometimes. Abram had been her best friend, not another girl, because she'd been a bit of a tomboy, but sometimes she'd missed being close with a girlfriend. Working here with these other women had fulfilled some of the lack.

So she smiled when the bell over the door rang, and she turned to greet the customer who walked in.

Her smile faltered when she saw Sarah Zook.

"*Guder mariye*, Sarah," she said, determined to be friendly in spite of her feeling Sarah had asked Abram for his help with her father's chores because she was interested in him. Rachel Ann had been trained that way—when you lived in a small community where you held church in each other's homes. You worked to live according to your spiritual beliefs not just think about them in church on Sunday.

"My *mamm* gave me a list of some things she needs," Sarah told her, pulling it from her purse. "I dropped my *dat* off at the doctor, so I don't have much time to shop."

"I hope he's doing better," Rachel Ann said. "Why don't we divide up the list so we can get you out of here quickly. Many hands make for light work."

"*Gut* idea."

Rachel Ann hoped Abram had asked another friend or two to help the family so he wouldn't be spending so much time there.

The two of them picked up shopping baskets and soon found the thread, yarn, fabric, and more on the list. They rechecked the list to make sure they hadn't missed anything and then walked to the front counter so Rachel Ann could ring up the purchases.

"*Mamm* and I have been so grateful Abram's been helping us," Sarah told her. "It's been nice seeing him every day. He's such a *gut* man."

Rachel Ann lost her concentration for a moment, wondering if she was being sent a message, and had to go back and check to make sure she hadn't charged for a spool of thread twice. Sarah handed her the money, Rachel Ann gave her change, and she tucked the purchases in a shopping bag.

"Well, time to go get *Daed* and get home," Sarah said as she took the bag. "We invited Abram to supper."

Shocked, Rachel Ann watched her walk away.

Anna had been straightening a shelf near the front door, and she held it open for Sarah and wished her a good afternoon. She walked over to Rachel Ann standing at the counter. "Everything *allrecht*?"

"I—*ya*, everything's fine."

"Did Sarah say something to upset you?" Anna tilted her head to one side. "She was smiling in a rather smug way on her way out."

She just dropped a bomb, Rachel Ann wanted to say. Abram wasn't leaving the Zooks' house early to have supper with her tonight. Not according to Sarah.

"*Nee*, I think she was just happy she got everything she needed quickly," Rachel Ann said.

"Well, she always reminds me of someone who enjoyed gossiping about me years ago."

Rachel Ann took the two shopping baskets and deposited them near the front door and thought her words had probably been accurate—Sarah had wanted to let her know she was the one who had plans with Abram this evening.

The day went downhill from there. Rachel Ann found herself thinking about what the doctor had said to her, and it seemed as if she had never seen so many babies and children come into the store.

Many of the mothers oohed and aahed over the caps Anna knitted and had to try them on their children. Yes, she agreed with a little pang in her heart, there was nothing so adorable as the baby or child modeling a cupcake cap or one in the owl or teddy bear cap. Anna's creations flew out the door almost as fast as she could knit them.

Rachel Ann wasn't hungry, but she forced herself to take a lunch break to get off her feet for a while. She sat with her sandwich uneaten on the table before her and wished the day would just get over. Each time she looked at the nearby clock, only a few minutes had gone by.

It was the afternoon that would not end.

She picked up half of the sandwich, forcing herself to eat, knowing she wouldn't have enough energy to get through the afternoon if she didn't.

Leah walked in, got her lunch out of the refrigerator, and sat down opposite Rachel Ann.

"You're looking sad again, *kind*," she said as she unwrapped her sandwich. "It seems to me you've been looking sad since you came back from the doctor's office the other day."

Rachel Ann's sandwich slipped from her suddenly nerveless fingers. "You remembered." Her mother hadn't. She knew her mother cared, but it had slipped her mind to ask her about it.

"Do you want to talk about it?" Leah asked gently, looking at her over the tops of her wire-rimmed glasses. Her faded blue eyes were kind.

Tears welled up, and she furiously blinked them away. Her hands fluttered as she tried to find the words. "The doctor says I have something wrong with me, something I never even heard of, and it means I probably can't have *kinner*. It's what's been causing my periods to be so bad."

"Oh, Rachel Ann, I'm so sorry." Leah reached over and touched Rachel Ann's hand. "I know this is hard news for you especially when we have so many *kinner* in our community. But I want to remind you the doctor doesn't decide if you'll have a *boppli*. God does."

Rachel Ann reached for a paper napkin from the holder in the center of the table and wiped at her eyes.

"Who's going to want to marry me knowing I might not be able to have *kinner*?"

"A man who loves you."

"But—"

"A man who loves you," she said firmly. "I know women who have thought they couldn't have *kinner* and they were wrong. Have you talked to your mother?"

Rachel Ann shook her head. "I haven't have a chance yet. But . . . I don't know . . . sometimes it's not as easy to talk to her as it is you for some reason."

"Talk to her, Rachel Ann. Promise me you'll do it right away, *allrecht*?"

She nodded and wiped at her cheeks again.

"And your young man, too."

She tried to summon a smile. "My young man? You think I have one?"

"*Ya*, I do," Leah said, and there was a twinkle in her eyes. "Now, finish your lunch. I have the feeling we're going to be busy this afternoon."

"We've been busy every afternoon for weeks."

"*Ya*, so it's how I know we'll be busy this afternoon."

Rachel Ann found herself laughing for the first time in days.

15

Rachel Ann was stunned to see Abram sitting in his buggy in his drive when her driver pulled in front of her home after work.

She gathered her purse and lunch tote, got out of the van, and thanked the driver, all the while watching as Abram climbed out of the buggy and walked toward her.

"What are you doing here?"

He grinned. "I live here."

"But I thought you were having supper with Sarah and her family tonight."

His grin faded, and his eyes searched her face. "I told you last night I was taking you out for supper tonight. Why would you think I'd change plans without calling you?"

"Sarah said—" she stopped as an awful thought occurred to her. "When did you see her?"

"Today. She stopped by the shop."

He frowned. "I hitched the buggy for her to take her *dat* to the doctor."

"She said she was going to go pick him up after she got some things for her mother at the shop."

"Sounds like she found time to make a little mischief," he muttered. "I'm sorry."

She shrugged. "I shouldn't have believed her."

"Well, are we still having supper? You didn't make other plans, did you?"

"*Nee*. I'll go put my tote in the house and tell *Mamm* I'm going out."

"*Gut*. I'll be waiting."

Rachel Ann walked up the drive and chastised herself for listening to Sarah. Then the other woman's words came back to her. *We invited Abram to supper.* Sarah hadn't said, *Abram is coming to supper.* She'd obviously asked and Abram had turned her down because he had plans with Rachel Ann.

So Rachel Ann had allowed Sarah to upset her for hours. She walked into the house and tossed her lunch tote down on a counter, disgusted with herself. But she hadn't been able to sleep much because of the news from the doctor, and face it, she was just plain tired from working so much. It hadn't taken much to upset her.

Something smelled wonderful. Rachel Ann peeked in the oven and saw a pan of stuffed pork chops browning beautifully. Her mouth watered.

"Hungry?"

Rachel Ann jerked in surprise, and the oven door slammed.

"*Gut* thing I'm not baking a cake," her mother said, smiling.

She laughed. "Sorry. I was being nosy. *Ya,* I'm hungry, but I'm going to supper with Abram. Did I forget to tell you?"

"*Ya* but it's fine. Tell him I said hello."

"I will. I won't be out late. Four a.m. comes early."

Her mother nodded. "Enjoy yourself."

"*Danki*." *Would she enjoy herself?* she wondered. She and Abram had argued last night about him not spending time with her lately, and there'd been tension between them. Then he'd insisted something was bothering her, and she'd felt too raw inside from the visit to the doctor and hadn't been ready to talk about it yet.

Abram had always been able to sense when she was upset like no one else did—and understand her like no one else did. It was one of the things she loved about him. But how would he feel about being married to her if he knew they might never have *kinner*? If they didn't complete their love as God intended? It was one of the reasons why God put a man and a woman together, wasn't it?

"Where shall we go?" he asked her as he helped her into the buggy.

"You choose."

He named a restaurant some distance away. "Unless you're too hungry and want to eat right away?"

"I'm fine."

"Are you feeling better today?"

"*Ya.*"

He told her he'd contacted some friends and would have help with the Zook chores until Melvin got on his feet. She felt better because he'd taken the step, and he'd cared about her feelings after their argument last night.

"*Gut.*" Afraid he was going to ask again what was bothering her as he'd done last night, Rachel Ann immediately plunged into a recounting of the day at the shop.

They didn't have long to wait for a table at the restaurant. Abram ordered his favorite spaghetti and meatballs, and Rachel Ann decided to join him. She hadn't had much lunch and was so hungry.

Rachel Ann glanced around as they waited for their salads to arrive. So many diners were concentrating on their cell phones around them, checking messages or texting. Even little kids were playing games on them. And it wasn't just *Englischers* or younger people. Rachel Ann saw two Amish men checking messages on their phones and one elderly woman text while her husband ate dessert.

It was the same thing she'd seen one day when she'd gone to the movies with Michael. *Didn't anyone talk to each other anymore?* she wondered.

She looked back at Abram and found him watching her. Disconcerted, she almost wished he had pulled out his cell phone and busied himself with it rather than concentrate his attention on her right now. She felt so . . . exposed. But he had never made it more important than spending time with her. "What?"

"I—"

Their server brought their salads, interrupting Abram. He waited for her to set them down and leave then looked at her again. "Everything *allrecht?*"

"*Ya*, the salad looks *gut.*"

"That's not what I'm talking about. I told you last night I thought something was bothering you, and I still feel the same way looking at you tonight."

"Why do you say that?"

"When you're worried about something you get this cute little frown and your attention wanders. And you won't look at me."

She stabbed a fork in her salad and began eating. "I'm fine. I told you last night. Eat. This is *gut.*"

He sighed and shook his head. After a long moment, he began eating.

Rachel Ann cast about for a safe topic to talk about. "Sam was decorating a Christmas drawing for you when I left. He was using lots of the glitter you bought him. *Lots.*"

"Glad he's enjoying it. He's quite a special *kind.* I hope we have one like him one day."

She froze, her fork halfway to her mouth. The salad suddenly became tasteless. "Don't let *Mamm* hear you say so," she said lightly. "He's been so cranky lately because he wants the cast off. She might offer to lend him to you."

"You're not going to finish that?" he asked, gesturing at her salad. He grinned when she pushed it toward him to finish.

Their spaghetti and meatballs came. Rachel Ann forced herself to eat a little, but the meatballs seemed to bounce around with the butterflies in her stomach. She finally set her fork down and nodded when the server stopped to ask if she wanted a box to take the food home.

Abram looked at his plate. "Nothing left for me to take home."

"There seldom is," she said, forcing a smile.

"Want dessert?"

She shook her head.

"*Mamm* was baking a cake when I left," he told her as he pulled out his wallet. "Chocolate. Nothing better than her chocolate cake. I'll have a piece when I get home."

He asked for the check, and after he paid they climbed into the buggy and began the ride home.

She turned to him. "Abram, I have something I need to tell you."

⇛

Shocked, Abram stared at Rachel Ann. "What?"

"You heard me," she said, her voice shaking. She let out a shuddering breath. "I don't want to date anymore."

"I thought we worked out our problem." Confused, he tried to take her hand, but she shook her head and shrank away from him.

"We did."

"Then what—?"

"I've been thinking about it a lot and I decided I don't want to get married. Since we date someone we think we might want to marry, well, then there isn't any point in our seeing each other that way."

"Oh?" Abram felt an unexpected surge of anger at how matter-of-fact she was being, when it felt like she'd just reached inside his chest and pulled out his beating heart.

"I'm sorry, Abram," she said gently, and he could see tears in her eyes. "I don't mean to hurt you, but I think there's someone better out there for you than me."

"This isn't about Sarah, is it?"

She shook her head. "I just don't want to get married after all."

It was a good thing his horse knew the way home. Abram was in such a state of shock he was glad he didn't have to concentrate on directing him home. When the horse slowed and turned, he was disconcerted to see that they were home.

"How can I fix this if you won't tell me what's wrong?"

"I did tell you. You just don't want to hear it." She pressed her fingers to her mouth. "I didn't mean it the way it sounded. I know how you like to fix things, but you can't make someone want to get married, Abram."

They sat there in the buggy in front of Abram's barn. Ned pawed the ground, eager to be unhitched, and led into his warm stall for the night.

The noise startled Rachel Ann. She looked around and seemed surprised they were home. "I need to go. *Gut nacht*, Abram." She slipped out the door and ran to her house.

Abram didn't know how long he might have sat there if Ned hadn't lifted his head and neighed at him. He climbed out, un-hitched the buggy, and shook his head as the horse hurried to his stall.

"Sorry," he said. "My girl just broke my heart." He pressed his face into Ned's neck. "I wish you could talk. Maybe you could tell me what just happened. Did I push her too hard to get married? I thought she felt the same way I did. I thought she was the one God set aside for me."

He walked out of the barn, shut the door, and stopped to stare up at the heavens. "Why?"

Hearing no answer, Abram shook his head and let himself into his house. He saw a light burning in the kitchen. His steps slowed. He loved his mother, but he didn't want to talk to anyone right now.

"Abram?"

"*Ya.*"

His mother sat at the kitchen table, stationery spread out in front of her. "You're home early."

"Rachel Ann couldn't stay out late. She has work early in the morning."

"Help yourself to a slice of cake. It's your favorite."

"Not hungry. I'll have some tomorrow."

"Do you want some tea? The water's probably still hot in the kettle."

He shook his head. "Had coffee at the restaurant. I think I'll go on to bed. Kind of tired."

She held out her hand, and he took it and squeezed it. "See you in the morning."

On impulse, he bent and pressed a kiss to her cheek. If nothing else, tonight had taught him how quickly things could change.

"Is something wrong? You look upset."

Abram shook his head. "I'm fine. Just a little tired."

She nodded. "You've been working hard helping the Zooks."

"*Ya.*"

He climbed the stairs to his room and got ready for bed.

He was still awake hours later when he heard the van pull into the Miller drive to pick Rachel Ann up for her bakery job. Slipping from bed, he peeked out the window hoping to catch a glimpse of her. He wondered if she had slept last night, comfortable with her decision, or if she'd tossed and turned as he had. Even though he was upset with her, he didn't wish her any ill.

He climbed back into bed and stared at the ceiling, going over and over the conversation he'd had with Rachel Ann earlier, then the one the night when they'd argued. Rachel Ann wasn't a flighty, impulsive person. He knew she cared for him. What could have happened to make her decide she didn't want to date him any longer?

She'd done it.

Rachel Ann felt sick to her stomach every time she thought about the way Abram had looked when she told him she didn't want to date anymore . . . just another way of saying she didn't want to get married in the future.

He'd looked stunned.

She hadn't meant to blurt it out, but how did you break up with someone? It was for the best. Abram wanted *kinner*, and she couldn't have them. She had seen how unhappy couples who couldn't have a *kind* were. How could she do it to him—to them?

Of course, she'd thought about telling him her news . . . for about one minute. Who wanted to have someone insist they still wanted to marry you because he felt it was the right thing to do. She didn't want his pity. She wanted—she felt tears rushing into her eyes. *Nee,* she couldn't break down here in the bakery. Linda worked out front, but you never knew when she would walk back here to ask a question or get something just out of the oven.

So she blinked back the tears and told herself to stop being a crybaby. She'd done enough crying over Sam. She had to find a way to get through this. To be happy somehow. A few minutes later she was glad she had gotten herself under control when Linda walked back to tell her she had a visitor.

"A visitor?" Surprised, Rachel Ann stared at her. The timer went off and she jumped.

"I'll get them out," Linda told her. "Mmm, Snickerdoodles. I might have to have one of these with a cup of tea."

Rachel Ann wiped her hands on her apron and walked out to the front of the bakery. Saul stood gazing into one of the glass bakery cases with a look of wonder.

"What a selection," he said when Rachel Ann approached him. "I'm trying not to drool all over the glass case."

She laughed. "This is a surprise."

"Elizabeth said she wanted something sweet. Now that the morning sickness has worn off, she's hungry a lot. I offered to get her something from here. Give me a dozen of the cinnamon buns and four of the gingerbread cookies. She liked the cookies last time she got them."

"You're a *gut mann*."

"It gave me chance to ask you for a favor."

She looked up from the box she was filling with the rolls. "*Schur*. What is it?"

"You say yes so quickly. It might be something bad."

She laughed. "I doubt it."

"I need to make an overnight trip, and I don't want to leave Elizabeth by herself. I thought I'd see if you could spend the night with her."

"I'd love to."

"Great. We'll stop by Stitches after work and pick you up. Unless you need to go home and get anything."

"*Nee*, I'll borrow a nightgown from Elizabeth. I don't work tomorrow, so I don't need another dress."

He lifted his head and sniffed. "What do I smell?"

"I just baked Snickerdoodles. They're cooling in the back."

"My favorite. Can I get a dozen of those?"

"*Schur*." Rachel Ann got the cookies and boxed them, then packed everything into a shopping bag.

Linda returned to the front of the shop and regarded the shopping bag and money being exchanged.

"Stop by anytime, Saul," she said with a chuckle.

"You're the best in town," he told her.

"Just the town?"

"Lancaster County."

"I was just joking," she said. "We are not supposed to have *hochmut*." She lowered her gaze modestly, but when she lifted it her eyes sparkled mischievously.

"See you later, Rachel Ann," Saul said as he lifted the bag and strode for the door.

She made a quick call to her driver to cancel her ride home, left a voicemail on the phone at home for her parents, and went back to work.

The afternoon passed quickly, full of customers coming and going, leaving her little time to think about what a detour she'd taken last night in her relationship with Abram.

A sleepover sounded like a nice change. It would be fun to spend the evening with Elizabeth and not chance running into Abram.

Rachel Ann stood waiting by the shop door at quitting time.

"It's not your usual ride," Leah remarked as she stood making out the day's deposit at the front counter.

"I'm going to spend the night with Elizabeth while Saul goes out of town. Have a good evening."

"Are you sure we're not taking you away from anything tonight?" Elizabeth asked her when she climbed into the van.

"I'm sure."

Elizabeth slipped her arm through Rachel Ann's. "*Gut*. We'll have a girl's night."

"What do you do on a girl's night?" Saul wanted to know.

"That's for girls to know and boys to find out," she told him pertly.

The driver stopped at Saul and Elizabeth's home and waited while Saul went inside for his overnight bag. Rachel Ann went on into the kitchen and started a kettle of water boiling so the couple could have privacy for a good-bye kiss.

She had mugs of hot water sitting on the table when Elizabeth joined her. Elizabeth settled into a chair and dunked a decaffeinated tea bag in hers.

"I'd have been fine by myself," she told Rachel Ann.

"You're probably right. But this way Saul doesn't worry, and I know you don't want him to worry."

Elizabeth sighed. "Aren't you clever?" She stirred sugar into her tea. "I know he's worried about me since I got pregnant, but the doctor has assured us even though I miscarried once it doesn't mean I will again."

"*Gut.* Now, what shall I make us for supper?"

"I should cook. You're my guest."

"I want to. What do you feel like having?"

"Something simple. How about grilled cheese sandwiches and tomato soup? And those gingerbread cookies Saul bought for dessert."

"Sounds good on a cold night." Rachel Ann put the soup on to simmer while she heated a cast-iron skillet for the sandwiches.

"I let Saul take the Snickerdoodles with him."

She glanced at Elizabeth. "Kind of like the guy, huh?"

"So how are you and Abram doing?"

The question caught Rachel Ann by surprise. She took her time adding several pats of butter to the skillet, then added slices of bread in when the butter melted.

"Rachel Ann?"

She laid cheese on the bread, topping it with another slice of bread before turning to look at Elizabeth. "We're not," she confessed. "I broke it off last night."

"Why on earth would you do that? You were happy last time we talked. What happened?"

Rachel Ann bit her lip as she used a spatula to flip the sandwiches. She found bowls, ladled the hot soup into them, and set them on the table. A check of the sandwiches showed that they were a nice golden brown on both sides. She put them on plates, cut them into sections, and served them. "Things just weren't working out."

"But—" Elizabeth subsided when Rachel Ann bent her head and started saying a prayer of thanks for the meal. She joined her, and the minute they were finished she put her hand on Rachel Ann's. "Come on, talk to me. What happened?"

She sighed. "I—went to the doctor and got some upsetting news."

Elizabeth turned pale. "Not—cancer?"

"*Nee*, I'm sorry, I didn't mean to scare you," she rushed to say. "You know what bad periods I have? I finally saw a doctor, and she said I have a condition that will probably mean I can't have *kinner*."

Elizabeth's hand splayed protectively over her abdomen. "Are you sure?"

"The doctor believes so. She wants to run some tests."

"So it's why you broke it off with Abram?"

She nodded. "Abram wants *kinner*."

"I don't understand. You told him and he didn't react well, so you broke it off?"

"*Nee*. You know Abram. If he knew, he'd still want to marry me. I couldn't do it to him."

"So you decided for him? How is that fair?"

"He deserves to be with someone who can give him *kinner*. He has a farm he'll pass down to a *sohn* or *dochder* like his *dat* passed it down to him. You of all people should know how important *kinner* are. I remember how devastated you and Saul were when you miscarried, how you worried you might not get pregnant again."

"Doctors aren't always right. If God wants you to have a *boppli*, you will. And there's always adoption."

"He deserves to have *kinner* of his own. He just talked the other day of how much he's looking forward to having them."

"Do you love Abram?"

"*Ya,* but it's not enough—"

"It's everything," Elizabeth insisted fervently. "Saul showed me how important *I* was to him when I miscarried. Don't you think you owe Abram the truth?"

Rachel Ann shook her head. She picked up her spoon and dipped it into her soup. "*Kumm*, eat your soup while it's hot."

16

*P*leasantly full of soup and sandwiches and cookies, Rachel Ann and Elizabeth sat up talking for hours in front of a blazing fire in the living room.

"This is nice," Elizabeth said with a sigh.

"You should go to bed. A mommy-to-be needs her sleep."

"We can sleep in tomorrow. We don't have to work."

"You don't have to be at the store?"

"Saul asked the twins to work," Elizabeth said as she leaned back on the sofa. "He was afraid I'd overdo if he wasn't around."

"He's probably right."

"Hey, whose side are you on?" Elizabeth tossed a throw pillow at her.

"His."

"He's a *gut mann*," Elizabeth said meditatively as she stared at the fire. "A little over-protective, but the miscarriage scared him. And me."

"And those who love you." She gazed around the room, dimly lit by fire and half a dozen little votive candles flickering here and there among fragrant evergreen boughs piled atop the mantle. "You've done a wonderful job making a home."

"*Danki.* The place needed a lot of work when we moved in. Every room had to be painted. Saul and Isaac had to rip out a lot of rotten wood."

Rachel Ann ran her hand over the back of the sofa they were sitting on. "I love this."

"The sofa's been in the family for years. I learned how to upholster to save money buying a new one."

She thought of her own limited sewing skills. "I'm impressed."

"Any talent I have in upholstery was born of necessity. Fixing up this old house was expensive. But it felt like home the minute we walked into it."

Elizabeth reached for the tote bag sitting on the floor near her feet. "I should be working on Saul's Christmas present while he's not around." She dug in it and pulled out the sweater she was knitting. For a few minutes the only sounds were the crackling of the fire and the clacking of her knitting needles.

Rachel Ann thought about the present she'd bought for Abram from Elizabeth and Saul's store. Now she doubted she'd be giving the funny little carved frog to Abram for Christmas. She didn't imagine Abram would want to exchange presents with her now they weren't seeing each other.

"Are you *allrecht*?"

"*Schur.*"

"Thinking about Abram?"

"I was just thinking some hot chocolate might taste *gut* right now," she said, avoiding the question. "Do you have cocoa?"

"*Ya.* I can make it."

"You stay put. I'll be right back."

"The cocoa's in the cupboard near the stove. There should be some marshmallows in there, too, unless Saul's been into them. He's like a big kid with marshmallows."

Rachel Ann stood watching the milk heat in a pan on the stove and thought about how well the couple got along even though they only knew each other for a year before they got married. They hadn't grown up in the same community as most Amish couples who married did. The fact that couples knew each other so well was said to be the reason for the longevity of the marriages here. For a moment, she let herself imagine sharing a home with her *mann* like Elizabeth did with Saul. Working together to build a future together. Looking forward to starting a family together.

"Still thinking about hot chocolate?" Elizabeth asked, breaking into her thoughts.

Startled, Rachel Ann dropped the spoon she'd been stirring the chocolate with into the pan. She pulled another spoon out of a drawer, fished the first one out of the pan, and put it into the sink.

Elizabeth opened a cupboard. "Look here, Saul left the marshmallows alone."

Rachel Ann poured the hot chocolate into mugs and watched as Elizabeth sprinkled a generous amount of mini-marshmallows into one. "Are you having hot chocolate with your marshmallows?" she asked wryly.

"I guess Saul isn't the only one who likes them. Just give me a couple. *Danki.*"

Elizabeth opened the white bakery box on the table and chose a gingerbread cookie. She offered the box to Rachel Ann who shook her head. They returned to the sofa. Elizabeth put her feet up on the hassock in front of the sofa and balanced her cookie on a napkin on her baby bump. She blew on her hot chocolate to cool it, causing the mini-marshmallows to bob around.

"Mmm," she said with a sigh. "This is good." She looked at Rachel Ann. "So what are you going to do?"

"About what?"

"About you and Abram."

Rachel Ann stared into her cup. "There's nothing to do."

"I've never seen you so unhappy."

She shrugged. "I'll be *allrecht.*"

"Will you? I'm not so *schur*."

"I'm *schur* of one thing," Rachel Ann said.

"What?" Elizabeth bit off the head of the gingerbread man.

Rachel Ann picked up the paper napkin on Elizabeth's tummy and handed it to her. "You have a marshmallow mustache."

"When did you get so good at changing the subject?"

"When a certain friend got to trying to be nosy."

"You mean caring."

She looked at Elizabeth. "*Allrecht*. Caring. But I don't want to talk about it right now. Tonight's about having fun. As soon as you finish your hot chocolate I want you to show me what you've done to the baby's room."

Elizabeth frowned. "Are you sure?"

"Now who's being over-protective? You don't have to worry about me. I'd be a pretty selfish person if I didn't want you to share your excitement, wouldn't I?"

"I went through a time when I didn't think I'd ever get pregnant again," Elizabeth said quietly. "I just don't want to do anything to cause you pain."

"There's lots of *boppli* and *kinner* in this community, lots of moms-to-be. I'll have to get used to it. Now, finish that hot chocolate and let's see what you've done to the nursery."

❧

She didn't come home.

Abram kept checking the time and even opened the barn door to keep an eye out, but Rachel Ann never came home after work.

He went inside for supper, washed his hands, and sat at the table, trying not to glance at the clock.

"In a hurry to be somewhere?" his mother asked him.

He shook his head. After last night's conversation with Rachel Ann, he doubted she'd agree to go out with him and talk. Still, he wondered where she was. Just as he put a spoonful of stew in his mouth he thought he heard a car pull into the drive of Rachel Ann's house. He got to his feet and went to check, peeking out the window, feeling like a stalker. What he saw was a car backing out and driving on, evidently a driver who'd pulled into the wrong driveway.

When he returned to the table, his mother looked at him with raised eyebrows. "Expecting someone?"

"Rachel Ann hasn't come home yet." He sat, buttered a piece of cornbread, and took a bite. He knew his mother had probably figured out the two of them were seeing each other, but he hadn't shared how their feelings for each other had grown.

"Maybe she had something to do after work."

"*Ya*." He spooned up stew, and then a thought came unbidden: maybe Rachel Ann had decided to start seeing Michael again. Maybe she'd even decided not to join the church . . .

"You could go over and ask her mother if you're concerned."

"*Nee*," he said sharply, so sharply she blinked in surprise. "Sorry. It would make it look like I'm checking up on her."

He finished the bowl of stew but refused a refill, which surprised his mother. "Sorry, it's *gut* but I'm not hungry this evening." He got up and put his dishes in the sink. "I think I'll check on Ned and work for a little while on some special orders."

"Dress warm."

He grinned as he reached for his jacket hanging on a peg on the wall. "Yes, *mamm*."

Ned stuck his head out of his stall and neighed when Abram walked into the barn.

"Thought I'd keep you company," he told the horse, but Ned turned back to his feed and ignored him.

"Guess I'm just not popular with anyone lately," Abram said to him.

He got out the orders, chose one, and selected the wood. The work was good for him, forcing him to concentrate and push thoughts of what had happened last night to the back of his mind.

When he finished construction of the box and set it in the drawer of the storage cabinet, he saw the one he'd made for Rachel Ann. He'd done his best work on the carved violets on the top of the box. The flowers held a special significance for them. In the spring, violets bloomed along the banks of the pond. It was their secret, special place where they talked and shared secrets for so many years.

Inside the box, he'd placed a special surprise. He wondered what her reaction to it would be.

Abram wondered if he'd even be able to give it to her. It was possible even being neighbors they wouldn't see each other to exchange presents. If so, he'd set the box aside and let it be part of next year's batch for the furniture store.

He had to find a way to get her to talk to him again, find out why she wanted to break it off.

Finally, his shoulders aching with tension and from bending over the work, his eyes a little gritty from lack of sleep, he gave up the effort for the night. He straightened up his work area, cleaned up his tools, and turned off the battery lamp.

"'Night, old boy," he said, giving Ned a pat as he walked past him.

He couldn't help glancing up at Rachel Ann's window as he walked toward his house. It was dark. The whole house was dark. The family had apparently already gone to bed. He supposed it was possible she could have come home without him hearing, but he didn't think so.

Maybe it was best they didn't see each other tonight. Maybe they needed some space before they talked about something so serious. He didn't know what to do. He just knew he was so miserable he ached, his chest raw and hurting.

Abram rubbed at his breastbone, willing the pain away. Maybe it was just indigestion, a touch of heartburn from the stew, he told himself. He was a practical man. His heart wasn't breaking.

This time when he went to bed he fell asleep almost instantly, exhausted from a long day of chores, the special-order work, and emotional turmoil he wasn't used to. He woke at the time he always heard Rachel Ann's ride come for her. But there was no van pulling up in the drive. He remembered belatedly it was her day off. He turned over and fell back asleep.

Sometime later, he woke and sat up in bed. He heard footsteps outside on the gravel drive and got up to look out the window. Rachel Ann walking toward her house. So, she'd come home late . . .

As he watched, she suddenly turned and walked between their houses, and he knew where she was going.

He fairly jumped out of bed, pulled on his pants, and hurried out of the house. He'd walked the path Rachel Ann had disappeared down so many times he could do it with his eyes shut, but there, in the snow, he saw her footprints guiding him.

She stood at the edge of the pond they'd sat beside while talking so many times, staring at something he couldn't see. An icy wind swept through the bare tree branches, shaking the glittering icicles and creating a sound like wind chimes.

When she heard his footsteps crunching on the snow behind her she spun around, her lips parted in surprise.

"We have to talk," he said, and his voice came out louder than he intended. He stepped forward.

Rachel Ann backed up, and her feet slipped. Her arms flailed as she tried to gain a foothold on the frozen bank.

Abram ran toward her and their fingertips touched and then hers slipped free. She slid down into the water. He jumped in.

And woke, panting and sweating, his heart pounding.

It was a long time before he slept again.

Rachel Ann smiled when she saw Sam's little face peering out the front window of their home. He grinned and began waving at her when he saw her get out of the van.

She opened the front door, and he rushed toward her, his cast thumping on the wooden floor.

"Wachel Ann!" he cried, throwing his arms around her knees. "I missed you!"

She picked him up and hugged him. "I missed you, too! I stayed with Elizabeth last night. One day when you're older you'll get to go spend the night with a friend."

"It will be fun," their mother said fervently.

Rachel Ann looked up. She hadn't heard her approach. Her mother looked worn out. "Fun for who?" she asked with a grin. "Sam—or you?"

Her mother gave her a weary smile.

She set her little brother down. "Sam, can you carry my purse into the kitchen and put it on the counter for me?"

"*Schur,*" he said. He slung the strap over his shoulder and marched off toward the kitchen.

"How about I take Sam outside to play for a little while so you can take a break?" she asked in a low voice.

"It would be *wunderbaar,*" her mother said. "I was going to take him for a ride on his sled, but I'm tired. It's on the front porch. You'll have to cover his cast so it doesn't get wet."

"I will." She walked into the kitchen and found a plastic kitchen garbage bag. "Sam, do you want to go outside and play?"

His shriek of happiness pierced her eardrums.

"I guess that's a yes," she said with a chuckle. "We have to dress warm."

Rachel Ann found his jacket, snow pants, and one boot. He squirmed as she drew the plastic bag up over his cast and pulled snow pants up over it and his uninjured leg. "If you don't want to put this on we can stay inside," she warned him.

Sam gave her his most winning smile and sat patiently while she finished dressing him and covering his little hands with mittens. When she finished she pulled a stocking cap down over his blond head and grinned at him.

"You look like a little piggy," she said. "A little fat piggy." She leaned down and found his neck. "Oink, oink, oink. Munch, munch, munch."

He giggled. "Outside. Want to go outside. C'mon, Wachel Ann."

She pulled on her gloves and boots, put one of Sam's boots on his uninjured foot, then picked him up. "Oof, you're heavy, little piggy!" she exclaimed.

He just giggled and waved good-bye to her mother as Rachel Ann carried him outside. She sat him on the porch stairs, dragged down the sled, and loaded him onto it. She turned in the direction away from Abram's house, hoping he wouldn't see she was out in the yard. Around and around the yard they went, Rachel Ann starting to huff and puff at the effort.

"How about I push you on the swing?" she asked Sam, stopping in front of the one their father had hung from a tree on the far side of the yard.

Sam shook his head. "Wanna make a snowman."

So they made a snowman, rolling and patting snow into small, medium, and big balls. Rachel Ann assembled the balls, the biggest on the bottom, the medium sized one in the middle, and the smallest on the top. Then she straightened and caught her breath.

"Wish I'd known you wanted to do this before we came outside," she told Sam. "We don't have anything to make a face on him."

Rachel Ann glanced back at the house, frowning as she thought about putting Sam back on the sled, pulling the sled, and carrying him into the house so she could get a carrot and maybe a muffler for the snowman's neck . . .

She turned back to Sam. "Maybe we can do Mr. Snowman's face tomorrow."

He folded his arms across his chest, shook his head, and pouted. She sighed and resigned herself to trudging back to the house. He'd been cooped up so much with his leg being in a cast, she wanted him to enjoy himself.

She realized Sam was looking past her, a wide grin wreathing his face, and knew who was approaching before Sam cried, "Abram!"

"Sam!" he responded.

Rachel Ann didn't want to face Abram but it would have been rude, and she'd never been rude. She turned. "Hi."

"Hi." He studied her intently. "How are you?"

"*Gut*. You?"

He opened his mouth to speak, but Sam tugged on his hand, stealing his attention.

"Abram, we need a carrot for the snowman's nose and somethin' for his mouth."

"You do," Abram agreed. "The snowman can't talk without a mouth, can he? Not that we always get to say something, do we?"

"Huh?" Sam looked perplexed.

Rachel Ann felt color rush into her face. "If Abram will watch you for a minute, I'll go get a carrot and some other things."

"I'll be happy to watch him." His voice was as cool as the winter air.

She hurried away, went into the house, scooping up a carrot from the refrigerator and an old muffler kept at the back door, then started to rush back outside. Her steps slowed. She wasn't eager to have to face Abram again, hear him make a mocking reference to her breaking it off with him and not allowing him to talk to her about it. She was sorry he sounded bitter. The last thing she'd wanted was to hurt him.

She walked back to where Abram stood, holding Sam up so he could put some small rocks in place for the snowman's eyes. The snowman had sprouted small bare tree limbs for arms while she was gone.

"Here's a carrot for his nose," she said, holding it out to Sam. "You put the biggest end in the middle of his face."

"I know." Sam poked it in, and when it wobbled Abram helped screw it firmly into the snowman's face.

Rachel Ann gasped when Abram held Sam upside down. "Grab the rocks we found for his mouth, Sam."

Sam giggled as he picked up the rocks and Abram swung him upright. The snowman got a crooked grin made of rocks and a muffler wrapped around his neck.

"Nice job," she told them. "Sam, we need to go in now. We've been out a long time."

The corners of his mouth turned down. "Don't wanna go in."

"Sam, how about I find out if your *mamm* will let me take you for a ride on your sled tomorrow?" Abram asked him. "Then we can build a snowman in my front yard, too, if you want."

"*Allrecht*," Sam said in a plaintive voice. He sighed dramatically to let them know he wasn't happy about going inside.

"Say *danki*," Rachel Ann told her brother.

"*Danki*, Abram."

"You're *wilkumm*." He hugged Sam, set him on his sled, and picked up the rope to pull him.

"I can do it," Rachel Ann said, reaching for it.

Abram just kept walking across the yard. When he reached the porch stairs he picked Sam up, then bent to grasp the sled, depositing it to the side of the front door before he handed Sam to Rachel Ann.

"*Danki*," she murmured and started to pass him to go into the house, but Abram put his hand on her arm.

"We need to talk," he said in a low voice.

She shook her head.

"Please, Rachel Ann."

"I—can't."

Rachel Ann's mother appeared at the door. "Rachel Ann—oh, hi, Abram." She turned to her daughter. "Supper's almost ready. Can you take off Sam's jacket and sit him at the table?"

"*Schur*," she said and hurried toward the kitchen, grateful for the chance to escape Abram.

"Can you join us for supper, Abram?" she heard her mother ask him.

Rachel Ann froze and cast a panicked look back at Abram.

Their gazes met. Something in hers must have communicated a message to him. He shook his head as he tore his eyes from Rachel Ann's and looked at her mother.

"*Nee*, but *danki*," he said. "I told Sam I would ask if I could take him to play in my yard and maybe make another snowman tomorrow."

"That would be nice, Abram. Of course you may. *Danki*."

"See you tomorrow then."

Rachel Ann heard the front door close and breathed a sigh of relief. She stripped the jacket, hat, and snow pants from Sam. He patted her cheeks with his mittens, full of snow crumbs, and she shrieked. He laughed and she shook her finger at him. "Stop it!"

"Too bad Abram couldn't stay," her mother said she walked into the kitchen. "We haven't seen him for some time."

"*Ya*, too bad," Rachel Ann said, and she said a silent prayer of thanks to God. It would have been so hard if Abram had stayed for supper.

17

Abram was in the midst of building a snowman with Sam the next day when he heard a buggy coming up the road. He looked up and saw that it was Saul.

"Sam, get a snowball ready and let's throw one at Saul." He bent to scoop up a handful of snow and pack it into a ball.

"*Ya!*" Sam crowed. "Throw one at Saul." He watched Abram and then imitated what he'd done, his snowball smaller and a little lopsided.

Abram ducked behind the snowman, and Sam followed him. "Get ready. I'll tell you when to throw it."

Sam looked up at him adoringly. "*Allrecht.*"

The buggy pulled up into the drive.

"Steady." Abram said. "Not yet."

Saul set one foot out of the buggy, then turned when his cell phone rang and reached for it.

"Now?"

Abram shook his head. "Not yet."

Finished with the call, Saul turned and stepped from the buggy.

"Now!" Abram said.

He stepped out from behind the snowman and lobbed the snowball at Saul and hit him in the middle of the chest. Splat! Sam threw his, and it hit Saul's knee with a mild thump.

"Wha—?" Saul stared down at the snow on his chest, then he looked up and saw Abram and Sam. "Why, you!" he said to Abram. "Snowballs?"

"*Ya*, for the one you threw at me."

"That was when we were kids."

"There's no statute of limitations on snowball fights."

"Oh yeah? Well, look out!" Saul bent, scooped up snow, packed it, and drew back his arm like a baseball pitcher.

Abram picked up Sam and darted behind the snowman. The snowball hit him on the arm. "C'mon, Sam, we need more snowballs."

Sam made the snowballs and handed them to Abram who pelted Saul with them as fast as Sam could make them.

Saul scooped up snow and retaliated for several minutes, and then, laughing, he threw up his hands. "*Onkel*! Truce!"

"What do you think, Sam? Should we call a truce?"

"What's a truce?"

"Saul is giving up. We stop the snowball fight."

"Oh, but it was fun. I liked it."

"I know. Me, too."

Saul laughed. "Guys, it's cold out here, and I have things to do."

"Maybe we should let it go," Abram told Sam. "Bet we could get my *mamm* to make us some hot chocolate."

"With marshmallows?" Saul asked.

Abram looked at him. "With marshmallows."

"I want hot chocolate," Sam said. He stepped forward, tripped in the snow, and tipped over onto his back. He struggled to get up but lay there like a little turtle on his back. "Abram!" Sam flapped his arms. "Pick me up!"

Laughing, Abram scooped him up. "So, Saul, were you stopping by for the keepsake boxes I promised you?"

Saul brushed the snow from his chest. "I sure wasn't stopping by to get into a snowball fight."

"It was fun!" Sam cried.

Saul grinned. "It was."

Abram saw Rachel Ann walking toward them. He went still, watching her approach. She greeted Saul then Abram.

"*Danki* for staying with Elizabeth while I had to go out of town," Saul said.

"No thanks needed. We had fun," Rachel Ann told him.

So that was where she'd been the other night, thought Abram.

"Wachel Ann, we had a snowball fight!" Sam cried.

She looked at each of them. "I see."

"Abram started it," Saul said.

"He did," Abram said. He turned to Rachel Ann. "You remember, Saul hit me with a snowball after *schul* one day."

"Can you believe him?" Saul asked her. "He's bringing it up after all these years."

"It was fun!" Sam told her.

She smiled at him. "I'm glad you had a good time. You need to come home now."

"We were gonna have hot chocolate," Abram spoke up.

"We'll have some at home."

"*Allrecht*, Sam, let's get you home then." Abram swung him up on his shoulders.

"You don't need to walk us home," Rachel Ann said quickly.

"I want to."

"Don't want to go home," Sam cried.

"You have your hot chocolate and maybe your *mamm* will let you come over again sometime."

Sam sighed and leaned down to hug Abram's head. "I love you, Abram."

He climbed the steps to the porch and reached up to pull Sam down, bending to hug him. "I love you, Sam." He glanced at Rachel, but she wouldn't meet his eyes. He turned and walked back to his house.

Saul had his hands on his hips and was frowning when Abram returned to his front yard. "What's going on between you two?"

"What do you mean?"

"The two of you didn't look at each other once when she was over here. I could feel the tension between you."

Abram gazed over at Rachel Ann's house. He could walk the distance from his house to hers so quickly, but now it felt like there was this huge chasm stretching between them.

He sighed. "I honestly don't know what's wrong. She told me she doesn't want to see me anymore."

Shocked, Saul stared at him. "And you have no idea why?"

"None. She won't talk to me about it." He sighed. "Let's go have some hot chocolate or coffee to warm up."

Saul slapped him on the back. "Things will work out."

Abram wished he was as certain.

⁂

Rachel Ann never minded hard work, and as the days flew by, she was grateful she was busy so she could try to keep her mind off Abram.

The bakery got busier with every day, and Linda had to hire another baker who came in after Rachel Ann left in the mornings. Stitches in Time always bustled with customers when she walked in after her time in the bakery. She felt guilty she couldn't offer Leah more hours, but Leah refused to hear her apology.

"We do the best we can," she said firmly. "It's just going to be busy this time of the year, that's all."

A few days after she last saw Abram, his mother came into the shop. "Abram had to run an errand in town so I decided to ride along and get a few things," she told Rachel Ann. "I like to keep a few gifts for unexpected visitors."

Rachel Ann couldn't help wondering if Sarah would be getting a present from her. Abram was free now to pursue Sarah . . .

"I've made some food gifts, cookies and candy and such, but I have to hide them from Abram or there's nothing left to give by Christmas," she said. "You know what a sweet tooth he has."

Was it her imagination Lovina watched her for some reaction?

"*Ya*, he does," she agreed politely and smiled. "Do you need help today or would you like to browse?"

"I think I'll browse in the fabric section. Can't ever have enough fabric, especially if you don't make it to town often."

"You let me know if I can help you in any way," Rachel Ann told her and hurried away. She had no idea if Abram had shared with her they weren't seeing each other anymore. They'd agreed they wouldn't share anything with their parents just yet so she doubted Abram had said anything to her.

Elizabeth showed up at lunchtime, her cheeks pink from the cold. "Saul insisted I get away for a little while," she told Rachel Ann. "I know I should have called first, but I thought I'd take a chance you'd go to lunch with me. My treat."

Leah popped up behind her, hands full of bolts of fabric. "Take advantage of the lull, Rachel Ann. It won't last long."

They were no sooner seated at the restaurant and their orders taken than Elizabeth turned to Rachel Ann. "Saul said he stopped by to see Abram last week and saw you."

Rachel Ann nodded and took a sip from her glass of water. She knew what was coming.

"He said the two of you wouldn't look at each other."

"And?"

"I didn't tell him why you weren't seeing Abram anymore. It's your business."

"*Danki.*" She picked up half of her chicken salad sandwich and took a bite.

"He said something interesting, Rachel Ann."

"What?"

"He said he could tell both of you were unhappy and he couldn't figure out what happened, because he couldn't imagine a couple who should be together more than the two of you."

She tried to swallow the bite of sandwich, but it stuck in her throat. She took a sip of her water and forced it down. "It can't be helped. Breakups aren't easy."

"It *can* be helped, Rachel Ann. I still feel you're not being fair to Abram by not telling him."

"I told you why, Elizabeth."

"There are two people in a relationship," Elizabeth told her, looking at her with concern. "I hurt Saul by not talking to him when I was grieving after I miscarried. I don't want to see you throw away a life with Abram by bottling this up and not sharing it with him. You and he were best friends before you dated. You have a long history together. I don't think having his own *kind* means more to him than having you as a *fraa.*"

She paused, looking earnestly at Rachel Ann. "Please, think about what you can have, not what you can't with Abram."

"Elizabeth? Are you going to eat your lunch? Because you need to eat for the baby, you know. And we don't have a whole lot of time left of our lunch hour."

Elizabeth sighed and picked up her fork. "Fine. I'm not going to say another word." She narrowed her eyes at Rachel Ann. "Stop smirking. You think I can't stop talking to you about this?"

"Nagging me, you mean?"

She drew herself up and tried to look offended. Then she grinned. "I'll show you. I won't say another word. It'll be hard not to try to keep you from making a big mistake, but if it's what I have to do—"

"*Danki,*" Rachel Ann said with a grin. Her grin faded. "I *do* appreciate your concern. I'll think about it, *allrecht*?"

"You mean it?"

She nodded.

They spent the rest of their lunch hour talking about the upcoming holiday, about the presents they'd made for family and friends, and about Elizabeth's prenatal checkup. Then Elizabeth was ordering Saul a sandwich.

They walked back to Stitches and hugged, then Rachel Ann watched Elizabeth wend her way through the tourists on the sidewalk.

The afternoon went by in a blur of shoppers who looked increasingly more frantic the closer it got to Christmas. They didn't just need presents—they needed ideas for them. Worn out, Rachel Ann caught herself nodding off on the drive home, her head falling forward and waking her up.

"You're chicken pecking," Mary Beiler said with a chuckle.

Mary worked at a store a block down from Rachel Ann, and they frequently sat together in the rear seat of the van. She yawned. "Just a few more days," she said with a sigh as she leaned back against the seat. "We'll make it."

"I wish I felt as sure," Rachel Ann told her.

Home never looked so good. The van had barely stopped before she was stepping out and hurrying to the front door.

"Don't worry about the dishes tonight," her mother told her later as they sat sipping a cup of tea after supper. "You look exhausted."

"You mean because I almost fell asleep in the mashed potatoes?" she asked with a wry smile.

"I'm glad Sam wore down early tonight. It'll give me a chance to get one of his presents finished and wrapped."

They cleared the table, and her mother reached into a cupboard for the navy sweater she'd been knitting. All she had to do was sew on the buttons.

"Abram said he made Sam a little wagon."

She knotted the thread and clipped it. "Abram's so good with Sam."

"Can I ask you a question?"

"May I?" her mother corrected her.

Rachel Ann chuckled. Sometimes she forgot her mother had taught *schul* before she married and had *kinner*. "May I? Were you ever sorry you and *Daed* only had two *kinner*?"

"You've never asked me that before," her mother said with surprise.

She couldn't tell her mother that she tended to be a little remote and didn't invite the closeness and girl chats her friends had confided they enjoyed with their mothers. Maybe it came from her being more of a stern schoolmarm back when she was younger.

"I'd like to have had more *kinner*," she admitted, with a faraway look in her eyes. "But it took five years before I got pregnant with you and then, my goodness, more than fifteen before I had Sam. Just before I got pregnant with him, the doctor did a procedure and I was able to have him. She said I had something called endometriosis, making it difficult to get pregnant." She sighed, threaded her needle, and started sewing on another button.

Rachel Ann started at that. "I didn't know. *Mamm*, that's what the doctor told me I have."

Her mother gave her a sharp look. "Well, the doctor told me I might have trouble getting pregnant, and it did take a long time. But as you can see, I did have Sam after what he said. God decides, not doctors."

Rachel Ann watched her mother finish sewing a third button, and then she held up the sweater and nodded. She fetched the Christmas wrap, tape, and ribbon and set it on the table for her mother before going to the sink and filling it with water and dish-washing liquid.

"I told you, you don't have to do them tonight."

"It's *allrecht*. You have enough to do." She stood at the sink and couldn't help looking over at Abram's house. He wasn't out in the yard. She wondered what he was doing tonight.

She felt tears slipping down her cheeks, falling into the dish-water. She missed him so much, it was a physical pain in her chest.

❦

"Wachel Ann! Wachel Ann! Is it Chris-mas yet?"

Sam bounced up and down on Rachel Ann's bed. She opened her eyes and saw it was still dark. Groaning, she pulled her pillow over her head.

He turned on the battery-operated lamp on her bedside table and shook her arm. "What time is it?"

She squinted at the clock. "Sam! It's only four o'clock! We are not getting up now." She lifted her quilt. "C'mon, get in and we'll sleep a little while longer and then we can get up."

He gave her a big sigh but turned off the lamp and climbed in.

She jerked when she touched his feet as she tucked him closer. "Oh, my gosh, Sam, your feet are freezing!"

He giggled and snuggled closer. "Love you, Wachel Ann."

"Love you, Sam."

He wiggled a bit but within minutes fell asleep. She smiled, remembering how impatient she'd been for Christmas when she was little. Her parents had been firm about what time they would get up and let her open presents, so she was just protecting him. On the other hand, as a late baby, both her parents tended to overlook some behaviors she remembered getting into trouble for. And of course, ever since the accident, he'd been indulged much more.

She shuddered at the memory of the accident as Sam snuggled closer, wrapping his little arms around her, comforting her in his sleep. Tears slipped down her cheeks. Oh, he was so adorable. She sent up a silent prayer of thanks to God for the gift of this child. The family had been given Sam four years ago, and now he was here to celebrate the birth of Christ another year.

Rachel Ann didn't join Sam in sleep but lay there thinking about what her mother had said earlier, thinking about Abram . . .

The thin pale light of dawn was blooming when her mother tiptoed into the room. "So this is where he is," she whispered. "Did he have a bad dream?"

She smiled. "*Nee*, he was looking for Christmas. I told him it was too early and to get some more sleep. Should we wake him up now?"

"*Nee*. You didn't get back to sleep? Are you *allrecht*?"

She nodded. "I was just thinking about things. People. God is so *gut*. He gave us Sam a second time instead of welcoming him into heaven."

Her mother's eyes filled with tears, and her lips trembled. "And He gave me a special daughter who reminds me of His love." She blinked back her tears and smiled. "I'm going to start breakfast. Get some more sleep. No need to get up early. No work today."

Rachel Ann drifted off, and when she woke next Sam was gone. She dressed and went downstairs.

"Wachel Ann! *Mamm* says it's Chris-mas!" Sam cried when he saw her walk into the kitchen. "It's finally here!"

"So it is," she said.

"There are pancakes keeping warm in the oven," her mother told her.

Rachel Ann bent to hug her mother. "Where's *Daed*?"

"In the barn. He said no one's to come out there. I suspect he waited until the last minute to finish—" She stopped as she saw Sam listening. "Finish some chores."

Rachel Ann got a plate out of the cupboard, served herself some pancakes, and sat at the table. She poured syrup over the pancakes and cut herself a bite.

"Chris-mas," Sam said with a sigh. He leaned over and gave his mother a kiss on her cheek that left a syrupy imprint. "Merry Christmas, *Mamm* and Wachel Ann!"

Tonight, they'd gather in the living room before the fire and *Daed* would read the story of the night Jesus was born from his big Bible. It would be a special time just for the family to celebrate the spiritual meaning of Christmas. Tomorrow, extended family and friends would come to visit, bearing gifts and joy.

"Merry Chris-mas, Sam," she said, smiling at her baby *bruder*.

18

Rachel Ann was pulling a pan of pumpkin muffins from the oven on Second Christmas when Lovina opened the back door, letting in a gust of cold air. She was the first visitor on this day when family and visitors came bearing gifts.

"If the mountain won't come to Mohammed . . . " she said, handing Rachel Ann a present before shedding the woolen shawl she'd tossed over her shoulders to keep her warm as she walked over from her house next door.

"Pardon me?"

"I wasn't sure if you felt comfortable coming to the house, so I decided to come over here."

Rachel Ann blushed. She didn't know what Abram had told her, but now wasn't the time to discuss it when her family sat in the next room and might overhear.

"Why don't you go on into the living room and I'll bring you some tea or coffee?"

"Tea would be lovely, *danki.*"

Rachel Ann smiled as she listened to Lovina greeting her parents and Sam. She carried the tea and a plate of cookies and pumpkin muffins into the living room and set them down on the coffee table.

Sam sat on Lovina's lap, helping her unwrap the present his parents had gotten her. Typical Sam, he couldn't keep a secret. "It's towels!" he announced before she pulled off the last piece of wrapping paper.

Lovina smiled as she held up the embroidered kitchen dish towels. "These are lovely, Martha. *Danki.*"

Rachel Ann reached for the present she'd gotten for Lovina and handed it to her. "Sam can't tell you what it is because he didn't see me wrap it," she told her wryly.

Lovina gave her a delighted grin when Sam pulled off the paper and she saw the package of assorted specialty teas they sold at the bakery.

"I can't wait to sample one of these! There's nothing better than a special cup of tea." Her gaze was warm on Rachel Ann . . . and she wondered if she saw a hint of sadness in her expression or if it was her imagination. Lovina had always been so welcoming to her when she was growing up.

She visited with them for a while, and she'd no sooner left than other friends and family came bearing presents.

But as the hours wore on and Abram didn't come, Rachel Ann's spirits sank.

Rachel Ann took empty cups to the kitchen to wash them and stood there staring out the window. Lovina's words suddenly came to her: *If the mountain won't come to Mohammed, Mohammed will come to the mountain.* Could she summon up the courage to go try to talk to Abram?

She dried her hands on a dish towel and ran upstairs to her room for Abram's present. Her mother walked into the kitchen with more cups and looked surprised when she saw Rachel Ann buttoning her jacket.

"I'm just going to take Abram his present."

Her mother nodded. "Tell him I said Merry Christmas."

"I will." She had no idea what his reaction would be to her.

The temperature had dropped at least ten degrees since she'd been outside sweeping the snow off the front porch earlier. She was glad she'd put on her jacket instead of just snatching up a shawl as Lovina had done.

She knocked at the front door. Abram opened it and stared at her, looking surprised.

"I wasn't expecting you," he said after a long moment.

"I know." She hated the way he stood there so remote, so reserved, but she didn't blame him. She thrust his present into his hands. "You didn't come over with your *mamm.*"

"I didn't think you'd want to see me."

"You were wrong."

He looked at the present, then at her. "*Danki.*"

"Can we talk?"

"*Now* you want to talk?"

She nodded and found herself holding her breath. He sounded so bitter. So . . . final.

"I don't want to talk," he said at last. "I—"

She turned and ran down the stairs, tears streaming down her cheeks.

"Rachel Ann!"

She got as far as the steps to her back door and stopped. There was no way she wanted to go inside and have her parents and their guests see her this way. But where to go? She found herself heading down the path to the secret place by the pond where she and Abram had shared so many special times talking.

The secret place looked stark and beautiful, the pond frozen over and icy white, the surrounding trees leafless against the gray winter sky. Icicles hung from the branches, glittering in the late afternoon sunlight, tinkling like wind chimes when a chill wind blew through them.

Miserable, she sank down on the fallen log Abram had dragged over for them to sit on and look at the pond. Memories rushed at her: the one that always came to mind was ten-year-old Abram thinking she was going to be a scaredy-cat girl and scream when he chased her with a frog. She remembered picnics of bologna and cheese sandwiches and whoopie pies and lemonade; wading in the pond on hot summer days and skating on it when it froze over in the winter.

Her tears grew chilly on her cheeks as she sat there wondering how she had made such a big mistake and caused herself such heartache.

She didn't know how long she sat there, but she became aware she was shaking. It was too cold to sit here. What had she been thinking? She should have hidden in the barn where it was warm. She brushed the tears from her cheeks and stamped her feet. They felt like blocks of ice. Like her heart.

With luck she could slip in the kitchen door, sneak up the stairs to her room, and avoid questions from her parents.

She heard footsteps crunching through the snow behind her and spun around.

⬿

Abram stood at the front door feeling like a heel. Rachel Ann had come to give him a present and asked to talk and he'd said no.

Almost immediately, he'd been sorry and called her back, but she either hadn't heard or she'd been too upset at his rejection to turn and walk back . . .

Schur, she'd hurt him more than anyone had done in his life, but she'd evidently come to explain or apologize or who knew what—he hadn't given her a chance to say a word. It wasn't like him. And it certainly wasn't the way he should have behaved on a day like today.

"Abram?"

He turned to see his mother standing there staring at him.

"Why are you standing there with the door open?"

Shaking his head, he closed it.

"Was someone at the door?"

He nodded, his eyes on the present in his hands. "Rachel Ann."

"Why didn't she come in?"

"Because I'm *ab im kop*."

"You're not crazy."

"I am."

"Are you going to open the present or just look at it?"

He ripped off the paper and chuckled when he saw the carved wooden frog. He knew why she'd chosen it—to remind him of how he'd chased her with a real one years ago. It was the perfect present.

His mother took it from him and gave it a look-see. "Cute little guy. Why a frog?"

He grinned. "Years ago, when she was a little girl, I chased her with one, thinking she'd run and scream like other little girls. But she just took it from me and chased me."

"She's special. Always has been."

He nodded.

"So what happened, Abram? It's obvious something has. Both of you have been looking miserable."

He didn't like the idea she thought he'd looked miserable, but he guessed mothers could sense these things no matter how hard you tried to hide them. Then he realized what she'd said. "Her, too? Rachel Ann looked miserable when you went over with her present?"

"*Ya*." She handed the frog back to him. "Why did you call yourself an idiot, *sohn*?"

"She wanted to talk to me and I said no."

"Why?"

"She hurt me. I—didn't want her to hurt me more."

"You don't think she came over to apologize?"

He sighed and ran an impatient hand through his hair. "*Ya*, I think she did, and I didn't give her a chance."

Lovina nodded and folded her arms across her chest. "So, now what are you going to do?"

Abram handed her the frog. "I'm going to go talk to her." He headed for the kitchen for his jacket, shrugged it on, and opened the door. "Back in a while!" he called.

He crossed the distance between the two houses quickly and took the back porch stairs two at a time. Martha came to the door.

"Can I see Rachel Ann?"

She frowned. "I thought she was at your house. She took over your present." When he shook his head, she invited him in. "Let me see if she came in and went up to her room."

He waited in the kitchen as she climbed the stairs, and when she returned she looked worried. "She's not there. Where could she be?"

"I'll go check your barn. If she's not there maybe she took a walk."

"As cold as it is? That doesn't sound like Rachel Ann."

"I'll find her." He handed her Rachel Ann's present. "Would you put this somewhere for her?"

"*Schur.* Let me know. It's not like her to go somewhere and not tell me."

Abram checked the barn, but she wasn't there. He started to turn to walk down the drive when something caught his eye—footsteps in the snow between the houses, down the path leading to the pond. Had she walked down that path to their secret place?

An icy chill ran down his back that had nothing to do with the weather. The bad dream he'd had earlier in the week flashed into his memory, the one where he'd gone looking for Rachel Ann and seen *her* footprints in the snow, guiding him. He'd followed them and seen her standing at the edge of the pond they'd sat beside talking so many times, staring at something he couldn't see.

An icy wind swept through the bare tree branches, shaking the glittering icicles and creating a sound like wind chimes. But instead of sounding musical, the sound was ominous. His footsteps quickened, and he began praying as he found himself remembering how in the dream she'd heard him approaching and spun around, her lips parted in surprise.

"We have to talk," he'd said, and his voice had sounded louder than he intended. He stepped forward.

Rachel Ann had backed up and her feet slipped. Her arms flailed as she tried to gain a foothold on the frozen bank. Abram ran toward her, and their fingertips touched and then hers slipped free. She slid down into the water. He'd jumped in and woke, panting and sweating, his heart pounding. It had taken him hours to sleep again that night.

He wasn't psychic. He didn't believe he'd had the dream to warn him of something happening to Rachel Ann. But fear made him rush down the path.

There she was, just ahead, sitting on the log in front of the pond. She heard his footsteps and turned. Her lips parted in surprise as he stopped a few feet in front of her.

"Abram!"

&

At first, Rachel Ann thought the cold had gotten to her and she was seeing a mirage. *Nee*, she told herself—mirages were from the heat in a desert.

"What are you doing here?"

"I went to your house looking for you and got worried when your *mamm* said you didn't make it home."

"Yes, well, I'm *allrecht*. I just didn't feel like going home yet."

"I understand. It's such a beautiful day," he said dryly.

"It's beautiful here," she said, looking around.

"And cold. C'mon, Rachel Ann, you're shaking. Let's get you inside before you catch your death of cold."

She stood, but when she stepped forward she discovered she couldn't feel her feet and she pitched forward. Abram caught her and looked at her, concerned.

"My feet fell asleep," she said, downplaying it. She stamped her feet, trying to warm them up.

He frowned and muttered something she couldn't understand under his breath. "I hope you haven't got frostbite. Here, let me carry you."

"Don't be dramatic," she told him, secretly pleased at the idea of him carrying her in his muscular arms. "I can walk."

Rachel Ann trudged down the path, and he followed her. When they reached her house, he touched her arm.

"You wanted to talk earlier and I turned you down," he said quietly. "Can I have another chance?"

She looked at him. "You mean it?"

"Please."

There were two buggies parked in the drive. "We still have company at my house."

"We can talk at my house. *Mamm* is in the *dawdi haus* and won't disturb us. But let me tell your *mamm* where you are. She was concerned when I came over here looking for you earlier."

He told her to go ahead to his house while he went in to talk to her *mamm,* but she waited for him, hugging herself for warmth. When he emerged a few minutes later with a package wrapped in Christmas paper in his hands, they walked over to his house and went inside. Abram set the package on a table and shed his jacket, but she left hers on for a while until she warmed up. He pulled a hassock up close to the fireplace and insisted she take a seat. Then he knelt and took off her shoes. "Your feet are freezing. Let's take these stockings off so I can check your toes."

"I can't do that!" she said, scandalized.

"Would you rather lose a few toes?" he asked her bluntly.

She pulled off her stockings and wiggled her toes to show him they were fine. Cold but fine.

He rose, pulled a quilt from the back of the sofa, and wrapped it around her shoulders. "I'll be right back."

When he returned he carried two mugs. He set hers down on a nearby table and handed her a pair of socks.

Rachel Ann plucked them from his hands before he had a chance to try to slip them on her feet. "*Danki.*"

She picked up the mug and found he'd brought her hot tea. She warmed her hands with the mug before taking a sip. It was tough to decide which was better—the warm socks or the hot tea.

He dragged a chair over and sat next to her. "So, you wanted to talk."

She took a deep breath for courage. "I thought I was doing the right thing. But I've come to realize maybe I wasn't being fair to you."

"I figured you decided to start seeing Michael again."

She stared at him. Was it possible he felt some insecurity like she sometimes did? It couldn't be. He always seemed so confident; he'd been self-assured even as a young boy.

"I hope I've grown up a lot." She studied the mug in her hands, afraid to face his direct gaze. "*Nee,* it was because I had some bad news at the doctor."

Remembering how alarmed Elizabeth had been when she'd blurted out her news, she hurried on. "The doctor said she doesn't think I can have *kinner.*"

"You stopped seeing me because of *that*?" He set his mug down so hard the crack of pottery on wood startled her.

"I know how important having *kinner* is to you, to everyone in our community."

"It's not more important to me than you!"

He sounded so vehement it surprised her. "I—"

He got to his feet and paced the room. "How could you decide such a thing for me? For us?"

"Abram? Is everything *allrecht*?" Abram's mother called from her room.

"Excuse me for a minute." He walked swiftly to the back of the house, and Rachel Ann heard the murmur of voices, Abram speaking to his mother, but she couldn't hear what was said.

A door shut, and when he returned he was alone. "She was worried when she heard me raise my voice. It tends to be rather quiet around here."

"Not like at my house. Sam's always making a racket."

Then she wished she hadn't said it. It just served to bring up the subject of *kinner*. "I've watched you with him," she said quietly. "Heard you talk about how your *dat* passed his farm down to you and you hoped to do it with a *kind* of your own one day. I didn't want to take it away from you."

"Do you think I couldn't love a *kind* we adopted if it came to it? Do you think I'd only want one if it was biologically mine? It doesn't say much for what you think of me."

She set her mug down. *Nee*, maybe it didn't, she reflected.

"I thought we shared everything, that we were friends, if we weren't more these past few weeks. I can tell this is upsetting you and causing you pain."

"I wanted to be your *fraa*, to have *kinner* with you." Tears rolled down her cheeks. She brushed at them furiously with her free hand.

"You'll be my *fraa*, and if God wills it, we'll have *kinner*. And we'll love them however God brings them to us."

She stared at him, becoming lost in his eyes. He was such a good man. Why had she been so afraid to tell him, to believe any man God set aside for her would love and cherish her no matter what?

"I don't deserve you." She gave him a tremulous smile.

Abram took her face in his strong hands and touched his forehead to hers. "Don't you say that. Do you hear me?"

He didn't raise his voice, but he didn't need to—she heard him. Believed him.

"So are we *allrecht*?" he asked.

She nodded.

"*Gut*." He drew back a little and touched his lips to hers, in a brief but tender kiss. "I didn't get to thank you for the Christmas present. I can't wait to see what you think of yours." He got up to retrieve it from a nearby table and handed it to her.

She unwrapped it and found a little wooden keepsake box, the type she could keep her covering pins and little treasures in. He'd carved delicate little violets on top and painted them pale lavender. She ran her finger over them, thinking how much they looked like the ones near the pond in the spring.

"It's beautiful," she breathed. "*Danki*."

"There's more. Open it."

She lifted the lid and laughed. Inside he'd tucked a little carved green frog—much like the one she'd given him.

"I think I found him at the same store you got my present."

"He reminds me of the day you chased me."

"And you chased me back. Best day ever," he said with a grin.

"'Til now," she said with a sigh.

He nodded. "'Til now."

RECIPES

Gingerbread Cookies

3 cups all-purpose flour
1 ½ teaspoons baking powder
¾ teaspoon baking soda
¼ teaspoon salt
1 tablespoon ground ginger
1 ¾ teaspoons ground cinnamon
¼ teaspoon ground cloves
6 tablespoons unsalted butter
¾ cup firmly packed dark brown sugar
1 large egg
½ cup molasses
2 teaspoons vanilla
1 teaspoon finely grated lemon zest (optional)

Directions:

Preheat oven to 375 degrees.

Prepare baking sheets by lining with parchment paper or grease baking sheets with a little shortening.

In a small bowl, whisk together flour, baking powder, baking soda, salt, ginger, cinnamon, and cloves until well blended. In a large bowl beat butter, brown sugar, and egg on medium speed until well blended. Add molasses, vanilla, and lemon zest; continue to mix until well blended. Gradually stir in dry ingredients until blended and smooth.

Divide dough in half and wrap each half in plastic and let stand at room temperature for at least 2 hours or up to 8 hours. (Dough can be stored in the refrigerator for up to 4 days, but in this case it should be refrigerated. Return to room temp before using.) Place one portion of the dough on a lightly floured surface.

Sprinkle flour over dough and rolling pin. Roll dough out to a scant ¼-inch thick. Use additional flour to avoid sticking.

Cut out cookies with gingerbread man cookie cutter. Space cookies 1 ½ inches apart.

Bake one sheet at a time for 7 to 10 minutes (the lesser time will give you softer cookies—very good!). Remove cookie sheet from oven and allow the cookies to stand until firm enough to move to a wire rack to cool.

After cookies are cool, decorate them any way you like. Rachel Ann likes to decorate them as gingerbread men, women, and children.

Roasht (Chicken Filling)

½ stick butter (4 tablespoons)
1 cup chopped celery
1 loaf bread, cubed
1 ½ cups cooked and diced chicken
3 eggs, beaten
½ teaspoon salt
Pepper to taste

Directions:

Preheat oven to 350 degrees.

Melt butter in large skillet. Add celery and sauté until soft. Toss bread and chicken together in large bowl. Pour celery and eggs over bread mixture. Sprinkle with salt and pepper. Mix well.

Pour into greased roaster or a large baking dish. Bake uncovered for 1 ½ to 2 hours. During baking, stir occasionally, stirring bread away from sides of pan to prevent over-browning or burning.

Red Velvet Whoopie Pies

2 cups all-purpose flour
2 tablespoons unsweetened cocoa powder
½ teaspoon baking soda
¼ teaspoon salt
½ cup butter, softened
1 cup packed brown sugar
1 egg
1 teaspoon vanilla
½ cup buttermilk
1 1-ounce bottle red food coloring (2 Tbsp.)
1 recipe Whoopie Pie Filling (recipe follows)

Directions:

Preheat oven to 375 degrees.

Line baking sheets with parchment; set aside. In medium bowl combine flour, cocoa powder, baking soda, and salt; set aside. In large mixing bowl, beat butter on medium to high for 30 seconds. Beat in brown sugar until light and fluffy. Beat in egg and vanilla. Alternately, add flour mixture and buttermilk, beating after each addition just until combined. Stir in food coloring.

Spoon batter out in 1- or 2-inch diameter rounds, about 1/2-inch high on prepared baking sheets, allowing 1 inch between each round. Bake for 7 to 9 minutes for 1-inch cookies or 9 to 11 minutes for 2-inch cookies, or until tops are set.

Cool completely on baking sheets on wire rack. Remove cooled cookies from baking sheets. Dollop Whoopie Pie Filling on flat sides of half the cookies. Top with remaining cookies, flat sides down. Makes 60 one-inch or 42 two-inch cookies.

Whoopie Pie Filling

¼ cup softened butter
½ 8-ounce package softened cream cheese
1 7-ounce jar marshmallow crème

Directions:

In medium mixing bowl, beat butter and cream cheese until smooth. Fold in marshmallow crème.

Snickerdoodles

1 ½ cups sugar
½ cup butter or margarine, softened
½ cup shortening
2 eggs
2 ¾ cups all-purpose or unbleached flour
2 teaspoons cream of tartar
1 teaspoon baking soda
¼ teaspoon salt
¼ cup sugar
2 teaspoons ground cinnamon

Directions:

Preheat oven to 400 degrees.

Mix 1 ½ cups sugar, butter, shortening, and eggs in large bowl. Stir in flour, cream of tartar, baking soda, and salt. Shape dough into 1 ¼-inch balls. Mix ¼ cup sugar and the cinnamon. Roll balls in cinnamon-sugar mixture. Place 2 inches apart on ungreased cookie sheet.

Bake for 8 to 10 minutes or until set. Remove from cookie sheet to wire rack to cool. Makes approximately four dozen cookies.

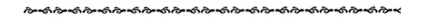

Pumpkin Bread

1 ½ cups all-purpose flour
½ teaspoon salt
1 cup sugar
1 teaspoon baking soda
1 cup pumpkin purée* (see below)
½ cup olive oil
2 eggs, beaten
¼ cup water
½ teaspoon nutmeg
½ teaspoon cinnamon
½ teaspoon allspice
½ cup chopped walnuts

Directions:

Preheat oven to 350 degrees.

* To make pumpkin purée, cut a pumpkin in half, scoop out the seeds and stringy stuff, and place face down on a foil or Silpat-lined baking sheet. Bake until soft, about 45 min to 1 hour. Cool and scoop out the flesh. Freeze leftover puree for future use. Or, if you are working with pumpkin pieces, roast or boil them until tender, then remove and discard the skin.

Sift together the flour, salt, sugar, and baking soda. Mix the pumpkin purée, oil, eggs, water, and spices together, then combine with the dry ingredients, but do not mix too thoroughly. Stir in the nuts. Pour into a well-buttered 9x5x3-inch loaf pan.

Bake for 50 to 60 minutes until a thin skewer poked in the center of the loaf comes out clean. Turn out of the pan and let cool on a rack. The recipe is easily doubled.

Glossary

ab im kop—off in the head. Crazy.

allrecht—alright

boppli—baby

bruder—brother

Daed—Dad

Danki—thank you

Dat—father

Der hochmut kummt vor dem fall.—Pride goeth before the fall.

dippy eggs—over-easy eggs

Englischer—what the Amish call us

grossdaadi—grandfather

grosseldere—grandparents

grosskinner—grandchildren

grossmudder—grandmother

guder mariye—good morning

gut-n-owed—good evening

haus—house

hochmut—pride

kaffe—coffee

kapp—prayer covering or cap worn by girls and women

kind, kinner—child, children

kumm—come

lieb—love

liebschen—dearest or dear one

maedels—young single women

mamm—mother

mann—husband

nee—no

newhockers—wedding attendants

Ordnung—The rules of the Amish, both written and unwritten. Certain behavior has been expected within the Amish community for many, many years. These rules vary from community to community, but the most common are to have no electricity in the home, to not own or drive an automobile, and to dress a certain way.

Pennsylvania *Deitsch*—Pennsylvania German

rumschpringe—time period when teenagers are allowed to experience the *Englisch* world while deciding if they should join the church.

schul—school

schur—sure

schwesder—sister

sohn—son

verdraue—trust

wilkumm—welcome

wunderbaar—wonderful

ya—yes

zwillingbopplin—twins

Group Discussion Guide

Spoiler alert! Please don't read before completing the book as the questions contain spoilers!

1. Rachel Ann is excited that she's traveling a new path for her—she has a new job and a new boyfriend. Has there ever been a time when you embarked on a new path? What was your predominant emotion? Excitement? Apprehension?

2. While Rachel Ann is watching her younger brother, he darts out into the road and gets hit by a car. She feels responsible. Do you think it was her fault? Was there anything she could have done to prevent the accident?

3. Sam, Rachel Ann's brother, sustains serious injuries from the accident. Have you or any member of your family ever been hospitalized for a long time? What kind of stress did this place on you or your family? How did you deal with it?

4. Rachel Ann and Abram have been good friends for years, yet they never dated. Have you had a friend of the opposite sex for a long time? How was this friendship different from your friendships with women?

5. Abram feels more than friendship for Rachel Ann but doesn't act on his feelings before she starts seeing another man. Have you ever experienced such feelings? What did you do about them?

6. The staff at the Stitches in Time shop is made up of a mixture of family members and unrelated women, but they have formed a bond and encourage each other. Do you work at a place where the staff has formed a bond? Is a working atmosphere like the one at the shop important to you?

7. Abram lets Rachel Ann know how he feels about her when she has a personal crisis. Have you ever had a male

or female friend offer to help you with a big personal crisis and it changed the friendship?

8. Couples in the Amish community keep their dating private. Why do you think that is?

9. Amish parents often live in a *dawdi haus*—kind of like a mother-in-law apartment—at the rear of their adult children's homes. Is this an arrangement you would ever consider?

10. Amish young people get to experience *Englisch* life during a period called *rumschpringe*. While some youth use it as a chance to break out of the strict rules of the Amish community, most do not. Do you think teens of either culture need a period of unrestricted time to mature?

11. Many Amish believe God has set aside a marriage partner for them. Do you believe this? Do you believe in love at first sight?

12. The Amish do not believe in divorce. They usually know their prospective spouse for many years before they marry since they grow up together in the community. Do you think this helps them to have happier and longer-lasting marriages?

13. Rachel Ann loves children, but her doctor tells her that she may not be able to have children of her own. She chooses not to tell Abram and breaks off their relationship. Do you think she should have done this? What did you think of his reaction when she finally tells him?

14. Do you feel God has a plan for you? Do you know what it is?

If you enjoyed *One True Path*, we hope you enjoy these samples from the first two books in the series, *A Road Unknown* and *Crossroads*.

A Road Unknown

1

Some people say if you look at a map of Goshen, Indiana, you'd see almost all Amish Country roads lead into the town.

But as Elizabeth stood waiting for her bus, all she could think about was the road leading out of the town.

The big bus lumbered into the station. Under her watchful eye, the driver put her suitcase in the storage area. She didn't have much and wanted to make sure it made it to her next home.

She winced at the word. *Home.* She was leaving everything and everybody she knew to go to a place she'd never visited in her life. It was exciting. It was terrifying.

"You getting on?" the driver asked, studying her curiously as he waited for other passengers.

Elizabeth nodded and taking a deep breath, she climbed up the steps into the bus. She walked toward the back of the half-empty bus and found a seat. She hoped she'd get a chance to sit by herself and not make conversation with a stranger. Especially an *Englisch* stranger. So many of them were curious about the Amish. She didn't want to talk about why she was walking—riding?—away from a community many of them thought was idyllic.

Oh, they liked the idea of a simpler life, but in the next breath they would shake their heads and say they couldn't imagine living without electricity or television.

She settled into her seat and tucked her small shoulder purse to her left between the seat and the window of the bus. Most of her money was pinned in a little pouch inside her dress but there were so many important things in her purse: a little address book, the resumé the job coordinator at the women's center had helped her with—everything she'd need for this new town where she'd be making her home.

Feeling a little self-conscious, she smoothed the skirt of her dark blue dress over her knees. Paula had said they could go clothes shopping at some thrift stores when she got there. Elizabeth had saved some money from her part-time job in Goshen, but things would be tight until she found a job. Paula hadn't wanted to take any money from her for her share of the rent until she got a job, but she really didn't have any choice. Things were tight for her as well since she was attending college.

Paula had sent her photos of the apartment she'd be sharing. Elizabeth drew them from her purse now and looked at them. So much space just for two people. Imagine. And imagine having a bedroom of her own. She hadn't had one for . . . eight brothers and sisters. As the oldest of nine *kinner* in the family, she hadn't had a room of her own or any peace and quiet in years and years.

A baby cried at the back of the bus. It was a familiar sound to Elizabeth. Too familiar. She loved babies, but she became exhausted taking care of someone else's. She'd read once the average Amish family had seven children, but she guessed her parents hadn't heard it. Stop, she told herself. Children were a gift from God. But, oh, had He blessed her family.

Exhausted, she leaned back in her seat and closed her eyes. She'd worked extra hours at the fabric shop this week to help the owner who hadn't been happy she was leaving. Angela had said she thought she'd finally gotten someone dependable and now she was losing her. Someone else to make her feel guilty.

Lately, she'd begun to feel like everyone depended on her and it was all too much. She'd tried to talk about it with her best friend, but Lydia was getting engaged and didn't understand. With working during the day and spending so much time helping her *mamm* when she got home, Elizabeth didn't get to go to singings or other youth activities. She knew she was hardly an *old maid* at twenty but she was beginning to despair of ever being able to date and get married. And who would help her mother then? Fourteen-year-old Mary, the next oldest, didn't seem interested in helping as she should.

Now, she would have to, thought Elizabeth. She opened her eyes as a woman in the next row of seats complained loudly about the bus being a few minutes late leaving the station. Elizabeth found herself biting her thumbnail as she pondered the selfishness of leaving home now.

The driver climbed on board, closed the door, and started up the bus, but he didn't immediately pull out. The woman in the next row who had been complaining turned to Elizabeth and shook her head.

Elizabeth turned to stare out the window. Goshen was the only place she'd ever lived. She'd never left it. Never wanted to. Now she felt like the woman who complained. When were they going to leave?

A thought suddenly struck her. Maybe it was a sign. Maybe she wasn't supposed to leave. Maybe it wasn't a part of God's plan for her. Hadn't one of the ministers at church once cautioned his listeners about fighting God, swimming upstream against His plan?

Maybe He thought she was selfish, too. Maybe He thought she should stay here with her family.

The bus began moving. Relief washed over Elizabeth. Dilemma solved.

She turned away from the window. Everyone knew what had happened to Lot's wife when she looked back . . .

Instead, she glanced around at fellow passengers, feeling a little curious about them. Were they making big life changes like her? Going on vacation?

She realized the woman who'd complained about the bus not leaving the station on time was watching her. Elizabeth pulled her gaze away and glanced out her window. She had always been shy. She didn't want to talk about herself, answer questions about why she was on the bus. It might have been a good idea to change into *Englisch* clothes before she left home, but she didn't have any, and she didn't want to upset her parents more.

"So where are you going?"

Elizabeth blinked at the sudden intrusion into her thoughts and looked over. The woman across the aisle was regarding her curiously.

"Paradise."

The woman laughed and looked incredulous. "Paradise?"

"Paradise, Pennsylvania."

"Oh, right, there is a city named that there. You know people there?"

Elizabeth nodded.

"I was wondering if you were in your rum—rum—" the woman flapped one hand. "I can't remember what it's called."

"*Rumschpringe.*"

"Yeah, that's it. When you get to be like a girl gone wild."

Elizabeth wondered where the *Englisch* got their ideas about *rumschpringe.* Like the mother of a friend had once said, "You think we suddenly let our kids run wild and don't know where they are?"

In reality, *rumschpringe* was something rather tame in her community. Oh, sure, she'd heard stories occasionally about some of the boys she'd gone to school with buying beer and having wild parties. But those stories were few and far between. And most Amish youth ended up becoming baptized into the church and stayed in the community.

"I'm just going there to visit," she said.

It wasn't the total truth, because she knew she was going to stay there longer than a visit. But she wasn't sure how long she'd be there and besides, she'd been cautioned not to talk to strangers.

A big yawn overcame her. She clapped her hand over her mouth. "I'm so sorry. I was up late last night getting packed. If you don't mind, I think I'll take a nap."

The woman nodded and didn't seem offended. "We can talk later."

Elizabeth smiled and nodded. What else was there to say? She leaned back against her seat and closed her eyes.

And when anxiety rolled over her like the tiredness in her body, she told herself to stop thinking about where she'd come from and instead forced herself to focus on where she was going.

❧

Saul nodded at the driver, handing him his ticket before climbing onto the bus. He'd made the trip from Pennsylvania to Ohio and back many times and felt a little bored as he looked for a seat. Then he saw the attractive young Amish woman sitting with her eyes closed.

Indiana, he mused as he walked down the aisle. The man ahead of him stopped at the woman's row and leaned down.

"Hey, pretty lady, dreaming of me?"

Startled, she woke and stared at him. "Excuse me?"

"How about I sit next to you?" he asked.

Saul could tell from the way she recoiled from the man it was the last thing she wanted.

On impulse, he stepped closer. "*Gut,* you saved me a seat," he said loudly.

The man turned and gave him a once-over. "Oh, you two together?"

Saul looked at Elizabeth and lifted his brows.

"Yes," she said, her voice soft at first and then she said it louder: "Yes."

Shrugging, the man moved on and found a seat a few rows back.

"Did you decide I was the lesser of two evils?" he asked her as he sat down.

"Yes," she said honestly, but the shy smile she gave him took away any sting he might have felt.

He knew from a glance at her clothing, she was from Indiana. It was easy to distinguish one Amish community from another by the style of the *kapp* and the dress the women wore. The Lancaster County women wore prayer head coverings made of a thin material with a heart shape to the back of them. This woman wore a starched white *kapp* with pleats and a kind of barrel shape. The stark look of it suited her high cheekbones and delicate features.

He studied her while she looked out the window. Her skin seemed almost alabaster. Her figure was small and slender in the modest dark blue cape dress she wore. She'd looked away before he saw the color of her eyes; he wondered if her eyes were blue—sometimes women wore dresses the color of their eyes.

A baby cried at the back of the bus. Its mother tried to shush it, but it kept crying, its voice rising.

The woman turned away from the window and frowned slightly as she glanced back toward the rear of the bus. Then, when she sensed him watching her, she looked at him and he saw her eyes were indeed blue—the blue of a lake in late summer.

"Poor mother," she murmured. "The baby's been crying for hours."

"Poor us if it continues," he said, frowning at the thought of listening to a baby cry for hours. Surely, the kid was tiring and would sleep soon? "So, you're from Indiana?"

"What?"

"You're from Indiana?"

She nodded.

"I'm from Pennsylvania. Paradise, Pennsylvania."

She turned those big blue eyes on him and he saw interest in them. "Really? How long have you lived there?"

"My whole life. Is it where you're going?"

Her eyes narrowed. "How did you know that?"

"The way you perked up when I said the name." He moved in his seat so he could study her better and smiled at her. "There's no need to be suspicious. My name's Saul Miller."

When she hesitated, he smiled. "Just tell me your first name."

"Elizabeth."

"Are you called Beth? Liz? Lizzie?"

"Elizabeth."

"Ever been to Pennsylvania?"

"Once. For a cousin's wedding."

"Ah, I see. So, you were there in the fall." When she just nodded, he tried not to smile. Getting her to talk was like pulling teeth.

"Well, can't be the reason this time. Not the season for weddings."

He watched her glance out the window at the passing scenery. There was a wistfulness in her expression.

"So are you going to Pennsylvania for vacation?"

"Vacation?"

"You know, the thing people do to relax."

Her mouth quirked in a reluctant smile. She glanced around her, then whispered, "Now how many Amish do you know who go on vacation?"

He shrugged. "There are some I know who go South for the winter for a few weeks."

"*Daed* would think you were crazy if you talked about a vacation," she scoffed. "Why, when I—"

"When you what?" he prompted when she didn't go on.

She frowned and shook her head. "Nothing."

Saul fell silent for a few minutes, waiting to see if she'd say anything else. It felt a little strange to be doing it all—to be carrying the conversational ball. But he'd had no trouble attracting the opposite sex. Usually, women let him know they were attracted, and then went out of their way to engage him in conversation.

Elizabeth was being no more than polite.

"So, Elizabeth, if you're not on vacation, are you on your *rumschpringe?*"

Elizabeth was beginning to think maybe it wasn't so bad back home—even if she'd seldom gotten out. But since she had now, it seemed everyone wanted to talk, talk, talk.

Really, whether Amish or *Englisch*, people certainly were a nosy bunch. First, the *Englisch* woman had asked questions, then Saul had picked up where she left off.

She immediately chided herself for being judgmental. People who judged others often were guilty of the same thing as the person they judged. And goodness knew, Elizabeth possessed a deep curiosity about other people. Her leaving home hadn't just been because she was tired of her confining, unsatisfying life. She'd wanted to know what was out there—trapped as she'd felt being stuck at home as a caretaker of her brothers and sisters, she'd loved her time working at the fabric shop where she could interact with others.

Personal decisions were just that . . . she didn't want to discuss it with someone who was a stranger.

The bus ate up the miles and she blessed the fact Saul had fallen silent and appeared to be watching the road. The woman across the aisle now sat, nodding, a magazine unread in her hands. Even the crying baby at the back of the bus fell silent.

The weariness of body and mind, which caused her to drift off earlier, returned. Her eyelids felt weighted; her body seemed to melt into the comfort of the padded seat.

"Give in," Saul said softly. "You look exhausted."

She frowned at him. "How can I when you keep talking to me?" she asked and heard the tartness in her tone. When he chuckled, she glared at him. "You know, you're acting like I'm here to entertain you."

"No," he said, obviously trying not to smile. "I just find you refreshing."

Refreshing? Her? "Are you mocking me?"

His smile faded. "No, Elizabeth, I wouldn't do that. You're just not like any of the women I know back home."

"I'm different from the women of Paradise? How?"

"You're not talking a lot. You're not trying to impress me."

"So you're used to being . . . pursued?"

He had the grace to redden. "I wouldn't say that."

Now it was her turn to try to hide a smile. There was no question he was attractive with mahogany-colored hair, strong, masculine features. And those dark brown eyes looking at her so intensely. She'd seldom gotten much interest from the young men in her community. It felt exhilarating. It felt a little scary. This was a very different experience for her, this enclosed, enforced intimacy of riding in a bus, conversing with a stranger and feeling he was expressing interest in her.

Maybe she was dreaming. After all, she was so very tired. She'd been sleeping and then woken up to see him looking at her. It was entirely possible she was dreaming.

So, when Saul wasn't looking, she pinched herself and found she wasn't dreaming.

No, she wasn't dreaming, but it was certain his interest was flattering. She drew herself up. Being Amish didn't mean you didn't know what went on in the world, you were aware of bad people, and knew bad things could happen.

It was entirely possible this Saul wasn't even Amish . . .

"What?"

She blinked. "Excuse me?"

"Suddenly you're looking at me like I'm the Big Bad Wolf."

"I don't know what you're talking about." But Elizabeth had never been able to hide what she was thinking.

"*Schur*," he drawled.

She focused on the billboards on the side of the road. They were quite entertaining to someone who mostly traveled in a buggy on roads not big and crowded like this highway. Most of the signs advertised restaurants and shopping, but there were a few to raise her eyebrows. It took her a moment to understand what an adult store was, but once she did she averted her eyes quickly at the next one they passed.

Her stomach growled. She reached for the lunch tote she'd carried on board, pulled out a sandwich and unwrapped it. She'd packed several sandwiches with her mother's grudging permission—her *daed* had been out—but she didn't know how long they would last and she had to be careful with her money.

As she did, she felt rather than saw, Saul come to attention. She glanced at him, saw he was looking at her sandwich and not at her. Well, she thought, I found a way to make him stop asking questions.

She took a bite and chewed and tried not to notice his attention then shifted to her mouth.

Manners kicked in. "Would you like half?"

"I wouldn't want to take your food."

"I have more," she said, handing him half the roast beef sandwich and a paper napkin.

She watched him take a bite and his eyes closed with pleasure as he chewed. "Terrific bread," he said. "Nothing better than Amish bread."

"It's just bread," she told him mildly. But she felt an unaccustomed bit of pride, since she'd made it.

"Almost don't need the meat," he said, his strong white teeth finishing the sandwich in several big bites.

Elizabeth ate a little faster when she noticed he was eyeing her sandwich. She popped the last bite into her mouth and wiped her fingers on her own napkin. Then she reached into the tote, pulled out a thermos and poured coffee into the plastic cap. She handed it to him, pulled a cup from her tote, and poured some coffee for herself.

When she'd tucked the cup into the tote earlier, it hadn't been because she'd anticipated offering some of the coffee to a stranger. She'd simply brought it because the cap didn't hold much coffee and could get hot.

"Coffee? You brought coffee?" He inhaled the steam rising from the cap and sighed. "Elizabeth, will you marry me?"

She laughed and sipped. "Don't be ridiculous."

"You're right. It has to be good coffee to get a proposal." He took a sip, closed his eyes as if in ecstasy, then opened them. "Well, let's set a date."

Elizabeth pressed her lips together. "Are you always this way?"

"Romantic?"

"Ridiculous."

"You have no idea how wonderful this coffee is, do you?"

"I do. But it's not worth a marriage proposal."

"Let me be the judge."

She finished her coffee and before she tucked the thermos back into the tote, topped off Saul's cup.

"I'm thinking this is a blessed day," he told her.

Elizabeth thought the coffee would help her wake up, but a big yawn overcame her. She covered her mouth and felt color creep up into her cheeks.

"Sorry."

He just chuckled.

"What's so funny?"

"You," he said.

"How am I funny?"

"You're being so polite, but you're going to drop off any minute."

"I know. I was up late getting ready for the trip last night."

"Be my guest," he said. "Would you like a shoulder to rest your head on?" It was then, in that moment, he fully understood the saying, *If looks could kill* when she glared at him.

She turned farther away from him, placing her purse under her cheek for a pillow. It couldn't have been very comfortable, but in a few minutes her breathing became slow and even and she slept.

Her cool manner toward him should have served to dampen his enthusiasm for getting to know her but perversely, he found himself wanting to know her better. He knew a few people in Goshen. Pulling out his cell phone, he texted a friend of his and asked if he knew an Elizabeth.

Lamar responded he knew only one Elizabeth. "IS IT ELIZABETH BONTRAGER?" he texted. "MARY AND JACOB BONTRAGER'S OLDEST *KIND*?"

"DON'T KNOW," he texted back. He thought about snapping a photo but told himself it was a bigger invasion of privacy than watching her sleep. Besides, she was turned too much away from him . . .

"ODD YOU SHOULD ASK," Lamar texted. "HEARD ELIZABETH LEFT TOWN TODAY. WHERE ARE YOU?"

"HEADED HOME."

"HOW'S LAVINA?"

"FINE. WHY?"

"Wondered if it was over since you're asking about another woman."

"Curiosity," Saul texted. "And confidential."

"Got it," Lamar wrote back.

"Talk to you soon." He put his phone back in his jacket. Elizabeth stirred in her sleep and turned toward him. He studied her while she slept and chided himself for the invasion of privacy. But he was a man, after all, and she was an attractive woman.

She moved closer, murmuring something unintelligible, then she sighed and put her cheek on his shoulder. Saul bit back a smile and tried not to move and wake her.

But the baby cried again and she whispered, "Give him to me" and her eyes opened. Struggling to focus, she stared at Saul, then she pulled back and sat up. "What did you do? I didn't put my head on your shoulder!"

2

Elizabeth had never felt so mortified.

She reached for her *kapp*, straightening it, and drew back into her own seat until she was shoved into the metal of the interior bus wall.

"I didn't touch you," Saul was saying. "You just turned and put your cheek on my shoulder while you slept."

"Why didn't you wake me up?"

"I don't know what you're so upset about," he said. "It was no problem."

"No problem," she muttered. He'd probably enjoyed having a strange woman putting her head on his shoulder. A good-looking man like him probably had women finding a way to get close to him all the time.

She glanced around furtively, but none of the bus passengers was watching them. They were too busy napping, reading, or staring out their window. Elizabeth sent up silent thanks the nosy woman from earlier in the trip had gotten off the bus. She wouldn't have wanted to deal with comments from her about Saul . . .

"Honestly, no harm done," he said, spreading his hands.

She glanced out the window, but it was dark and she couldn't see anything. "How long did I sleep?"

"Only about an hour."

Gathering her sweater closer, she tried to relax.

"Cold?"

"I'm fine. It won't be much longer."

"Someone meeting you?"

She nodded. "My new roommate."

"So you're going to stay for a while?"

"Yes," she said reluctantly. "What do you do?" she asked politely, more to deflect him from asking about her.

"You mean besides ride buses and get women to rest their heads on my shoulder?" he asked, a glint of mischief in his eyes.

She frowned at him. "Yes."

"I work in a store. We sell Amish crafts."

It was so tempting to ask him about a job at the store where he worked. After all, she needed one and it wasn't such a stretch in imagination to go from selling fabric to selling things like crafts. Yes, it was so, so tempting. But how would it be to work in a place with someone who acted attracted to her?

Attracted. It was a stretch. He'd just been friendly to her, saving her from the man she didn't want sitting beside her. Maybe Saul had flirted a little. Guys did it. He might not even realize how he came off. And she was pathetic, so lonely for contact with someone her own age, because she never got out but for work.

But still, she felt some attraction and wondered if he did, too.

Well, didn't matter. They'd be in Paradise very soon. They would probably never see each other again. And maybe it was best. She needed to settle into her new home, find a job, and learn to take care of herself—when all she'd ever done was take care of others.

A list. She needed to make a list of everything she had to do. She'd been in such a rush to leave she hadn't done much planning. And if she was honest with herself, she knew it was also because she was scared—scared of finding there was so much to do to have a break, she'd frighten herself into staying. She pulled a pad of paper and a pencil from her purse.

"Folks, we'll be making an unscheduled stop for a few minutes," the bus driver came on the intercom to say. "You can get off and stretch your legs, get some coffee if you like."

He pulled into the parking lot of a fast-food restaurant.

"You're not getting off?" Saul asked her.

She shook her head.

"Want anything?"

"I'm fine."

She watched him disembark and thought about eating the last sandwich she'd packed but decided to save it since she wasn't real hungry yet. She wasn't sure of exactly when they'd arrive in Paradise and she might need to stretch her food. Then she happened to glance out the window and found herself watching several birds pecking at some crumbs from the restaurant.

His eye is on the sparrow.

She blinked. Where had the thought come from? They weren't even sparrows.

But it was an intriguing thought. She wasn't sure where it had come from—she hadn't been consciously thinking about it.

Look at the birds of the air, for they neither sow nor reap nor gather into barns; yet your heavenly Father feeds them. *Are you not of more value than they?*

The book of Matthew. She'd always found comfort in it. Sparrows didn't worry about their next meal. God provided for them. Why wouldn't He provide for her? It didn't mean she could just lie around and not work, but she didn't intend to do that. God would help His child to find a job to feed herself, wouldn't He? Everything she'd had growing up hadn't really come from her parents, but from her heavenly Father.

Feeling a little relieved, she found herself doodling on the paper. She was so busy sketching when she felt movement beside her she was startled to see Saul was sitting down, and in fact, the bus had filled again.

"I know you said you didn't want anything, but I thought you might when you saw what I got," he told her as he held out a paper sack.

She tucked the pencil behind her ear and laid the pad of paper on her lap. "You didn't have to do that."

"You gave me part of your sandwich," he said, shaking the bag.

Elizabeth opened the bag and found a Big Mac and French fries. "Oh, a favorite of mine," she breathed.

"Good. Diet Coke okay?" he asked, holding out a drink carrier. "I don't think you need to save the calories, but every woman I know drinks diet instead of regular."

She had to admit he was right.

He set the drink carrier on the floor between his feet and pulled his own Big Mac from his bag.

She felt him lean over and look at the pad of paper before she could juggle things in her hands to cover it.

"Nice," he said. "How long have you been sketching?"

She shrugged. "Couple of years. Not much time for it."

"You're good."

Elizabeth blinked. Very few people had seen her sketching, but she'd never had anyone actually compliment it. Her teacher had done so years ago, but it didn't count. Besides, Lydia had told her she had to stop sketching in class and concentrate on her lessons.

She knew she had a problem with staying focused and it hadn't gone away when she got older. Hadn't she just taken out her pad of paper to make a list and then started sketching birds? But as she munched happily on her hamburger and fries, she refused to chide herself for her inattention.

Hadn't she just been given a sign all would be all right? His eye was on the sparrow . . . He was already showing He was taking care of her by bringing her a meal she hadn't had to pay for. She smiled.

He'd brought her a Big Mac just like He'd brought the sparrows—er, pigeons—their crumbs.

⌦

Saul ate his Big Mac and was glad he'd bought one for Elizabeth when he saw how happy she was to get it. He got the impression she didn't go to McDonald's often.

The unexpected stop there had been welcome. Usually Lavina packed him food for his trip home on the bus, but he'd decided to leave a day early and she'd acted a little upset with him over it. Which was strange because things hadn't gone well with this last visit. He was beginning to think absence hadn't made the heart grow fonder—the physical distance between them since her parents had moved the family to Indiana had caused an emotional gulf as well.

There had been a way to fix it. He could have asked her to marry him. They'd been headed down that road for a long time now. But something had held him back.

She hadn't said anything even though the visit before this one she'd hinted so broadly he began to wonder if she'd ask him to marry her, reversing the usual role. But then she didn't.

He'd brought the subject up with his father just before he left this time. "How do you know if the woman is the one God set aside for your wife?"

His father had stopped stocking a shelf and turned to study him, stroking his beard thoughtfully, as his eyes seemed to gaze inward.

"It's just a feeling you get," he'd said finally. "You just know. And if you're not certain, well, she's probably not the right one."

His father had thumped him on the shoulder in an awkward gesture of support and urged him to make another trip north. He'd insisted he could get along without Saul.

"No one's indispensable," he'd said gruffly.

Saul felt a mixture of gratitude and consternation. "You'll miss me when I'm gone," he'd called after his father's back as the older man headed for the stockroom.

But he grinned as he turned back to the order form he'd been working on. Thank goodness his father wasn't insisting his duty lay here helping run the store. Each time Saul had left, there had been no pressure about only staying a few days.

It was likely his father would be surprised to see him when he walked into the store tomorrow.

He'd cut his visit short, making an excuse to Lavina, and returning to Paradise a day ahead of the date he'd told his parents.

Elizabeth made a noise with her straw, draining the last of the Diet Coke. She wriggled her nose and grinned when she realized what she'd done. "Sorry! It was so good. I don't drink them often."

"Glad you enjoyed it." He watched her put the empty hamburger wrapper back in the bag. "Maybe we could go get lunch there sometime after you get settled?"

She paused and stared at him. "I—guess."

"You don't have to feel like it's a date," he rushed to say as silence stretched between them. "Just friends."

Elizabeth nodded.

"How long do you think you'll be here?"

"I don't know." She looked away from him, folding down the top of the bag.

He frowned, hearing a curious mix of sadness and indecision in her voice. What was it about? he wondered. Was this really a visit or had she left her home in Indiana for some reason?

"How much longer will it be before we get to Paradise?" she asked him.

Saul glanced out the window and calculated. "About a half hour," he told her.

Elizabeth sat up straighter and her eyes sparkled. "I can't wait."

There it was again, he thought. The mix of emotions. She looked excited, sounded excited. But her hands shook as she put her pad of paper back in her purse.

As much as Saul was ready to get off the bus, inhale some good fresh air, and climb into his own bed, he wanted more time to figure this woman out. She was a mystery he wanted to solve.

"Where will you be staying?" he asked, trying to sound cool and polite since she'd been wary of him asking personal questions earlier. "I need to know where to call for you. When we go for that Big Mac."

"Maybe you could give me your number," she said.

He nodded. "Good idea." He pulled a business card from his jacket. "May I?" he asked, gesturing to the pencil behind her ear.

She looked surprised it was still there and handed it to him. He wrote his cell phone number on the back of the card with the store address and phone number on it. He gave it to her, she looked at it for a moment, and tucked it safely into her purse.

"So tomorrow you have to work?"

Startled she had initiated conversation, he nodded.

"A job's a good thing."

"True." He inclined his head and studied her. There was a wistful note in her voice. "What did you say you did in Goshen?"

She smiled. "I didn't." After a moment, she said, "I worked in a fabric store."

Too bad she was just visiting, Saul thought. They could use someone like her since Miriam was taking maternity leave soon. Then he realized what she'd just said.

"Worked? Does that mean you left your job?"

She touched her mouth with her fingers and looked chagrined. Then she nodded. "I needed a break."

"I guess so," he said gravely. "I mean, you must have been there forever."

"You're laughing at me." But she said it tentatively, as if she was unsure if he was teasing.

"No. You just make it sound like you've been doing it for so long you had to retire or something."

"I just need a break. Vacation. Whatever you call it." She frowned. "*Rumschpringe.*" She paused and glanced around. "I hate to use the word. *Englischers* seem to think we turn into wild things and run around getting drunk."

He winced. "Well, some guys I was friends with did, but I know what you mean."

The bus slowed and moved into the lane to the exit ramp. Passengers who were getting off at the next stop began shifting in their seats, looking out the windows.

Saul watched Elizabeth pull on her jacket and loop the strap of her purse over her shoulder. He'd seen her tucking her purse on one side of her between her body and the bus wall, guarding it carefully. She lifted her tote bag and put it on her lap.

"Thanks again for the sandwich and the coffee."

"Thank you for the Big Mac."

They were turning into strangers again now the enforced intimacy of the bus ride was nearly over.

"Don't forget we're meeting for another once you get settled."

She nodded but her attention was riveted on the front of the bus as it came to a stop.

Saul remembered his mother once complaining his father, anxious to be on his way for a hunting trip, had already left them before he walked out the door. Now he knew what she meant; he felt the same way about Elizabeth. She was already mentally out the bus door, so eager to be at her destination.

He stood and gestured for her to precede him, and they joined passengers in the line to disembark from the bus.

"Who's meeting you?" he asked her when they were standing by the side of the bus where the driver was getting their luggage.

"My new roommate." She scanned the crowd of those waiting for bus passengers. "Oh, there she is!"

"I'll see you soon, Elizabeth No Last Name."

She smiled at him. "Yes, Saul Miller. Have a good night."

He watched her wend her way to a woman her age waiting for her and then turned to look for the driver who waited for him.

"Good trip?" Phil asked, as he loaded Saul's suitcase into the van.

"It was okay," Saul said. "What's been happening here?" he asked, knowing the man would fill the drive with chatter about the latest goings-on and he wouldn't have to contribute anything.

He didn't feel much like talking now that Elizabeth wasn't near. He wondered if he'd see her again or if she'd forget about him once she was settled.

And he wondered why he was thinking about her instead of Lavina . . .

❧

Elizabeth held onto the armrest on the passenger side of the car and prayed as she caught a glimpse of the speedometer while Paula chattered a mile a minute.

"Did you have a good trip? I got a little worried when the bus ran a half an hour late."

"I'm sorry if you had to wait—"

"Didn't! I checked before I drove to the bus station."

"Oh. That's good."

Elizabeth studied Paula. They were so different in looks and personality: Paula's chin-length blond hair curled madly all over her head, she wore bright lipstick and jeans with holes at the knee and a big blue men's chambray shirt. They'd met when Paula's family had visited Goshen earlier in the year. They'd written dozens of letters since then—Paula had once called them pen pals. Elizabeth had grown to feel safe enough to feel she could talk about her frustrations and dreams, and when she had, Paula had invited her to visit.

She'd accepted the offer immediately, hoping Paula was sincere. Paula had written back and invited her to come as soon as she wanted. Elizabeth was on a bus to Paradise a month later.

"You're sure it's not a problem to stay with you for a while?"

"I told you it isn't! My parents wanted me to get a roommate."

"I don't know how long I need to stay."

Paula reached over and patted her hand. "Don't worry about it. When you decide, I'll just advertise at the college for a roommate."

They couldn't have been more different: Elizabeth was Amish, Paula was *Englisch*. Elizabeth had dark hair. Paula's hair was a streaky blond mass that made Elizabeth think the sun had run its rays through it. Paula had laughed and said the streaks came from a bottle.

It was another way they were so different. Elizabeth was shy and quiet. Paula fairly bubbled with exuberance.

"You're being quiet."

Elizabeth smiled. "That's me. Quiet."

"The deep ones are always quiet."

A laugh escaped before Elizabeth could stop it. "I'm not deep. You're the one who's going to college."

"Yeah, well, I'm not doing so well," Paula said.

It suddenly got very quiet in the car.

"Why?"

Paula shrugged. "I'm having trouble with my English class. Math, no problem. But if I have to do any writing like I have to do in English and history, I'm in trouble. College is harder than high school. A lot harder than I thought it would be."

Elizabeth bit her lip. "English was my best subject in school. I'd love to help you, but we only go to school to the eighth grade and then we go to work."

"I appreciate the offer." Paula sighed. "I just have to buckle down and work harder. Maybe go to the tutoring center at school."

Back home, Elizabeth had often helped the teacher with the younger students. Later, she helped her brothers and sisters with their homework while their mother cooked supper. But it wasn't going to help Paula.

"It doesn't sound easy but you'll be glad you did it. There aren't many jobs for people without a college education. Not in your world and not even in mine." She smoothed her skirt. "Several people in the shop I worked in had college educations. I'd never be promoted to senior clerk or manager there no matter how long I stayed."

"But I thought most Amish women worked at home."

"After they're married."

"You're too young to get married," Paula said firmly. "Women shouldn't get married until they're at least in their middle twenties. You're only twenty, right?"

"Yes."

Paula pulled into the drive of an apartment building. "We're here. Welcome home!"

They got out of the car and Paula got Elizabeth's suitcase out of the trunk. "I've got it," she told Elizabeth. "You look tired."

"I shouldn't be. All I did was sit on the bus."

"Traveling is tiring."

Elizabeth doubted Paula had ever traveled on a bus. When she and her family had visited Goshen, they'd come in an expensive looking SUV.

"Hungry?"

"I have a sandwich left," Elizabeth said, holding up her tote.

"I'm not sure it's safe to eat anything you've been carrying around your whole trip."

"It's insulated."

Paula reached for the bag. "C'mon, I'll make us some soup and sandwiches."

"I don't want you to go to any trouble."

"No trouble. My mom brought some stuff over as a welcome present. Does a turkey sandwich and homemade vegetable soup sound okay?"

"Sounds great."

Paula warmed the soup in the microwave while she made them sandwiches. They sat at the kitchen island and ate while she peppered Elizabeth with questions.

"Who was the cute Amish guy who got off with you? Do you know him?"

Elizabeth nearly choked on her soup. She'd seen Saul?

"He was just someone who was on the bus."

"Oh, so you didn't know him? Seemed like you two knew each other when you were talking."

"We talked on the ride. He's from here."

"Are you going to see him again?"

Elizabeth felt her cheeks warming. "We might. It's not a date or anything."

"Sounds promising, though," Paula said. She spooned up some soup.

"What about you?" Elizabeth asked shyly. "Are you dating?"

"I've been going with Jason since we graduated from high school. But he wanted to serve in the military. He got shipped to Afghanistan and I have no idea if he's signing up for another stint, when he's coming home . . ."

She sighed. "Everyone tells me I should look for another guy. But *he's* the guy I love. We've been staying in touch by e-mail but it hasn't been easy with Internet connections where he is. Besides, I don't think anyone realizes there aren't many guys like Jason. This guy in my Algebra class asked me out for coffee and I thought, hey, it's just coffee. Turned out he just wanted me to let him cheat on the next test."

"Oh, my! How wrong!" Aghast, Elizabeth stared at her.

Then, just as suddenly, it occurred to her she shouldn't have said anything. What if Paula felt it was okay to let the man cheat from her test? What if she felt judged? What if she kicked her out? Would she tell her to get back on a bus and go back to Goshen? She couldn't do that, she—

"Well, of course, I told him to stuff it!" Paula said, sounding disgusted. "How dare he even ask such a thing. What kind of a person does he think I am, anyway?"

Relieved, Elizabeth spooned up more soup. Why had she been worried? she chided herself. Paula had seemed to her to be a good person and she was seldom wrong about this sort of thing. Jumping to conclusions Paula would order her out . . . well, she was just plain silly. She was letting her fears get to her.

It was a big step to leave her home, her life back in Goshen. She'd been so scared. But she'd packed her suitcase, walked on shaking legs out of the only home she'd ever known, and climbed aboard the bus to bring her here to a new life—for however long she stayed.

She could do this with some faith and confidence or she could do it in fear. Warmed by the welcome she'd received from Paula, the soup she'd reheated, and now eager for the comfort of some rest in bed after trying to catch some sleep on the moving bus, Elizabeth stood. She gathered up her empty dishes and those in front of Paula.

"This was so good," she said. "I'll wash up."

Paula got up and walked over to the kitchen counter. "Let me introduce you to my dishwasher," she said, grinning. "I think you're going to like it as much as I do."

She showed her how to load the dishes and where to pour the dishwashing powder in the receptacle in the door. Then she closed the door, pressed a button, and the machine began making a swishing sound.

"That's it?"

"That's it. Let me show you your room."

The room looked huge and even had a bathroom attached. Elizabeth set her suitcase on a padded bench and let out a sigh. The bed had a brass rail headboard and a thick, soft mattress. Elizabeth sat on the bed and bounced.

"It's beautiful!" she breathed as she glanced around the room.

"I'm glad you like it," Paula said with a grin. "Mom helped me decorate. You probably have better quilts back home. This is the one she bought me for college."

She yawned. "I better get to bed. Let me know if you need anything else."

Elizabeth looked up at her. "I don't need a thing. Thank you for making me feel welcome."

"You're welcome. I think we'll have fun, roomie. 'Night."

Elizabeth got up and wandered around the room, touching the carved wooden bedside table, the little scented soaps in a dish on the bathroom vanity sink, the crisp white pillowcase. A big yawn overcame her, but she was too excited to sleep. She opened her suitcase thinking she'd hang her few clothes in the closet—no pegs like at home!—and then she saw what lay atop her two dresses.

A worn brown teddy bear stared up at her with his one good eye.

"Oh, Brownie!" she cried, picking him up and clutching him to her chest. "Why did Sadie put you in here? She can't sleep without you!"

She felt tears slipping down her cheeks at the thought of her youngest sister—just four—slipping her favorite toy into her big sister's suitcase, so she'd have something of home with her.

Curling up on the bed, Elizabeth pushed her face into her pillow, trying to cry quietly so she didn't wake Paula. It was hours before she slept.

Crossroads

1

"Pretty sweet sound, don't you think?" Isaac turned up the volume of the CD player in his buggy. Heavy metal music came pouring out.

Emma gritted her teeth and wished she felt brave enough to plug her ears with her fingers. Isaac called it music. It sounded awful to her. She wanted to ask him to turn it down because it was giving her a headache but instead, she smiled and nodded. Maybe it was wishful thinking but she hoped his taste for such music was just his going through his *rumschpringe*.

Joe, Isaac's horse, shook his head as he pulled the buggy down the road and Emma bit back a smile, wondering if horses got headaches.

Another buggy approached at a fast speed from the opposite direction. The driver leaned out and waved. It was Davey, one of Isaac's friends. As his buggy passed theirs, the sound from his own CD player blared even louder than Isaac's. A flock of chickens grazing inside a fence near the road squawked and scurried away.

She sighed. Sometimes she wondered whether Amish boys enjoyed music or beer more during their *rumschpringe*.

Well, perhaps she couldn't call Isaac Amish any more. She looked at him and wondered where the Isaac she'd loved since she was ten had gone. He wore jeans and a polo shirt.

And an *Englisch* haircut.

"Where are we going?" she asked him.

"It's a surprise."

"I don't know if I can stand another one," she murmured.

"What? I didn't hear you."

"Never mind," she said, raising her voice.

Now, as Emma sat beside Isaac in his tricked-out buggy, she remembered how she and her older sister, Lizzie, had argued the night before.

"I think Isaac's enjoying being a bad boy right now," Lizzie told her as they prepared for bed in the bedroom they shared.

"If he is, I can change him," Emma said with a confidence she didn't entirely feel.

"You think a good girl can reform a bad boy? It doesn't work," she said with the wisdom of someone only two years older than Emma's twenty-one. "You shouldn't try to change another person."

The buggy hit a bump in the road, bringing Emma back to the present. Isaac was driving into town, away from their homes. She thought about their recent conversations and tried to guess what kind of surprise he'd planned.

The day was perfect for a drive. She sighed happily. The breeze coming in the windows was cool, but the sun felt warm. Late spring weather could be iffy here in Paradise, Pennsylvania.

A week ago, Puxatawny Phil, the funny little groundhog the *Englischers* watched for a prediction about winter ending, had emerged from his burrow and seen no shadow, so spring would come early.

They passed the Stoltzfus farm and she saw the "For Sale" sign in the front yard. She waited with bated breath. Were they going to turn into the drive? Isaac had always worked in construction as a roofer and a carpenter . . . maybe Isaac had decided he wanted to be a farmer after all. He hadn't seemed upset when his father told him one evening he was selling the farm to Isaac's brother, not to him. But Isaac didn't share his feelings about things as much lately.

Well, she'd been raised on a farm and liked the idea of helping run one. They'd have *kinner*, lots of them if God willed it and they'd help as they grew older . . .

Lost in her daydream, it took her a moment to realize they were driving past the farm.

Okay, well maybe the farm wasn't where he was taking her. Maybe it was a different one. Maybe it wasn't a farm at all. Maybe it was a house he'd found and wanted to fix up. They didn't have a lot of money saved and property was so expensive in Lancaster County. He was so good with his hands, could build anything, fix anything. They could buy something run-down. A fixer-upper, she'd heard them called. They could buy one and make it theirs. Hopefully, they'd get it in good shape before a *boppli* came along to crawl in the sawdust.

She studied his profile, never tiring of looking at him, being with him. As scholars, they'd passed notes in class and the minute their parents had allowed it, they'd attended singings and gone on buggy rides together. He'd been the cute little boy with blond hair and mischief in his big blue eyes who'd grown into a handsome man.

Lately, though, he seemed different. He spent hours working on his buggy after he got off work, and this was the first time they'd been out in a week. When he picked her up he hadn't noticed she was wearing a new dress in the color he liked best on her—robin's egg blue—and he hadn't asked her about her new job.

"Can't stop looking, can you?" he asked, winking at her and giving her a mischievous smile. "Like it?"

"I—I don't know what to say," she told him honestly, staring at the short, razored cut replacing his Amish haircut. "You look so different."

"That's the idea."

"You never said you were going to cut your hair like an *Englischer.*"

He shrugged. "Decided to try it. If I don't like it, it'll grow back."

"Have your parents seen it yet?"

"*Nee.* I mean, no."

She winced as he corrected himself. It was a small thing but he seemed to be ridding his talk of Pennsylvania *Dietsch.* "When did you get it cut?"

"Two days ago."

"How could they not have seen it by now?" she wondered aloud. "Isaac? Isaac?"

"What?"

Emma reached over and turned the volume down. "How is it your parents haven't seen your haircut when you had it done two days ago?"

"I moved out."

Her eyes widened. "Moved out?"

"Yeah. I got my own place. I have a job. I can afford it."

"But I thought we were saving to get married in the fall."

He pulled the buggy into the drive of a run-down looking little cottage, stopped, and turned to her. "We don't have to wait to be together. You can move in with me."

❦

The minute Isaac saw Emma's expression, he knew he'd made a bad decision.

Shock mixed with horror on her face as she stared at him. "You're *ab im kop*," she said finally.

"I'm not crazy," he said, frowning. "You keep saying you want to be with me."

"I do. I want to be *married* to you!"

He bent his head and stared at his hands. "I know."

"You know, but you bring me here and say this?"

There was no easy way to say it. Isaac looked up. "I'm not sure I'm ready to get married."

No, it wasn't the truth, he told himself. He owed her the truth.

"I'm not ready to get married," he said more firmly.

She pressed her fingers to her lips to stop their trembling. "But we've talked about it for . . . forever."

He sighed. "Maybe that's the trouble. We got too serious, too soon."

Emma drew a handkerchief from her pocket and wiped at her eyes. "Are you saying you don't want to be engaged anymore? You want to date other women?"

"*Nee!*" he said quickly. "If I did, would I be asking you to move in with me here?"

She straightened, tucked her handkerchief away, and straightened. "I think you do want to see another woman, Isaac Stoltzfus. Because this woman isn't interested in living with you without being married."

He watched her look around her, at the fields just planted, and felt a stab of guilt when she took a shuddering breath.

"Would you take me home, please?"

"Emma—"

"Please." She twisted the handkerchief in her hands and avoided his gaze.

"*Allrecht*. I just need to put a box or two inside. Are you sure you don't want to look around?"

"It's the last thing I want to do," she said quietly.

He climbed out of the buggy, stacked the two boxes on top of each other, and carried them into the cottage.

When he came back outside, she was gone.

He had other boxes he wanted to put inside the cottage, but they weren't important now. After he ran back to lock up the place he jumped into the buggy and retraced the route he'd taken. He looked up one side of the road and down the other, but there was no sign of Emma.

How could she have just disappeared? He hadn't heard another buggy or car as he carried the boxes inside the cottage. Had someone picked her up? She wouldn't take a ride with a stranger, would she? Surely not. She was too smart, too sensible.

But she'd been so upset with him. More upset than he'd ever seen her about anything.

"C'mon, Joe, help me find Emma. Where'd Emma go?"

The horse whinnied when he heard his name, but, of course, he couldn't answer Isaac. The horse's hooves echoed rhythmically on the pavement, but the sound was hardly soothing. Isaac called to Joe and shook the reins. Joe picked up the pace, and the buggy rolled faster back toward Emma's home.

Isaac pulled into the drive, and the wheels had barely stopped turning when he jumped out. He pounded on the front door.

Lizzie, Emma's sister, opened the door and blinked when she saw him. "Isaac! I thought you just left."

"Emma! Where's Emma?"

She just stared at him. "She went with you."

"Did she come back?"

"Isaac, you're not making any sense."

Frustrated, he ran his hand through his hair. "Lizzie, could she have come home and you didn't see her?"

"I guess." She glanced around her. "I'll check. Do you want to come in?"

"No. *Danki*," he added, aware he sounded impatient.

She shut the door and was gone for a few minutes. When she returned she wore a frown as she opened the door. "She's not anywhere in the house."

"You're *schur?*"

"Of course, I'm *schur.*" She stared at him. "What did you do to your hair?"

"Cut it," he said curtly. "It's not important now."

"What did you argue about?"

Isaac met her gaze and he looked away. "I'd rather not say."

Lizzie crossed her arms over her chest. "I told her you were a bad boy, and she shouldn't try to change you."

Shocked, he shook his head and opened his mouth to protest. But she was right. He wasn't a boy, but he had been selfish in the way he'd treated Emma. How had he thought she'd just go along with moving in with him because he wanted it?

Well, maybe because Emma had always gone along with what he wanted. She was sweet, smart, and above all, his best friend.

Had he ruined everything?

He turned and walked back to his buggy. Maybe she'd decided she wanted nothing to do with him and it was why she had left the buggy. He wouldn't blame her.

But he was going to find her and make sure she was safe if it was the last thing he did.

"Emma!"

She turned and saw Elizabeth Miller waving to her from her buggy.

"Can I give you a ride?"

Emma nodded quickly and fairly jumped into the buggy before Elizabeth brought it to a complete stop. "*Danki.*"

"Where were you going?"

"Just out for a walk."

"Long walk," Elizabeth commented.

She took a surreptitious glance back and didn't see Isaac coming out of the cottage. Still, she was relieved when Elizabeth got the buggy moving again.

"So how are you and Isaac doing?"

"Fine. You and Saul?" She turned and focused on Elizabeth. "I don't need to ask. You're glowing. Married life is *gut*, *ya*?"

Elizabeth laughed and nodded. "Very *gut*. But you'll find out for yourself soon, I think?"

The question hit Emma with a force every bit as physical as a blow.

"I know, I'm being nosy," Elizabeth went on without waiting for an answer. "But it's so obvious the two of you are a couple and have been for years. You're not going to surprise anyone when you decide an announcement should be made."

Emma felt grateful who dated who wasn't discussed—or, at least, not encouraged. At least if it turned out she and Isaac were not going to be married in the fall she might not get as many questions from others.

Fearing Elizabeth might ask more questions, Emma decided to ask some of her own. Though it pained her greatly after what Isaaac had just done to her dreams, there was one topic which would take Elizabeth's attention completely from Emma: her new life.

"Have you been able to do much getting your household settled since you work at the store with Saul?"

Elizabeth sighed. "Not as much as I'd like. But there's time. I—oh!" she stopped and pressed her fingers against her lips, then pulled the buggy off the road and stopped.

"Are you *allrecht*?"

After a long moment she took a deep breath and nodded. "*Ya*, I'm fine. I feel like I'm having heartburn. Must be something I ate. I'm sorry, I'll get us back on the road in a minute."

"Don't rush, I'm in no hurry," Emma told her quickly. "Why don't you take a drink of water and see if it helps?" she asked, indicating the bottle of water on the seat between them.

"Why didn't I think of that?" Elisabeth uncapped the bottle and took a drink, then recapped it and set it down on the seat.

Emma thought about how much time had passed since Elizabeth's wedding the previous fall and tried to hide a smile. She doubted it was heartburn affecting her friend. By the time the next fall rolled around, she suspected Elizabeth might be a new *mamm*.

Next fall, when she'd hoped to be married. She sighed.

"What's the sigh for?"

"Oh, just thinking about something. Nothing important."

Elizabeth checked traffic, then shook the reins and her horse pulled the buggy back onto the road.

"You didn't have to work today?"

"I take one Saturday off a month to do bookkeeping at home. This afternoon I thought I might work in the kitchen garden." She sighed and looked rueful. "I'm still getting used to the differences in weather between here and Goshen, trying to figure out what I can plant this time of year."

"Talk to my *mamm*. Or Katie and Rosie, the twins at the store. They're wonderful gardeners."

"Tell me about it." Elizabeth pulled into the driveway of Emma's house. "I told Saul we're going to lose them one day. Their Two Peas in a Pod jams and jellies sell out constantly at the store."

She brought the buggy to a stop. "I'm so glad we had a chance to talk."

"Me, too," Emma said. Once she'd led Elizabeth down a different conversational path, she'd enjoyed it. "*Danki* for the ride," Emma said as she got out of the buggy.

"Be sure to tell Lizzie I'll see her day after tomorrow."

"I will."

Emma felt depression weighing her down as she climbed up the front porch steps and went inside.

"There you are!" Lizzie cried as Emma walked into the kitchen.

"*Ya*, here I am," Emma muttered as she filled the teakettle, set it on the stove, then turned on the gas flame under it. She rubbed her hands for warmth. She'd felt so cold since Isaac had blurted out how they could live together.

"What happened?"

She turned. "What do you mean?"

"Isaac came looking for you."

"Oh." She turned back and stared at the teakettle, willing it to boil.

"Did you two have an argument?"

"I don't want to talk about it."

"Are you going to call him? He was worried about you."

She shrugged.

"Emma—"

"I don't want to talk about it."

An uncomfortable silence fell over the room.

"How did you get home?"

"I got a ride with Elizabeth Miller. She saw me walking home."

The front door opened, then closed. Their mother came in carrying several tote bags. "Will you put these things in the refrigerator? I'm going to go lie down. I don't feel so well."

"I told you it was too soon to be up and about," Lizzie scolded, acting like the *mamm* instead of the grown child. "The flu really took it out of you."

She helped her mother take off her sweater and hang it up. "You go change and get back into bed. I'll make you a nice hot cup of tea and bring it to you"

The teakettle began whistling as Emma finished putting away the items her mother had bought. Lizzie fixed a cup of tea for their mother, adding milk and sugar, and went to give it to her.

Emma fixed a cup of tea for herself and sat at the big kitchen table to drink it. When Lizzie returned, she carried the cup of tea. "She was already asleep when I got there." She sat at the table. "Guess I'll drink it."

"You don't like milk in your tea."

Lizzie shrugged. "No point in it going to waste." She stirred it then took a sip. "Now tell me what happened with Isaac."

"I said—"

"I know what you said. But it's obvious you're upset about something."

Emma rubbed her forehead and tried to fight back tears. "There's nothing I can do."

"Are you saying you're going to break off the engagement?" Lizzie asked, her eyes wide.

Restless, Emma got up, dumped her cold tea in the sink, and poured more hot water into her mug. She sank down into her chair and dunked another tea bag in the water. "It's more like Isaac is breaking it off with me."

She told Lizzie what Isaac had said. Lizzie went white and when Emma finished she listened to the clock ticking loudly.

"Well," Lizzie said at last. "Was that why you came home?"

Emma nodded. "I saw a buggy approaching and got a ride."

"So what are you going to do?"

Emma stirred her tea, studying the pattern the spoon made in the liquid. "I don't know," she said finally. "I'm not willing to live with him without us being married."

Lizzie stood. "I should say not!"

She reached out and grabbed her sister's arm. "You can't tell anyone."

"I wouldn't dream of it. Him asking you to do such a thing is too insulting for words." She paced the room. "Are you going to tell *Mamm* and *Daed*? I think they're expecting you and Isaac to get married after the harvest. When we were talking about the kitchen garden the other day she was saying she was thinking about planting extra celery."

Then Lizzie stopped. "Oh, Emma, I'm sorry. The last thing I need to be talking about is *Mamm* planting celery in case both of us are getting married."

"I'm going up to my room."

Lizzie hugged her. "You'll feel better after you've had some rest."

Emma doubted rest was going to make her feel better but she didn't have the energy to disagree. She just wanted to be alone.

As she started up the stairs, she heard a knock on the front door. She turned and looked at her sister. "If it's Isaac, I don't want to talk to him."

"You don't have to," Lizzie announced, a determined look on her face as she started for the door.

Emma couldn't help herself—she stood on the stairs and waited to hear who the visitor was.

It felt like a hand squeezed her heart when she heard Isaac's low, deep voice. Her lips trembled but she stayed where she was until Lizzie sent him away. Then she climbed the stairs to her room, feeling decades older than her age and threw herself on her bed.

She rolled over and punched her pillow to be more comfortable and her hand encountered her journal. Pulling it out, she flipped through the pages and began reading what she'd written a few days before: "I'm worried about Isaac. I think he's still grieving over his brother drowning when he was a little boy, but he says he's fine and he won't talk to me. We were friends before we decided we wanted to be married. I want my friend back."

Tears slipped down her cheeks. She closed the book and held it to her chest. From the time she was ten she'd loved Isaac. She couldn't bear the thought of him not being in her life.

2

Isaac stared at Lizzie. "What do you mean she doesn't want to talk to me?"

"She doesn't want to talk to you."

"It's not possible—" He put out his hand to stop her from shutting the door. "Lizzie, come on. You know how I feel about Emma."

"I know how you used to feel about her," Lizzie said, her eyes blazing. "She told me what you said today, Isaac. How can you think she'd want to have anything to do with you after what you said?"

"I didn't say we wouldn't get married!"

"Isaac, Emma doesn't want to talk to you and I don't either."

She shut the door firmly in his face.

He backed away, shaking his head and started to walk to his buggy. Then he stopped and glanced up at Emma's bedroom window. His gaze fell to the pebbles on the edge of the drive. He scooped up a handful and tossed them at the window. They bounced off the glass and fell back to the ground.

But Emma never came to the window.

So close . . . and yet so far.

His shoulders slumped. He walked back to his buggy and climbed inside. He called to Joe and the vehicle began rolling down the drive. His hand reached for a CD and then he paused, a little ashamed to remember the pained look Emma had worn when he played it earlier.

He paused at the end of the drive, looking both ways before letting Joe pull the buggy onto the road. The drive to the cottage seemed to take longer than it had earlier. Maybe it was because his spirits had been higher.

When he arrived he disconnected the buggy and freed Joe of the harness before putting both into the ramshackle barn behind the cottage. Lost in his thoughts, he almost forgot to feed and water his horse but Joe sensed his distraction and butted his arm.

The horse happily munched at his feed as Isaac closed the barn door behind him and started for the cottage. Just as he reached the back door, he heard a buggy pull up in the front drive. He walked through the house and opened the front door just as Davey reached to pound on it.

"Hey, man, thought I'd see what you were up to tonight." Davey looked over Isaac's shoulder. "Emma here?"

"No," Isaac said shortly.

Davey glanced each way. "I have a six-pack in the buggy. You got anything to eat?"

"We could order a pizza." Isaac had money in his pocket he'd planned to use taking Emma out to supper, but since that wasn't going to happen tonight—maybe even in the near future—he decided to blow it. "Go on into the living room and I'll call the pizza place. Pepperoni, right?"

"Yeah. Extra cheese."

When Isaac walked into the room a few minutes later, he found Davey sitting in a lawn chair, his legs stretched out in front of him.

"Hey, man, love the furniture." Davey waved his hand at the room. "Who was your decorator? The Patio Store?" He chuckled and popped the top of a can of beer.

"Not funny!" Isaac kicked at the metal leg of the lawn chair Davey sat in, making it sway.

"Hey, man, I was just joking!" Davey protested, drawing his legs up and and planting them on the floor for balance. "Geez, look, you made me spill my beer," he complained, brushing drops off his lap. "You're in a mood. What, did you have a fight with the old lady?"

"Don't call her that." Isaac picked up a can of beer from the fruit crate serving as a coffee table. He sat in another lawn chair and popped the top on the can.

"O-kay." Davey took a long gulp of beer. "Want to catch a movie?"

Isaac shook his head. He took a long swallow of his beer, then another. He'd only been drunk once in his life and he'd been sick afterward. But tonight he felt like drinking until he forgot how it had felt when Emma refused to see him.

He was on his second beer when the pizza arrived. Isaac dug in his pocket for money.

"You fellas have a nice night," the delivery guy said, smiling at the tip Isaac gave him.

Isaac set the pizza box down on the crate and opened it.

"Hey, you get ESPN?"

"Yeah." He tossed the remote to him and watched him find the channel.

"Man, I love TV," Davey said. "So glad this place has electricity, huh?"

Isaac shrugged. "It's okay."

Davey finished his beer, burped, then leaned over to help himself to two pieces of pizza, putting the pepperoni sides together and eating it like a sandwich. "Aren't you eating?"

"In a minute." He reached for another beer, popped the top, took a long swallow, then stared at it moodily. "Davey?"

He tore his attention from the television. "What?"

"Do you ever see Mary?"

"Yeah. Now and then. Why?"

"Are you going to get married?"

"Her parents don't like me."

"So?"

"So we're giving it some more time. No hurry. Fall's a long way away."

Isaac took a gulp of the beer, then another. And then he set it down. Stuff tasted bitter. He watched the action on the television for a moment, and then he found his attention wandering. Davey wasn't the brightest, but he had a point.

Fall was a long way away.

Maybe he'd know what he wanted by then.

He hadn't prayed for a long time, not since things had gotten confusing for him. But he prayed now he would figure things out soon. Real soon.

∞∞

Emma woke, glanced at her alarm clock on the table beside the bed and started to get up. Then she remembered it was Saturday, the one day she could sleep in a little if she wanted.

And then she remembered how her world had come crashing down the day before . . .

She punched her pillow and lay on her side, watching the sun rising. Sleep had been a long time coming. It would have been nice to sleep in a little, but she'd woken at the same time she had to get up for work each day.

Lizzie slept in the other bed. The two of them had totally different personalities. Lizzie looked sweet, but she spoke up for herself—something Emma found difficult. She had opinions about just about everything, while Emma liked the middle of the road.

The only thing they'd agreed on was the color of the walls—a soft robin's egg blue. And sleeping in. Lizzie liked it as much as Emma.

Right now Lizzie had her quilt pulled over her head, blocking out the rays of sun coming in the room. They'd each sewn a quilt for their beds when *Daed* had let them move up to the third floor, away from the other *kinner*. Lizzie's stitching wasn't as tidy and careful as Emma's—Lizzie didn't have the patience and besides, Lizzie wasn't interested in quilting or sewing. She loved painting with watercolors where she could splash color with abandon on the canvas. Emma had surprised Lizzie on her last birthday by framing several of Lizzie's watercolors and hanging them on the walls.

Emma's gaze landed on a small, carved wooden keepsake box on top of their dresser. She slipped from the bed to get it, careful not to disturb Lizzie, then sat on her bed and opened it. She pulled out the little folded notes she and Isaac exchanged in *schul,* paged through her journal to sniff at the wild rose he'd given her. She'd pressed it between the pages where she wrote about her growing feelings for him. And felt her heart breaking again.

The edge of her bed went down as Lizzie sat beside her and hugged her. "Come on, Emma, don't cry. Everything's going to be *allrecht*."

"You don't know it for sure."

Lizzie patted her on her back. "*Nee*, I don't, she admitted with a sigh. "We just have to trust."

"Trust? I can't trust Isaac after what he said."

She blinked as Lizzie pulled back and put her hands on her cheeks. "Not trust Isaac. Trust God. We don't know what's happening here. Why it's happening. But God does. He's in every situation, Emma."

Emma reached for a tissue on her bedside table and wiped her cheeks. "I thought Isaac was the man God set aside for me."

Lizzie nodded, her expression sad. "I did, too."

There was a knock on the door.

"*Mamm* says breakfast is ready," one of their brothers called out. "She's making pancakes. Better come on now or Daniel and me are gonna eat yours."

Emma listened to the clatter of shoes descending the stairs to the lower level.

"Pancakes, Emma," Lizzie said as she got up and began dressing. "Your favorite."

"I'm not hungry. I have a headache."

She wasn't lying. An ache had formed behind her eyes and her stomach felt queasy. She began putting the things back in the box, then got up and put it back on the top of the dresser.

"What are you doing?" Lizzie asked, placing her hands on her hips when Emma climbed back into her bed.

Emma pulled the quilt up over her head. "Tell *Mamm* I'll be down in a while and clean up the kitchen."

When Lizzie didn't say anything Emma pushed the quilt down. Lizzie stood by the door, looking back at her uncertainly. "Go have breakfast, Lizzie. I'm just going to lie here for a little while and get rid of my headache."

With a nod, Lizzie left the room, shutting the door quietly behind her.

Emma lay there for a while, unable to go back to sleep because her mind kept spinning, spinning. Finally, afraid she was having a pity party, she got up, made her bed and Lizzie's, then dressed.

"There you are," her mother said when she walked into the kitchen. "Feeling better?"

She nodded, glanced at the sink, and saw it was empty. "I told Lizzie to tell you I'd be down to do the dishes."

Her mother patted her cheek. "I didn't do them. Lizzie did before she left for the library. Sit down, I saved you some breakfast."

"I'm not hungry. I just thought I'd have some tea."

"You—not hungry?" Looking concerned, her mother placed the back of her hand against Emma's forehead. "No fever." She narrowed her eyes at her daughter. "You're not . . ." she trailed off as her gaze dropped to Emma's abdomen.

Emma followed the direction of her mother's eyes and her cheeks flamed. "*Nee!*"

Lillian's expression cleared. "*Gut.* I wouldn't like to think you and Isaac—well, would become intimate. I'm not blind to the way you and Isaac have been."

She hesitated, wondering what—if anything—Lizzie had said to her.

Her mother pulled a plate piled high with pancakes from the oven and set it before Emma.

"I didn't think there would be any left."

"I hid them," her mother said with a smile. "Tea or coffee?"

"I'll get it—" she began.

Her mother put her hand on her shoulder. "Sit. I'm ready to have a cup of coffee with you."

So she subsided, poured syrup over her pancakes, and began eating. She hadn't thought she was hungry but once she put a forkful in her mouth she couldn't stop eating. Her mother made the best pancakes.

"So, what are your plans today?" her mother asked as she stirred her cup of coffee. "Doing something with Isaac?"

The bite of pancake Emma was chewing and about to swallow turned into a lump in her throat. She reached for her tea, found it too hot to drink, and jumped up to get a glass of water from the tap.

"*Nee,* I have some things to do," she said vaguely. Then inspiration hit her. "Could I use the buggy to go into town?"

"Check with your *dat.* I don't think he planned to use it."

Emma took her plate and cup to the sink and washed and dried them. Then she grabbed her sweater and went to find her father.

Her father looked up from checking the hoof of their mare and grinned at Emma. "*Guder mariye,* sleepyhead."

"*Daed*, could I take the buggy into town?"

He set Flora's hoof down and nodded. "*Schur.*" He tilted his head to one side. "Plans with Isaac?"

She bit her lip and shook her head. "*Nee.* I just have some things to do."

"*Ach.* I see."

Emma walked over and looked at Flora's hoof. "Is she okay?"

"*She* is," he told her. "I thought she was favoring this leg, but I can't find anything wrong." He peered at her. "What about you?"

Startled, she glanced up at him. "I'm fine."

His eyes were warm and concerned behind his wire-rimmed glasses. "I don't think so," he said after a moment.

She went to him then and hugged him. "Have you been talking to Lizzie?"

"*Nee,*" he said quietly, pulling back to look down into her face. "Should I?"

Afraid she'd lose what tenuous hold she had on her composure, Emma backed away. "*Nee.* I'm fine. I'd just like to take the buggy into town to do some things."

"So you said. I'll help you hitch it up."

He led Flora out of the barn and hitched her to the family buggy. Emma helped him, both of them silent as they performed the task they had done so often.

When she climbed inside the buggy, he waited until she got her skirts out of the way and then shut the door. She lifted the reins, and he reached in and touched her hands.

"Wait," he said, dug in his pocket and handed her a folded bill. "Buy yourself something."

"I don't need—"

"You work hard and always turn over your check to your *mamm* to help. Buy yourself something."

She blinked hard at the tears that threatened. "*Danki.*"

"Nothing is ever as bad as it seems."

"Really?"

He patted her shoulder then stepped back so she could leave. When she slowed the buggy before entering the main road she glanced back, and he waved.

She turned her attention to the road ahead. It was time to stop looking back at what might have been and think about her future.

～♨～

Isaac nudged Davey with the toe of his shoe. "Hey, wake up."

Davey rolled over on the floor and pulled the quilt covering him up over his shoulder. "Go way."

"Time for you to go home."

He yawned and sat up, wincing. "Next time I hope you have a sofa."

There wasn't going to be a next time. Last night had been a mistake. Drinking hadn't helped him forget Emma.

His friend got to his feet and tossed the quilt into a nearby lawn chair. He walked over to the cardboard box on the coffee table and looked inside. "We ate it all."

"You ate most of it."

Davey shrugged and checked his watch. "I'm starving. You got anything for breakfast?"

"There's cereal and milk in the kitchen."

He made a face. "Think I'll head home, see if *Mamm* will make me something to eat." He yawned and scrubbed his hands through his hair, making it stand up even more. "Thanks for the food last night. And the great accommodations. Feel like I'm as old as my *dat* today," he said as he rubbed his back with one hand. "See you later."

Isaac watched his friend stumble off to the barn, then turned his attention to the room. Beer cans littered the crate along with the empty pizza box. He got a plastic garbage bag and threw the box and used napkins inside it.

Rounding up the empty beer cans reminded him of how much he'd drunk the night before. He got the recycle box from the garage and tossed them inside. As he was carrying the container outside to the garage, he saw a buggy heading down the road toward him.

A familiar buggy.

He set the container down abruptly and ran toward the buggy, waving his arms. "Emma!"

Flora shied and tossed her head, but she stopped.

"Go away!" Emma yelled, but Isaac didn't let the skittish horse keep going. He grasped her bridle and talked to her, and she let him lead her into the drive.

"I don't want to talk to you!"

"Just give me a minute," he pleaded.

Flora shook her head, nearly breaking free. Isaac stroked her nose and talked to her softly. He had a way with horses, and Flora had always liked him.

She made a snuffling noise and looked down at one foot, then at him.

"Something the matter, Flora?" he asked her, bending to look at the foot.

"She's fine! Let go!"

"No, I think something's the matter with her right front foot." He lifted it and peered at it, frowning, before looking up at her. "Come on, pull in here and I'll check it out."

He watched her struggle with what to do and simply began to lead Flora over to the drive. When he stopped, Emma opened the door and climbed out. She stood watching him, her hands on her hips.

"I can't find anything wrong, but she was definitely favoring her one leg," Isaac said at last.

He patted Flora on the neck and turned to Emma who was watching him with a suspicious expression. "I don't think you should let her pull the buggy any more today."

"I just hitched her up."

Her tone was tart and defensive.

"I know you love Flora," he said quietly. "I wasn't implying you'd do anything not good for her. Now, we can do one of two things: you can call your *dat* and ask him to come get you both. Or I can take you home and we'll stable Flora here in my barn."

Emma bit her bottom lip, something she did when she was trying to make up her mind. Then she shook her head.

"I have to call *Daed*. It's his decision."

Isaac nodded and pulled out his cell phone.

"I have my own."

"Emma, just use it." He handed it to her and waited while she made the call.

Emma disconnected the call and gave him the phone. "*Daed* said if you would stable Flora until he gets over here to get her he'd appreciate it."

"And you? Do I keep you here as well?" he asked, smiling at her.

She stiffened. "Don't joke. *Daed* wouldn't want me anywhere near you if he knew what you'd suggested."

He had to admit he hadn't thought about what her parents would think. "I thought you'd want what I want," he said defensively. "You always do."

Emma's eyes widened. She stared at him for a long moment. "Yes," she said at last. "I do usually go along with what you want, don't I?" She heard bitterness in her voice, but she couldn't help it. She had a right to feel bitter after—she forced away the shameful thought.

"It's what you should do," he said. "A *fraa* should want what her *mann* does, right? If she loves him?"

"But you said you're not ready to get married. You can't talk about what a wife should want and yet not want to get married."

"I just said I'm not ready yet."

"Fall is months away. We weren't getting married right away, you know that."

He didn't know what to say. When he'd thought he'd lost her earlier, he'd reminded himself fall was months away and he had time to fix things . . .

Emma lifted her hands and let them fall. "I can't talk to you. I *won't* talk to you. I want you to take me home." She walked away and sat on the steps of the cottage.

Feeling defeated, Isaac led Flora back to the barn and unhitched the buggy. Then he led her to a stall and watered her, wondering the whole time if he was going to find Emma had bolted again like yesterday.

Cautiously optimistic, he hitched his horse to his own buggy and drove it to the front of the house.

She still sat on the porch steps. He let out the breath he hadn't realized he'd been holding.

"Ready to go?"

Emma didn't say anything, simply walked to the buggy and got in.

Isaac bided his time, letting the only sounds be the clip-clopping of the horse's hooves and the buggy wheels rolling on the road.

"Beautiful day," he said at last, stealing a furtive look at her. He frowned. Her bonnet hid her face from his view. "Where were you headed?"

"Town."

"I can take you there."

"*Nee!*" she said with such vehemence the horse shook his head.

She turned to him. "No, *danki*," she said in a quieter voice. "I want to go home."

"But Emma—"

"Isaac, I said no," she said, drawing herself up and looking at him with more determination than he'd ever seen her possess. "I'm not going to let you run over me like a steamroller. I let you do it in the past and look what happened. Now take me home or stop and let me out and I'll walk."

"Be reasonable, Emma. We just need to talk this out."

She reached for the door handle.

Isaac jerked on the reins and threw his arm across her to prevent her from opening the door and jumping out. "What are you doing? You'll hurt yourself if you try to get out when the buggy's moving."

Their faces were just inches apart. He couldn't mistake the fire in her eyes as she glared at him.

"*Allrecht, allrecht,*" he said. "I promise I won't try to talk to you the rest of the way."

She turned, folded her arms across her chest, and stared at the road ahead.

He did the same, although Joe didn't need his attention as he plodded along. Too soon, Emma's house came into view. Joe needed only a slight pull on the reins to know to pull into Emma's drive. Isaac figured as smart as Joe was he'd already figured out it's where they were going.

Emma had the door open the minute the buggy stopped. "I'll send *Daed* out to talk to you about Flora. *Danki* for the ride."

She walked away without looking at him again.

And coming in Fall 2015 from Barbara Cameron and the Abingdon Fiction team . . .

Twice Blessed

Twice Blessed is a Christmas novella collection about two sets of twins—one male, one female. The Amish love large families and have more multiples than the *Englisch. Twice Blessed* follows two sets of identical twins as they pursue life and love. When you've been together in the womb and all your life since then, it's hard to think about a job and a boyfriend without your twin tagging along. But these two sets of twins are determined to do it out of the shadow of their exact double.

Her Sister's Shadow

Katie and Rosie—the twins—who are secondary characters introduced in *Crossroads,* the second book in the Amish Roads series—work part-time in an Amish store and part-time in Two Peas in a Pod, their own business raising vegetables and fruits and canning them for sale. Although they are identical twins, their personalities are different: Katie has always been more outgoing, and boys have been more attracted to her. Rosie has always felt she was in her sister's shadow. Having to conform to a culture requiring community identity, not self-identity, it's even harder for her to be an individual. It will take an unexpected business opportunity and one special man to help Rosie see she's a unique woman of her own.

His Brother's Keeper

Ever since they were boys, Ben has trailed after his brother, Mark. Ben envies Mark because he's always been more adventurous than him. He envies him even more because he's engaged to Ruth, a woman Ben loves, too. Then the twins are involved in a terrible accident on Christmas Eve. When Ben wakes, he finds that Mark is seriously injured and everyone thinks *he's* Mark. Mistaken identity . . . envy . . . it's a dangerous combination. Ben has a chance at Ruth . . . and he takes it. It's a terrible deception, but the only chance he'll have to see what love would be like with the woman both men love.

Want to learn more about author
Barbara Cameron and check out other great
fiction from Abingdon Press?

Check out www.AbingdonFiction.com
to read interviews with your favorite authors, find tips
for starting a reading group, and stay posted on what
new titles are on the horizon.

And be sure to visit Barbara online!

BarbaraCameron.com
AmishLiving.com
facebook.com/barbara.cameron1

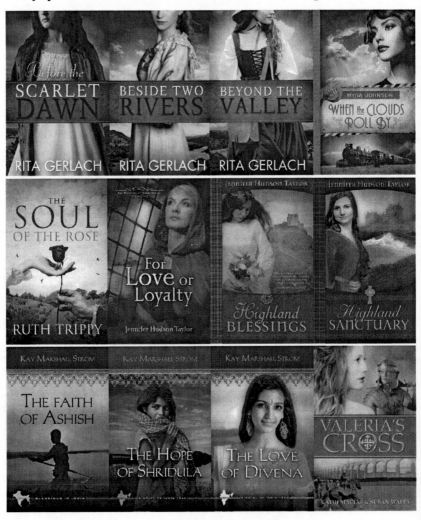

CPSIA information can be obtained at www.ICGtesting.com
Printed in the USA
LVOW07s0546110215

426524LV00001B/1/P